# a FRIENDLY Flirtation

A Friends First Novel

CHRISTINE WARNER

Entangled Publishing, LLC
2614 South Timberline Road
Suite 109
Fort Collins, CO 80525
Visit our website at www.entangledpublishing.com.

Select Contemporary is an imprint of Entangled Publishing, LLC.

Edited by Karen Grove
Cover design by Louisa Maggio
Cover art from iStock

Manufactured in the United States of America

First Edition February 2016

*For my awesome readers. My goal in all my stories is to leave you with a smile—an aww moment—that somehow my characters touch your heart. I hope this book accomplishes those goals. Happy reading!*

# Chapter One

"It's not like I asked you to devirginate me." Allison Hall's frustration level rose with the pitch of her voice. What the heck had made her say that? She wanted his help, but she didn't plan on asking him to extend his help quite that far. Of course, there was no denying that if he agreed to assist her, the virginity issue would take care of itself. Hopefully. But at the moment she had bigger fish to fry—as Gramps would say.

"Devirginate? Is that even a word?" Jared Esterly's eyebrows shot up toward his hairline, and he cleared his throat. Not often had she witnessed him out of his element.

"Does it matter?" Heat spread across her face as quickly as butter melted on warm toast. She pushed her glasses farther up the bridge of her nose and then locked her hands together in front of her, lacing her fingers so tight the muscles in her arms ached. "I know I don't approach you with stuff like this often—"

"Ever."

"I'm asking you because you're the one person I can trust. The one person I don't have to worry about laughing me out of the room." *The one person outside of my family I consider safe.*

He held up his hand, and she swallowed. "What about your brother?"

"Nick?" she squeaked. "Yeah. Already tried that. He told me in his overbearing brotherly way that I don't need to make changes. I'm perfect the way I am." *Just like I figured he would.*

He nodded, a glimmer of a smile touching his lips as he crossed his arms over his chest and rocked back and forth slightly in his chair. "I can almost hear him now."

"I'll bet." Her rib cage tightened, and she fanned her fingers across her chest as if that would calm her pounding heart.

"Colleen—"

"Wouldn't know the first thing about helping me with any of this."

"Have you thought about asking another friend?"

She laughed outright at the desperate look on his face. "Isn't that what I'm doing? You might be my boss and, although we aren't as close as you and Nick, we're friends. At least I thought we were."

His smile vanished to be replaced by a somber expression. One that hardened his jawline and made her legs rubbery.

"Like you said, I'm your boss. Hell, I'm your brother's best friend—"

"And my friend, too. We practically grew up together. Not that we share secrets, play poker, or hang out after work, but…" She shrugged, hoping in the process to shrug off some of her apprehension. "We are friends," she whispered, as if trying to convince herself.

She fumbled with the black and white penguin buttons on her black sweater, twisting one tightly as she blinked to clear her somewhat foggy vision. *Don't you dare tear up.* "I know our past conversations consisted mostly of is-that-software-ready, or pass-me-the-green-beans at Sunday dinner. That's my fault because I suck at conversation, but that alone should prove to you how much I need your help."

"So you decide instead of easing into some conversation, you'd jump in headfirst?" Humor flecked his eyes again.

*What the heck didn't he get?* She wasn't playing around. Her stomach did a little dance as she licked her lips. "I'd think you'd consider that I came to you a huge compliment."

"Compliment?" Jared's laugh came out hollow and uncertain. "I never expected anyone, especially you"—he ran one hand roughly through his hair—"to come to me with a request like this."

She'd laugh at the absurdity of this conversation if she didn't take it so seriously. "That's probably because you don't know anyone else who has my problem. You're surrounded by beautiful people, and none of them are in need of—"

"A makeover?" He stood and came around to the front of his desk. "You need a makeover about as much as I need to grow a few inches."

This time she did laugh. Not just any laugh, but the one that threw a soft snort in for good measure. She slapped her hand over her nose and gave him credit for acting like he hadn't noticed her less than gracious reaction to his comment.

Instead, he towered over her, regarding her through his incredibly blue eyes. Besides his confidence, height, complexion, and perfect hair, his eyes were his best feature.

"Please don't go into the same spiel as Nick. I can't take that speech two days in a row."

His lips twitched. "Nick's a smart man."

Even though she was standing, she actually had to tilt her head back to meet his gaze. Not that she was short by any means, but his six-three height and broad shoulders always made her feel small, and for the first time since she'd known him, a little breathless. How come she'd never seen him as intimidating until now?

"You're not looking at me as a woman—"

"Of course I am. I see you almost every day. I'm pretty sure I know you're a woman."

She shook her head and mentally rolled her eyes. "No wonder you fit into my family so well."

"Now that I take as a compliment."

"You drive me as crazy as Dad, Gramps, and Nick." Did none of them understand a woman's feelings or fears? Why would they? She'd only recently started to understand them herself.

"Al—"

"You need to stop looking at me as your best bud's little sister. An employee you see around the office day in and day out. The way everyone sees me, if they notice me at all." She pinched the penguin button until she winced, then rubbed her fingers along the seam of her pants to soothe the sting. "I'm tired of being the background noise that nobody really notices," she whispered. A tug of emotion pulled at her chest, and she swallowed the threat of tears at the back of her throat. She'd peptalked herself all the way to his office about not allowing her emotions to take control. She didn't want anyone's pity, especially Jared's. But she did need his help.

Maybe she'd been insane for thinking she could go to him. Confident people like Jared didn't get it. But he'd always seemed approachable and willing to lend a hand.

He rubbed the side of his neck and sighed. A sound so deep and full it resonated around the walls of his office and almost made her feel guilty for interrupting his work day.

She closed her eyes and forced herself to take a few deep, calming breaths. Last night, after Nick had shot down her request for help, she'd played around with her idea—her deepest wish—and had taken it one step further. Over her Lean Cuisine dinner for one, she'd jotted down ideas to implement a plan of personal change that would hopefully alter her life. She wanted, no *needed*, a chance to fit in and shine. But to do that she'd need help. An advisor of sorts. Someone the complete opposite of her.

Which is why she'd approached Nick first. He'd always been popular. The athlete, the man in charge, with charisma and friends from all over the world. But he'd shot her down—blah, blah, blah—and another picture formed in her mind.

A picture of Jared.

Although Nick was everything she wasn't—confident, good-looking, charming, funny, comfortable in his own skin—so was Jared. Maybe even more so. He oozed confidence. From the way he stood, walked, spoke, and even rode his motorcycle. And it didn't hurt that he was easy on the eyes. The perfect, unbiased person to help.

Then, while eating lunch—*had that really only been fifteen short minutes ago?*—as she studied several of her coworkers chatting and laughing in the break room, the idea she'd tossed around the night before hit her square between the eyes. Somehow, in that moment, it hadn't seemed too silly or crazy.

Desperation to fit in seized her as she sat at a round table for six—five of the chairs empty—in the center of the sun-filled room. She'd picked at her salad while groups around her chatted about happenings, made plans to meet after work to kick off the weekend with drinks, or talked about an upcoming date with someone new. Conversations and laughter swirled around the room, but nobody noticed her. Nobody ever did. Not at work or anywhere else. If she wanted to fit in, score an invite now and then—a date, for Pete's sake—she needed to get noticed. She needed change.

Now. Not later.

Before she could talk herself out of it, she'd chucked her barely touched salad into the trash and made her way to Jared's office. Now, here she stood. Her stomach growling and her heart pounding so hard and fast it just might punch a hole in her sternum. She studied his concerned expression and patted the small notebook in her pocket as if it would give her all the answers to persuade him to help. Instead her newfound and short-lived confidence fell away and puddled at her feet. Her head swam, and panic rose in her chest. She fought to gain some control, but the blood rushing through her body vibrated inside her ears, and she closed her eyes.

"I don't understand, Al."

His soft words—and the fact he used her nickname—dragged her back to the present. She let out a breath.

"You don't need my help. Or anyone else's for that matter. You can do anything you set your mind to. You've proven it again and again. You work in a male-dominated field, and you own it. You graduated from high school at the age of sixteen and then went on to college and earned not one but two degrees." He punctuated his statement by holding up two fingers, as if that would make his words more effective. "Those are two examples that take some level of confidence. You're selling yourself short."

She wouldn't bother correcting him. Not only had she double majored in computer science and information technology, but she had also minored in business. *Hello, I'm the biggest geek in the land.* Or maybe the fact that her nonexistent social life had left her plenty of hours in the day to study played into the equation of overachievement.

His intent gaze had her shifting her weight from one foot to the other. She'd never been comfortable being the center of attention. It was clear he hoped she'd suddenly realize he was right and she didn't need to be made over. She hated to disappoint him, but that wasn't going to happen.

She had to make him understand. Not that she didn't have a backup plan—because come hell or high water, *thanks for instilling another cliché into my life, Gramps*—she'd find a way. With or without help. But she'd prefer help.

"You need to look at me through the eyes of a stranger." Allison challenged him with the lift of her chin as she brushed her hand down the length of her body. Her own gaze flickered across the front of her beige blouse and even more beige slacks, then down to her feet. *What possessed you to wear white sneakers with slacks? To work no less. And beige clothes? Really?* At least her sweater gave her a splash of color. *Yeah, black. Loads of color there. And penguin buttons, too? How old are you? Six?* She'd taken over her mom's collection of penguins when she'd been a teen and over the years had grown to love everything about them.

As for the lack of color, she'd always dressed this way, blending into her surroundings like a chameleon. But lately it'd become a huge irritant—she didn't want to blend in. She took a step toward Jared, thanking her lucky stars her klutzy habit of tripping over her own feet when she was nervous didn't make an appearance. It was bad enough she'd snort-laughed. She rested her hands on her hips and squared her shoulders to give herself added height—and hopefully conviction. "Look at me. What do you see?"

Blood pounded in her ears as a heavy silence filled the room. His gaze took a leisurely walk down her front and then back up until their eyes locked. Heat devoured her flesh as if he'd actually touched her. And she liked it. She pushed her thoughts aside. Now wasn't the time to go all weak-kneed because someone looked at her longer than three seconds. *This is Jared, for Pete's sake.* He may be good-looking, but they were from opposite ends of the universe. All she wanted from him was his help.

She swallowed as she waited for him to say something. At the same time she feared hearing the *B* word. *Boring*. But that was exactly what she was.

"Allison Hall. Little sister to my best friend and business

partner. An exceptionally smart woman who always gets the job done. A hard worker. Dedicated. Loyal. Smart. A little quirky, master of mashed potatoes, and confident with a capital *C*." Jared dropped down onto the edge of his desk, folding his arms as he studied her through narrowed eyes. As if he dared her to argue his appraisal.

Silly man. Of course she'd challenge him—even though he liked her mashed potatoes.

"Then you're blind. I might be confident when it comes to discussions about computers, or anything to do with my job, because I know what I'm talking about, but when it comes to the real world, I'm lost. I need an extreme makeover. Maybe one of the extremist. And I've decided you're the person to help."

He grinned, shaking his head. His slightly too long dark brown hair rubbed against the collar of his striped shirt. "I think you're exaggerating."

"Would you have noticed me in a crowd?" Heck, there were days she didn't even see her own reflection in the mirror when she passed by one. Yes, she even bored herself. "I'm sure over the years there have been times when you've been at my dad's and forgotten I was in the room."

Her heart sank when he didn't deny it.

"If you were older, I'd think you were having a midlife crisis."

"And if you were funnier, I'd laugh."

The tension in her shoulders evaporated when he grinned. "Touché."

"Maybe I'm having my midlife crisis early." Her lips twitched as humor flecked the lines around his eyes. "I didn't come up with this idea over my lunch break, you know. It's been brewing for a while. Only I didn't know how to fix it until now."

"And I'm the golden-ticket holder?" He smirked.

She sighed. Her fingers ached to shake him until he could see her point. "Look at how I'm dressed. My makeup, or lack thereof. My hair. My nonexistent social skills…everything. This isn't normal; I'm not normal. But with your help, I can be."

"Bullshit. You're the most normal person I know." The laugh lines disappeared, and his face sobered.

"I don't feel normal."

He rubbed his chin. "I think—"

"Come on, Jared. I need to make some changes, but I have no clue how or where to begin, except to ask for your help." A thick curtain of hair settled across her face as she paced and then swung back around to face him. She refused to hide behind it, no matter how much she wanted to. She flung the long, unmanageable length over her shoulder and swiped her sweaty palms down the pleat of her pants. *I can do this.*

Maybe if she'd had a woman role model in her life things would have been different. But being raised by Dad, Gramps, and Nick—who was only a few years older but decades advanced in his ability to act like a protective adult—she hadn't stood a chance of learning anything remotely feminine. And the few friends she had weren't much help. They'd all been cast from the same nerd mold and were as socially inept as she was. None of them—including her bestie, Colleen—would be able to dole out advice on makeup, clothes, or flirting.

If only her mom were here.

Her heart clenched. Amanda Hall had been taken in a tragic car accident when Allison had barely been two. Although Gramps and her dad kept pictures around the house and shared stories, Allison had no memories of her own. She wished she remembered the woman with whom she shared the same hair and eyes. But there the similarities ended; all the pictures of her mother showed a woman who radiated confidence from the way she stood, smiled, and the look in her eyes. No wonder her dad still mourned her. She must've been extra special.

"You can't even fathom what it feels like to be me, Jared. I'm a total mess."

His eyes softened. He reached out as if to offer her comfort, but before he touched her his hand fell away, and he sighed. "You are not a mess."

"You should consider getting your eyes checked. I'm the stereotypical girl-geek that you see in every movie. If we were in a horror flick, I'd be the first to get the ax."

His laugh—deep, rich, and from the gut—gave her the courage to continue.

"I'm through being the predictable, boring woman you can set your clock by. If I want to get ahead in my professional life, as well as my personal life, changes need to be made. Those changes start with boosting my confidence. And confidence starts with looking and feeling better about myself. A makeover from head to toe."

He sat tall, his shoulders stiffening. "Like I said, you're fine and—"

"I'm not like you." She swallowed hard, her mind racing to find the words to convince him to help. She blew several wayward strands of hair from her eyes as she pushed her heels together. "I can't just walk into a room of strangers and win them over with a witty comment or a bright smile. People don't hang on my every word. The only reason I don't get yawned out of Firstline Security functions is because I'm related to one of the bosses. Who'd be crazy enough to offend Nick's little sister at the office Christmas party? I've considered doling out toothpicks so that people can at least look like they're awake when I'm talking." She sucked in a gulp of air in an attempt to lower the pitch of her voice. "But that wouldn't stop the way people's eyes glaze over whenever

I approach. That wouldn't stop me from eating lunch alone day in and day out."

He cleared his throat. "You have a great sense of humor. Use it to your advantage. You just need practice. You need more—"

"Confidence?" She shifted her weight to one leg, fighting the urge to tap her foot.

"It'll just take time. Nothing happens overnight."

His sympathetic voice gnawed at her gut. "Overnight? I've had my quota of overnights. Don't you think by the age of twenty-three some level of confidence and social know-how should've kicked in?"

"Our conversation right now is going just fine. You don't seem uncomfortable in the least." He held up his hands and stared at her wide-eyed. "And look, no toothpicks."

She rolled her eyes and choked out a laugh. "Of course I can talk to you. You're practically family. Plus, we don't have an audience." She spread her arms before her, encompassing the room with her glance. "What I need help with are social situations with coworkers, business associates, anything that involves a group larger than two and isn't business-related. You're the one who suggested I push for a few independent consultant jobs to add to my résumé, but how can I do that if I freeze up at the idea of approaching someone?"

"I've seen you conduct hundreds of meetings. You always sound confident."

She growled in frustration. "Because I'm talking shop. I know my job. I'm uber-confident there, but the whole idea of approaching someone on a personal level scares the heck out of me."

"I can help you get business contacts. I told you that already." He released a barely audible sigh when she pursed her lips. "As long as you don't let them lure you away once they find out how amazing you are at your job."

They stared at each other in silence until Allison plopped down in the chair before his desk and groaned, pushing her glasses up the bridge of her nose again. "You still don't get it."

"I don't. I can't help you with your confidence. It'll come with exposure. Keep putting yourself out there. Read some current events so you have something to talk about. Look up some jokes. Take the first step here at work. Don't wait for an invite but extend your own."

"You make it sound so easy. It's not." The mere idea of approaching her coworkers to ask them out for drinks or coffee sent her mind and heart racing out of control. Even now her palms grew sweaty. She'd always lacked confidence, but deep inside she knew if she made a few changes on the outside it would result in even bigger changes on the inside.

He rubbed the side of his neck. "I don't know. I'm no confidence expert. And what the hell would I know about makeup or women's clothes?"

The fact that he thought about it so seriously gave her hope, and she sat forward.

"You know what a man likes, don't you? I'd think a man would be the best shopping buddy in the world to help out a woman like me." She shrugged. "As for makeup, through the years you've dated some of the most beautiful, poised, and elegant women I've ever seen. The best part is that you've remained friendly with all your exes." She had no clue how he pulled it off, but none of his splits had been bitter. Once he dated a woman he had a friend for life. "Can't you introduce me to one or two of them who'd be willing to share some secrets?"

"I think—"

"With a new wardrobe and hair and makeup skills, I'd be golden. Ready to tackle the world in heels." She followed his gaze south. He lifted his brow as he took in her well-worn, white sneakers—complete with scuffs and bright pink shoelaces with dancing penguins. She rubbed one foot over the other as if that would hide them. "Or at least something besides sneakers or flats."

"Why now? After all these years, why are you so focused on making changes? You always seem happy."

A shiver wrapped around the length of her spine and squeezed. She swallowed the ball of emotion working its way up the back of her throat and closed her eyes for a second to stop the sting of tears from her own tortured thoughts.

"Like I said before, this didn't just pop into my head. I've lost count of the number of times I've embarrassed myself in social settings. I know that my fashion sense is about two decades behind. I tried to make changes on my own, but I don't know what to wear with what, which colors to put together, fabrics to choose, flattering styles..." She threw her hands out to her sides and fell back into the chair, focusing on the wooden beams crossing the ceiling to keep the threat of tears in check. She pulled herself up and sat forward. "Look at me. Beige is the safest color combo I know. But I don't want to be safe. Not anymore."

"But—"

"I want to eat lunch with my coworkers. I want them to ask me to meet after work for a drink. I want to walk down the street and feel awesome because I'm wearing something flattering, colorful. I want to feel like a woman, act like a woman, look like a woman. Not just any woman, but someone people won't forget three seconds after they meet me." She stood, pulling in a lungful of air. "When I enter a room, I'd like people to sit up and take notice. Respect me. I want them to *want* to talk to me, listen to me. Basically, Jared, I want to be the female version of you. When you walk into a room you command attention. You know what to say and do. How to dress. Not that I need to have all eyes on me all the time, but once in a while might be nice." Her insides felt inflamed with her wants and desires, her desperate need for acceptance. If she looked feminine, she'd act and feel feminine. She took another deep breath, twisting her hands in front of her as her attention shifted from the floor to his face. "I want to fit in."

"Everyone loves you. You fit in. Looks aren't everything."

"Looks aren't everything," she whispered to herself. Her chest tightened, and she laughed dryly, only registering the last part of his comment. "Maybe not in the long run, but you have to admit that first impressions are invaluable."

He opened then closed his mouth, and another tiny spark of hope filled her chest that maybe finally he'd get it.

"You're one of those people, Jared. I want a little of what you have. Come on, even the women you date prove that confidence wins. They all have beauty, brains, talent—you name anyone with those attributes and Jared Esterly has probably dated her, or will shortly. I've never seen you with someone like me. Quiet, mousy, invisible."

He furrowed his brow. "Are you calling me a snob?"

"No. I'm saying opposites may attract but not when it comes to confidence. Confident people stick together, and I want some of that." The air in the room grew thick. "All I'm asking for is your guidance. Teach me."

The hard edges of his face softened. "So you want me to take you shopping and then introduce you to some of my lady friends who'll help you with makeup?"

She nodded, trying to quash the excitement in her gut at the acceptance in his voice. Would he finally say yes?

"Yes. And there's one more thing." The idea to ask him for this added bit of help hadn't occurred to her until now. Her face roared with heat, and beads of sweat dotted the back of her neck. Her fingers automatically found one of her buttons again and twisted.

"What's that?"

"My life's been so involved in getting an education and

building my career I've barely dated."

"It's not like you're over the hill, Al." His eyes sparkled with mischief.

"I need to play catch-up. Not only am I asking for your help with a makeover, but..." She could feel her throat closing off. How could she say this?

His face sobered, but even his obvious interest and relaxed attitude didn't make what she had to say any easier.

*Just say it.* She took a steady breath and blurted, "I want to find someone special. I want to find love. Build a future."

"I can see all of that for you."

"Good, because I want you to give me some dating advice. Through example."

# Chapter Two

"You what?" His voice boomed, and he almost fell off the side of his desk, but managed to catch himself in pure confident Jared fashion. She'd never heard him raise his voice, but even through the boom he echoed strength and authority, and it gave her an odd level of comfort.

"Keep your voice down." She pressed her finger to her lips as she swung around to make sure his office door was closed. The last thing she wanted was for Nick and Jared's assistant, Maureen, to hear any part of their conversation. She'd never be able to look the older woman in the eye again. And she'd hate that, because she liked Maureen and their casual office friendship.

"You want me to date you?" His voice didn't just return to normal but went full-blown library level.

"Don't sound so thrilled. I'm not asking for a lifetime commitment." In order to defuse the situation she choked out a laugh, disappointed that she didn't have the skill required to sound flippant and at ease.

He released a lengthy sigh—at the same time raking his

fingers through his hair again, with the added element of white knuckles. His deep brown hair always had that tousled appearance, and she'd bet money the thick waves would be soft and tickle her fingers. Not to mention he'd smell good. From a distance he sure did—a soothing sandalwood—so up close and personal would probably be hypnotizing.

She calmed her racing mind, pressing her palms flat on her thighs. Why the heck was she thinking about Jared's hair or how he smelled?

*Nerves. Right?* Anything to take her mind off this awkward conversation. Her hand automatically slid into her sweater pocket, searching for her standard soothing Hershey's Kiss—the surefire remedy to pacify her nerves—but her fingers found only her tiny notebook and a balled-up wad of tinfoil wrappers. She'd used her reserves.

She opened her mouth and her lips moved, but nothing came out. Okay, at this point any type of chocolate would do.

"I didn't mean it as an insult. You know me better than that." Jared folded his arms. His shirt stretched taut over his shoulders, and once again the awareness of him saturated her senses. What would all that muscle hidden under his shirt feel like? She rubbed her palms along her pants.

She forced her eyes from his shoulders and met his face. His stoic expression suddenly became funny. Had humor become the easiest way for her to release some of her frustration? She grinned, holding his gaze as she gauged his reaction. "My makeover is kind of a two-parter."

"You don't say?" His lips compressed, and one brow rose at a harrowing angle.

She bit off her laugh, but he didn't bother as he released a throaty chuckle.

Allison cleared her throat. "The changes tie in together. Personal and professional."

"Really? I don't see how anyone's dating habits, or lack

thereof, affects their work or their confidence."

He had somewhat of a point, but so did she. No way could she just spew out her story. She had to lead into it. "Other than lacking confidence, my professional life is going fairly well. I love my job, I know I'm good at it, and the consultant idea will be a great addition to my résumé…if I can learn to function in a social situation without balling into a knot." She shrugged as if none of this mattered, when in reality it meant more than she'd ever be able to put into words.

"And?" He leaned forward as if she were about to answer the probing questions about what the universe was made of, Area 51, and why we dream.

"I also need confidence to achieve a personal goal. As in dating. Finding love."

"Finding love?" He mouthed the words more than spoke them.

She nodded. "I want a man in my life. Not because I need one, but because I want one. I want love, someone to share my life with…" Her voice faded away, and she swallowed. Hard. Her admission had become more difficult than asking him for makeover help. "And, to be clear, I'm not asking for you to be that guy—so you don't have to break out in a sweat or consider working remotely from another country—I only want you to teach me how to date."

Nervous energy bounced off him as he stood, picked up a pen from his desk, and began clicking. His tight shoulders and the way he paced back and forth in front of his desk told her just how much she'd taken him by surprise.

He stopped pacing, turned toward her, and groaned again, dropping his rear back onto the edge of his desk, his thumb working faster as he clicked his pen. "And what the hell would Nick say? Your dad? Hell, your grandfather? You think they'd just ignore us dating?"

His thick voice coated her like hot fudge on ice cream.

She dropped back down into her chair. For some reason, his agitation affected her on a whole new level. Was it because she'd shared a part of herself she'd never told anyone? Or was it because the idea of dating him more than appealed to her? Even if it weren't real. It gave her that rush of excitement her life lacked. Almost as much as the idea of sitting on the back of his motorcycle with her hands pressed flat against his six-pack. Because he would surely have a six-pack.

*Heck, you might be asking for more than you can handle.*

"I don't know. I didn't think that far ahead." Very unlike her. The tiny space between them seemed nonexistent, and she fought to keep her voice steady.

He shook his head, repeating her words under his breath before saying, "Why me, Al? I mean, to some extent I am flattered, but what made you think— "

"Because I'm comfortable around you. I have a good sense that you'd never judge me. Hurt me. You're patient and kind. And more importantly, I trust you. Not to mention you're pretty damn hot." Her hand flew to her mouth. She hadn't meant to say that out loud, no matter how often she'd thought it.

Surprise flecked his eyes, and he smiled. "You're not so bad yourself, you know?"

"Now I have no choice but to book that eye exam for you."

They shared a laugh. A short, kind of uncomfortable one that two new friends who were just getting to know each other might share.

His Adam's apple bobbed as he swallowed. "That doesn't stop me from considering your family. If I help you with a makeover, take you on dates… I know them. Not only is Nick protective of you, your entire family is. We'd be— "

"Opening an entirely new can of worms."

"That's one way of putting it." His low laugh warmed her

heart, and she followed the movement of his fingers as he rubbed his chin, slowly, as if he were considering her idea, or trying to find a way out of it.

"It's not like I live at home. Heck, sometimes I don't see my family for days." She shrugged, trying to keep the desperation out of her voice. "They'd never have to know. I hadn't planned on sitting down over leftover meatloaf and mashed potatoes to tell them you were going to be the Professor Higgins to my Eliza."

They sat in silence for what seemed an eternity before Jared exhaled a long breath. She scooted to the edge of her seat and touched his knee.

He swiped his palms down the legs of his trousers and gripped her hand. A serious shroud covered his face. "I don't like the idea of feeling like I'm doing something behind your family's back. Not after the way they've welcomed me into their lives and taken me in when I had no place to go during holidays. They've been there for major milestones—some that my own family didn't care enough about to support—and all the Sunday dinners, birthdays… Hell, everything." He released her hand as he flung his arms out to his side.

His steely-eyed glare made her pulse race and her eye twitch. She lowered her gaze to study the black scuff on the toe of her shoe. Uncertainty roared through her as he stood, turning away from her as the incessant click of his pen filled the room.

This had been a total mistake. *No it hasn't.* Her mind fogged over as her sneakers came into bright focus. Seeing her ugly shoes pushed a dose of courage through her veins. She had to make Jared understand. Get him to agree to help. All in the name of replacing her boring white and beige life for a pop of spicy salsa red. She needed a splash of color. She could do this.

Allison took a deep breath and met Jared's noncommittal

expression. She hated to beg, but she'd do whatever it took. "I've always been the brainiac nobody bothered to glance at twice. I kept my nose in a book all through school, never veered off the path toward being successful. I missed every school dance, only had a handful of friends who were all as bashful and as awkward as me. I've kissed one guy my entire life—and no, Gramps, Dad, and Nick don't count—and I'm tired of the path I'm on. I'm happy, but I know I can be happier. I deserve to have what's missing in my life. I want to up the ante on my career, make new friendships, get a social life, find love, and hopefully have a family of my own someday. It would be a lot easier if you'd agree but, with or without your help, I'm doing this."

She waved away his unspoken words when he opened his mouth.

"I'm being honest here, Jared, I need to make these changes as much as I need to breathe."

•••

*Shit, she has me pegged all wrong.* His life wasn't as perfect as the picture in her mind, and he wasn't the confirmed bachelor everyone thought. At least he didn't want to be that guy.

If only he could reach into his desk and grab one of those damn Hershey's Kisses. He could always think through a problem with a little chocolate. He blamed that on his mom.

He'd almost been swayed enough to help Allison with the makeover, but going deeper—as in dating each other? Not. A. Chance. He couldn't cross that line of trust between him and Nick without fists flying. Hell, Nick knew him better than most, and Jared was no fucking idiot. He'd be the last guy Nick would want dating his kid sister. No matter if it was strictly for the sake of advice or not. There were some lines that friends didn't cross. And this was a big thick line highlighted with neon and lit up with flashing signs.

The Halls were like family. And even though Allison remained on the sidelines, she came as a package deal with Nick. Although he'd learned more about her in the last ten minutes than he had over the last decade, he'd always respected her. Liked her because…

*Because she's Nick's kid sister.*

But something else held him back even more than his relationship with the Hall family. He wanted what she wanted: love. A future with someone special. And he had no idea how to make that happen.

What if he did agree to help her and she ended up in the same predicament as him?

Loveless. Alone. Searching.

All because he hadn't figured out the secret to that part of happiness any more than she had.

He studied her as she concentrated all her attention on her shoes and then glanced up to meet his gaze, adjusting her glasses and squinting at him through the clear lenses. She was cute, in a sister kind of way. He hated hearing her put herself down. She acted like she was the hunchback of Chicago—and she was far from it. She might not be the glamorous type he usually went for, but that didn't mean she wasn't right for someone.

He'd like to help her. But he couldn't.

"I can't help you find love." The words spilled out before he even realized he'd voiced them.

She frowned up at him with the most serious line marring her brow as she pushed the mop of hair falling over her forehead out of her face. Her big brown eyes studied him intently. "But you can give me the building blocks. You know what a man likes. What turns a guy on, gets his attention about the way a woman dresses and moves. You can help me find confidence. I don't want to be inadequate anymore and…"

The pain in her eyes nearly severed his heart. She looked away, but he lifted her chin with his finger. He needed to look into her eyes. Big and soft and passionate. Windows to her thoughts. "What happened that makes you think you're inadequate? Because you're anything but."

She pulled his hand from her chin and patted it softly before releasing it, as if she needed to comfort him instead of the other way around.

"Lance."

"The guy you dated from college?" His gut tightened. He'd only met the guy a handful of times and had liked him less with each meeting.

She nodded. "We were pretty serious for a while."

"I remember."

"Until the night we decided to do the deed and he laughed at me when he found out I was a virgin." Her voice faded away on the last word. "I can't believe I just told you that."

Jared's protective instincts rushed forth, and he curled his fists at his sides. Why would anyone laugh at Al? More importantly, what was so damn funny about being a virgin? Men dreamed of being a girl's first. And being a virgin as an adult was almost unheard of nowadays. For some reason her whispered confession kind of turned him on, and he hated himself for it. He could almost feel Nick's fingers wrapping around his throat.

He massaged his neck. "So I'm going to assume his laughter spoiled the moment?"

"That's an understatement. We had a huge fight and broke up. I couldn't believe he laughed at me. As if he had a bevy of beautiful babes waiting in the wings to sex him up on demand. Jerk."

"Did you tell him that you were giving him the biggest gift of all by sharing your virginity?"

She tilted her head to the side, and a smile tugged at the

edges of her lips. "Do you read historical romances on the sly?"

"No. No." His face burned, but he managed a strained smile. Since when had he become one to get embarrassed? Of course he'd never discussed virginity—sex in general—with Al. As a matter of fact, their current conversation had been the lengthiest they'd ever shared. With one of the most difficult topics. "I'm just saying that he should've felt honored. I can't tell you the last time I—"

"Met a virgin?" she whispered. "They're sort of like unicorns, right?"

They laughed, no discomfort like the last time.

She might be shy and quiet, but she'd never be the type of woman a man could walk over. "Don't you see how much confidence it took for you to break up with Lance after what he did?"

"I think that was due more to anger than confidence."

"Have you considered that you just haven't met the right guy yet?"

Her doe-like brown eyes grew large, and she smiled. "Most definitely. But in order to meet the right guy, I need to have the right tools."

"I think this entire idea is crazy. Are you letting one idiot from your past determine your future? I've always enjoyed our conversations, so I know you're okay in that department. As for your appearance, maybe you need to look in the mirror and not judge yourself so harshly. You have beautiful eyes, perfect teeth, and hair most women would kill for."

"You sound like you're buying a racehorse."

He shook his head and smiled. "Not to mention you're funny, smart—"

"You already went over those last items." She laughed a little self-consciously as she twisted her button so hard she pulled it from the thread and slipped it into her pocket in one brisk move. "Thanks for the pep talk, but the only thing you've convinced me of is that I want a makeover now more than ever. All of it combined will only help in my quest for love. And from there I'll be more confident when the time comes for me…"

A deep blush roared over her face, and she dropped her gaze.

"All of that will happen in time. No matter what Lance led you to believe, sex is special. Don't give it away." *Where the hell had that come from?*

"I don't need another brother." A slow, tenuous smile filled her face. "Don't try to tell me that every time you've had sex the woman was special."

"I've made mistakes. I have regrets. You don't have to."

Her shoulders slumped. "Lance told me that no man wants an inexperienced woman in his bed."

"Who made Lance the expert?"

She shot him a glare. "Well, I believe him. Why would any guy want some fumbling idiot making lame attempts to turn him on? I'm sure that'd have the opposite effect."

Jared shook his head, but before he could get a word out, she grabbed his hand and squeezed.

"I want to go into that part of a relationship knowing what the heck I'm doing. I want to turn on my man with a touch, a glance. Drive him crazy with a kiss, make him want more. I want the all-consuming relationship both inside and outside the bedroom. A good sexual relationship will enhance everything. The bond and closeness, those intimate touches and looks in public. I want it all. I want the man in my life to have it all."

For some reason her words took his breath away, and he sucked in a lungful of air to steady his heart. He'd never expected to hear anything like that from Al. Never.

It made his own wants and desires burn hot inside him.

He ached for all that she talked about—and more.

"Now who's been reading romance?" he teased in an effort to lighten the mood.

"Sorry to disappoint, but most of my info comes from magazines and articles I've read on the internet." She released his hand and then sat back in her seat, closing her eyes briefly as if collecting her thoughts.

He'd watched his parents struggle their entire married life. They had loved each other, but in an unconventional way. One that didn't involve them being in the same state—*hell, city for that matter*—longer than a few weeks a year. They'd been horrible role models, but he hadn't let them crush his deepest desire to have a woman he could love and worship above all others.

Al's words reminded him that he longed for the same thing she did. Not just the sex, but that intimate bond between a man and a woman.

A sudden weight settled over his chest, and he struggled to stay focused and do something as naturally as breathe. He'd almost lost touch with his own dream of a future. Thank God for Al, for making him come back down to earth. Deep inside he knew only one thing could make him whole. Complete.

The love of a woman. The ultimate bond.

Over the years he'd searched so hard for the perfect woman he'd turned into a serial dater. None of the women he'd met lasted longer than the latest electronic gadget, and as time went by he'd given up on finding Miss Right. Settling instead for Miss-Right-Now. Dating for fun, laughs, the short term.

Hell, if he were honest, all the women in his life had been amazing, but none had held his interest like he wanted.

Maybe he needed to make a few changes of his own. Omar and Roth had done it. They were two of the luckiest sons of bitches he knew. They'd never even wanted that type of love—and Jared had never shared with them that he had—but they'd found it. In spades.

He could, too.

But how? The very idea of trying again scared the shit out of him.

"Jared?"

He came crashing back to the moment as Al's eyes pleaded with him.

Although he liked that she had approached him—respected the fact she'd veered from her comfort zone, because he knew she had—how the hell could he help her when he couldn't even help himself?

Blood pounded in his ears as he moved toward the windows. He lifted a slat of the blinds and peered outside. His back stiffened, and he rolled his shoulders in an attempt to loosen the grip of the fabric. A stream of sunshine lit a path along his hand, and he turned to follow it across his desktop and farther still to where it spilled across Al's slacks.

She stood, brushing at the light that she couldn't really erase. "Well?"

"I'm beyond flattered, but I'm not the man for the job. Sorry, Al."

•••

Disappointment hit Allison like a tidal wave the moment Jared's office door clicked closed behind her. Her eyes flickered shut, and she took a few deep breaths.

"You okay, hon?"

Allison jumped at the sound of Maureen's soft voice. She'd forgotten where she was for a moment and pasted a smile on her face as she met the concern filling Maureen's mossy green eyes. She looked past her at Nick's closed office door. At least she didn't have to worry about him putting in an appearance, since he was out of town until next week.

"You look like you've seen a ghost."

The ghost of what her future held maybe? More humdrum boringness. "I'm fine. I think I just stood up too fast."

"You want me to get you a glass of water?" Maureen pushed her keyboard aside as she stood. "Maybe you need to have a seat."

Allison motioned her to sit down. "No. I'm okay." She eyed the abstract metal clock filling the wall behind the woman's desk. Time to make an exit before Maureen asked any more questions. "If I want to finish up the comparisons I'm working on before the weekend starts, I better get back to work."

"Okay..." Maureen's voice faded as she slowly reclaimed her seat.

Allison rushed from the airy room that had suddenly become suffocating. She made her way into the empty corridor and rounded the corner before she sagged against the wall to regain her composure. Her body grew numb, and she shook out her hands, as if that would shed the tension road-mapping her body.

Now what? *Plan B. I'll have to do this solo.* She'd made the decision to make some changes. She couldn't let one little bump in the road stop her.

More internet searches. Magazines. The library again. Everything sounded tiring and daunting, but she had no choice if she planned to make this work.

She reached inside her pocket, remembering the moment her fingers touched the ball of tinfoil that her reserve of Hershey's Kisses was used up.

The lack of chocolate was neither here nor there. Changes would be made with or without Jared's help or a dose of chocolate. As for the issue of dating—for now she'd comfort herself with the idea that once she changed her looks, confidence would build and dates would follow.

From there, being the oldest virgin in the land would fix itself. Right? *Definitely.*

*Maybe I could place an ad, conduct interviews? Check the yellow pages—or better yet, Google—for sex gods who moonlighted as sexual mentors?* No way could she be the only person on the planet who needed sexual mentoring. Could she? She giggled and snorted at the same time, covering her mouth as her eyes darted up and down the empty corridor.

Not that she was in a hurry to lose her virginity. And Jared was right, she didn't want to give it away, but she didn't want to keep it until it became an antique, either.

Allison massaged her temples. She'd think about the sex part later. She squared her shoulders and resumed her trek down the hallway.

Her steps faltered as she moved past the break room where some of the staff were eating a late lunch. A group of young women—all about her age—sat around the table she'd vacated not even an hour before. They all looked so happy, at ease, comfortable with themselves and one another. She jammed her hands into her pockets and tried to quash the pulling sensation tearing at her gut. She pinched the ball of wrappers, rolling the pebble-sized foil between her thumb and forefinger.

Determination with a smidgeon of desperation surged through her. *I can do this.* She'd start tonight, right after work. The entire weekend would be devoted to her efforts. Come Monday morning she'd arrive at the office, and there'd be some changes. Some noticeable changes.

Glenda and her cohort Andrea pushed past her. "Hey, Allison," they said in unison.

"Hey," she said.

They feigned friendliness, but Allison had seen their attacks on too many others to buy into their fake smiles.

Glenda learned your weaknesses, and Andrea helped her go in for the kill. She'd seen them both shred coworkers in the past, although they usually left her alone. More than likely because of Nick.

Allison squared her shoulders as she continued down the hall, forcing her steps to remain light. She swiped her badge to enter her secure work area, tripping over her loose shoelace as she stepped inside the dimly lit room abuzz with computers and rapid key tapping. Kenny, Pete, and Nate didn't even glance up. But that was nothing new.

She smiled to herself as she pulled out her chair and plopped into the seat, retying her laces and then typing in her password. The chocolate Kisses in the bowl beside her keyboard called her name. She plucked out a tinfoil-wrapped sweet, quickly unwrapped it, and popped the chocolate into her mouth. She dropped the wrapper into her pocket to be added to the ball later.

Her leg bounced quickly underneath her desk and she quieted it with her hand, gripping her knee so tight she actually winced. She glanced around to check if the guys had heard her knee hit the desk. They hadn't. Nate and Kenny had their earbuds ground so tightly into their heads they probably couldn't hear themselves think, and Pete always had a glazed expression and seemed to be in his own world.

The chocolate in her mouth grew smaller and smaller as she rolled it around her tongue. Today would be the first day of the rest of her life. Didn't she have a keychain that said something to that effect?

Gone were the days of dressing for comfort in outdated clothes. No more shopping the clearance rack or browsing the local secondhand store because she feared going into a fashionable clothing boutique.

She chuckled to herself as she sat taller, tucking a strand of hair behind one ear. And no more rushing past makeup counters because she had no clue what to do with lip liner, foundation, or skin toner. She'd ask the clerk for help. No matter how uncomfortable talking to a stranger might be.

The shy girl who broke out in a cold sweat when thrown into social situations would morph into the confident woman who claimed the room with her presence. Jared might have hit the nail on the head when he suggested she stay on top of current events. She'd have plenty of conversation topics. *How come I never thought of that?*

She knew she couldn't accomplish everything over one weekend. But she could start with something small. How about two somethings small? Both simple. The makeup counter. And she'd dig out the contacts from her bathroom cabinet and give them another try.

Change was exciting, and change was definitely in the air.

# Chapter Three

Allison's feet were cemented to the sidewalk outside the department store window a mere seven hours later. She could see the makeup counter with the well-dressed and perfectly made-up salesclerks smiling from behind the glass countertop, and all her backbone evaporated. They intimidated her. At this rate she'd never open the door and go inside. She shouldn't have worked late. For some reason, during those extra hours, she'd lost her nerve. The hype from her earlier pep talk forgotten.

She'd come off looking like a complete fool if she went in there. All her questions would probably drive them crazy, even though they'd smile and act polite. She didn't even know where to start, what she needed, how to use half—*no, make that 99 percent*—of all the items adorning the counters and shelves. Bottles and tubs and jars and vials full of mystery. At least a mystery to her. How did women know this stuff? Did the makeup gene skip her?

*But the salespeople will help.*

She pressed her hand to her throat, and her pulse pounded

against her fingertips. No way. She couldn't do it. At least not right this moment. She needed more time.

*Damn confidence. Or lack of confidence, to be exact. I'm a grown woman. A successful grown woman with a college education, an amazing job, and, according to Jared, a sense of humor. Quit being so shy.*

She pulled her sweater more firmly around her front and hiked up the strap of her purse as a light wind blew around her. Maybe she should call it day. Try again tomorrow after she slept on it, formed a better plan.

*Chicken.* The voice inside her head echoed.

*Damn straight,* she answered back.

Her phone jiggled in her pocket at the same time she tossed a chocolate into her mouth. She pulled it out of her purse and read the screen. Colleen. Should she let it go to voicemail, or confide her fears and ask for help? After all, if she couldn't count on Jared and didn't dare go into the department store, maybe at the very least Colleen could offer moral support, even if she couldn't give advice. Over the years they'd shared so much.

Except this little quirk into her own insecurities. Her friend probably had no idea how deep this issue ran.

"Hey, where are you?" Allison answered the phone as she sucked on the Kiss.

"I was going to ask you the same thing. Jerry's been gone all week, and I'm going half out of my mind. Conversations with the cats are getting old." Colleen's singsong voice filled her ears. A definite comfort in a moment of sheer panic.

"That's what you get for having a dream job that allows you the luxury of working from home."

"I know. I shouldn't complain. Anyway, are you home yet? Up for some company? I have wine. And I'm already halfway out the door."

Allison could picture Colleen's larger-than-life smile,

her short curly hair bouncing around her face as she hurried around her apartment turning off lights, tracking down her purse, and grabbing a jacket in preparation for her departure.

Allison took a big breath. She needed to confide in someone. "I'll be there shortly. Have to make a pit stop first. What would you think about helping me with a project?"

"What type of project?" Excitement bubbled across the receiver as the sounds of Colleen locking up her apartment door echoed across the phone.

"A makeover."

"Are you redecorating?" The drop of excitement in Colleen's voice made Allison smile. Her friend wasn't into Suzie Homemaker tasks like decorating, vacuuming, or any type of cooking that didn't involve a prepackaged meal and a microwave. How they'd remained friends for so long was a mystery. Maybe opposites did attract, because Allison loved all that homey stuff. She had more in common with Jerry—Mr. Homemaker—than her own bestie.

"In a manner of speaking." She moved away from the department store, her mind made up to take baby steps and shop for makeup at the drugstore down the block from her apartment. The people who worked there were more approachable. More like her. If things went well, and her confidence grew, she'd attempt the department store the next time. Maybe when she worked on her wardrobe.

"I'm not interested in painting, if that's what you have in mind." Colleen's grimace came through loud and clear.

"This makeover involves me, and the painting we'd be doing will be on my face."

"As in makeup?" Colleen laughed, all of her earlier distaste gone as the tingly sound in her voice returned. "Wouldn't that be like the blind leading the blind?"

Allison grinned. Colleen's aversion to makeup rivaled her lack of enthusiasm for most things domestic—actually to anything that she didn't want to do. Ever since they'd been kids, Colleen had played by her own rules, and she wasn't shy about it. "I know you're not a fan, but I could use the moral support."

"Then say no more. Where should I meet you?"

"The drugstore by my apartment. You can help me make some color choices."

"See you there."

For the first time since she left work, the tension skating between her shoulder blades eased. The night wouldn't be a total bust after all.

Allison whipped out the barrette binding the hair at her nape. She shook her head until all her hair fell across her face and then brushed it away from her eyes with her fingers. For some reason all the confidence she'd felt Friday night when Colleen stood at her side vanished with the Monday morning light.

She couldn't do this. Her vulnerabilities came crashing down around her as she stared at her reflection. Fear gripped her as if she stood naked in a crowd. Alone. Uncertain.

If all those feelings sliced through her in the safety of her own apartment, how would she handle herself once she set foot outside?

She sat on the edge of the tub, twirling her glasses between her fingers and staring at her shoes. Cute little red flats that Colleen had dug out of the back of her closet, along with a matching red button-down blouse. Allison didn't even remember buying them.

*I want to make changes. I need to make them. Damn it. Sit up straight and do it. Go for it.*

She gathered her breath, along with her courage, and stood in front of the mirror. Tossing her glasses onto the counter she put in her contacts, pulled back her hair, combing through it with her fingers, and then refastening the red clip at her neck. All her movements precise. She smoothed her palm along the side of her head to make sure every hair lay in the proper place, then spritzed on a little hair spray and pasted a smile to her lips.

Friday night—a little over forty-eight hours ago—Colleen had recommended she wear her hair back in order to show off the new look. Although at first Allison felt overexposed, and she automatically sought out her widow's peak—*Gawd, who came up with that term?*—her reflection had held her spellbound. She couldn't believe the woman staring back at her *was* her.

The effect this morning hadn't changed. She liked how she looked. The eyeshadow, lipstick, even the mascara that felt heavy on her lashes helped her square her shoulders with determination to meet the world with a smile. She really did feel good. She couldn't worry about what others thought, as long as her thoughts were happy.

*Right?*

She shook out her arms, wiggling her fingers as she met her reflection, rubbing her lips together. For some reason her eyes looked bigger, her red lips—bold red that matched her hair clip, blouse, and shoes—accentuated her face. Even her cheekbones looked more pronounced. Of course she'd shadowed them with a darker blush. A tip from one of the magazines.

Although she could see the difference in her appearance, would anyone else? And if they did, what would they say?

*Who cares? This is for your confidence and has nothing to do with anyone else.*

Maybe all of this was too much, too fast. She should start out slow. Little bits at a time. Foundation one week, switch up her hair the next, then the following add lipstick, mascara…

She reached for a facecloth and ran it under the faucet.

*No. I will not become my own worst enemy and talk myself out of this. I can do this.*

Gawd, she didn't know how to handle this part of her life. She had a great job, some good friends, and an amazing family, yet she couldn't throw on a little makeup and greet the day. She felt beyond beautiful, but her stomach spun, and she leaned over the counter, staring into the sink as she clutched her fist around the damp washcloth. She breathed in so deeply she coughed, then straightened, tossing the cloth into the hamper as she met her stern expression in the mirror.

"You are so doing this."

She jumped when her phone rang, and the "Space Odyssey" music that was Colleen's unique ringtone sliced through the silence in her apartment.

"Hey, isn't this a little early for a phone call from you?" Allison asked as she pressed the phone tightly to her ear. She loosened her death grip. *Relax. This is Colleen.*

"I set my alarm so that I'd wake with the roosters so I could check on you. You okay? Ready?"

Allison nodded as she answered, "Ready as I'll ever be."

"Don't overthink it. Just keep your head held high. You look fab, girl."

"I hope so." Allison concentrated on taking normal breaths. "And, Coll, thanks again."

"Love you."

They said their good-byes, and less than fifteen minutes later Allison stepped onto the E train. A tinge of self-consciousness strangled her chest. Maybe she should've worn her hair down. And the red blouse, maybe it was too much. She didn't wear a lot of color. Did she really want to attract so much attention right away? *But I have my black sweater. My shield.*

She couldn't—*wouldn't*—let doubt keep creeping in.

Enough was enough. The determination that gripped her in Jared's office the other day returned full force. Change could be hard, but she'd never been one to give up.

She forced back her shoulders and made herself meet the other commuters eye to eye. She got a few blank stares and some smiles. A couple of businessmen came aboard, and she gripped the pole as the train lurched forward. One of them gave her a lopsided smile, nudged his buddy, and they both gave her the once-over. The second guy said something to the other one and then chuckled, delivering her a wink.

Her confidence soared. Could a little makeup really make such a big difference? She'd been riding the El for years. Nobody had ever held eye contact, let alone winked. Of course, she'd usually spent her commute with her nose in a book and her hair falling over her face.

The train glided to a stop, and several more people stepped aboard. She earned more smiles, and one guy and girl stared at her for several minutes—until the train stopped at Allison's destination and she stepped off. She thought she heard them laugh, but she had to tell herself that it didn't mean they were laughing at her.

That little bit of interaction from a handful of people lifted her spirits. She practically floated along the sidewalk toward her office building, her heart light, and her footsteps lighter still. Maybe her coworkers would be as receptive as the strangers on the train. Wouldn't it be awesome if maybe one person invited her for a coffee, or a drink after work on Friday? Wouldn't it be better still if she dared to ask one of them?

She straightened her shoulders, biting back her smile. Heck, maybe she would.

She rode the elevator up to Firstline's floor, a bundle of energy as she tapped her foot. The doors slid open, and she stepped off, thankful to be greeted by an empty reception area. She wanted to work her way into seeing everyone. Her back stiffened, and she lifted her chin as she strolled down the corridor. The swing to her hips just happened and she grinned, biting her lip in hopes she could calm down enough to make her expression neutral. She didn't want to come off looking like a loon.

On the way to her shared office, she stopped at the break room to grab a cup of coffee. The moment she spotted Glenda and Andrea her feet stopped working, and she tripped across the threshold. They weren't the pair she wanted to see first. As a matter of fact, she preferred to not see them at all. In an instant her palms grew sweaty, and as she was about to turn on her heel and make a quick escape, Glenda—not the good witch as several other coworkers referred to her under their breath—turned and spotted her, nudging her cohort.

Allison had no choice but to continue to the coffee station. She looked straight ahead, but out of the corner of her eye she saw Andrea turn toward her and Glenda jabbing her in the ribs.

Andrea cleared her throat, and Allison glanced in their direction. The two other women smiled, and she lifted her chin, flashing a smile of her own, even though her stomach flipped.

"Morning, Allison." Andrea's gaze slid over her from head to toe, and her grin spread across her face.

Something in the way both women looked at her, wrapped around her confidence and squeezed, making her stomach somersault again. This time so hard she pressed her hand to her center.

"Have a good day," Glenda said as she breezed by, pulling Andrea behind her.

Allison sank against the counter, lifting a Styrofoam cup from the pile beside the coffee machine. With shaky hands she filled her cup, and her stomach rose in rebellion when she heard whispers on the other side of the break room entrance and then laughter.

She'd know the sounds of Glenda and Andrea's cackling anywhere.

"What the hell happened to her?"

"Looks like she put her makeup on in the dark."

More cackles, and then, as their voices lowered, Allison only picked up a few choice words. *Overdone. No clue. Awful. Feel sorry for her.*

Her legs wobbled as she swallowed air, depositing her coffee into the sink and tossing the cup.

Even though she didn't want to listen, she couldn't stop. Every fiber in her body grew taut, her stomach pinched and spun. She looked skyward, waving a hand in front of her eyes in hopes of stopping the waterworks already blurring her vision.

And their laughter. That was the killer.

Her entire life she'd been the nerdy girl, but she'd never been picked on. Laughed at. Maybe staying in the shadows wasn't such a bad thing after all. It certainly didn't hurt as much as people talking and laughing about her.

Her chin quivered, and she touched her face, her lips, and then dropped her hand down to her side. Defeat seeped through her, and she hated it. She'd never been one to let what others said get her down, but when it came to something she'd worked so hard on, something she wanted so much…

She hugged her middle as she heard another laugh—definitely Andrea—and then Allison went still when that same gritty sound stopped mid-cackle, and Jared's voice sifted through the room and wrapped a blanket of protection around her.

It had that same commanding boom from the other day. The one that she'd never heard him use.

"That's enough, ladies. You both have better things to do

than waste your morning on idle chitchat. Am I right?" His dismissive tone made even Allison fumble with her collar, straightening her shoulders in preparation to get to her desk.

Although she couldn't hear what the other two said, the quick tap of their heels on the tile told her all she needed to know. Her shoulders sagged as she released a long breath, and she swiped at the moisture beneath her eyes.

A glimmer of sunshine soared through her. She normally didn't need a protector, but that didn't stop her from looking overhead and sending a silent thank-you that Jared had come to her rescue. There'd have been no way she could've walked past Andrea and Glenda again, and now she didn't have to worry about it. At least not until she could regroup.

She ran her tongue across her upper lip as Jared entered the room, holding her gaze.

"They were laughing at me, weren't they?" She didn't even know why she asked. She knew deep in her gut they were, and the look on his face—tight lip and controlled anger in every line of his forehead—confirmed it.

"Does it matter?" His voice—restrained, deep, and authoritative—sent a chill down her spine.

He was right. It didn't matter. Nothing would change with a confirmation. She wouldn't stalk after them and have a confrontation. Her style was more *live and learn*. But she wouldn't alter her plan of change. She'd have to woman up and harden her heart. Some people liked to hurt others—be it from jealousy or their own insecurities—and that's what she'd attribute Glenda's and Andrea's reactions to.

*Nobody said this would be easy.*

He took the last few steps toward her and stopped, lifting her chin with his fingers. "What have you done?"

"W-what?" She bit the corner of her lower lip. For the second time in less than a minute, she didn't need an answer. All the stress from the last few days collided with her good sense. She dropped her face into her hands so hard she poked her eye with her knuckle. Now she really did have a reason to cry, and silent sobs shook her shoulders. The moment Jared put his hands on her arms—so soft and reassuring—she froze.

She hated being weak. She hated it even more that someone—Jared, to be exact—saw her at this low point.

It didn't matter that he'd come to her aid only minutes ago, she wanted to be alone in her misery. To compose herself, if that'd ever be possible. She gave him her back. "Leave me alone." She choked on her last word. "Please."

"No." His warm palms settled across her shoulders and squeezed, and for a moment a little of his strength seeped into her. But the warmth didn't last long as the last thirty minutes hit her like a ton of bricks. Everything played before her eyes as she blinked, unable to stop the tears from escaping.

The awkward smiles from the people she passed on her way to the E train. The woman who approached her as she waited on the platform, but then averted her gaze and moved past her. The people on the train. The men. Nudges. Smiles. Winks. Laughter after she got off.

Had everyone been making fun of her? Had the grand finale been the moment Glenda and Andrea spotted her? They hadn't even been able to get back to their desks before they'd started their rapid-fire round of insults.

She clenched her teeth so hard her jaw ached. What the hell had she been thinking using makeup tips from a few YouTube videos? And even more so, what made her think she and Colleen knew anything about choosing makeup? She needed professional help, at least when it came to a makeover. She should've gone into the department store. She should've taken more time, researched further before unveiling a new look. Her own desires and excitement had pushed, and she hadn't been ready. How come she hadn't seen that? She'd always been one to prepare, double-check, overanalyze. But not this time. Her heart had led instead of her head.

Her chin quivered as she turned to look up into Jared's blurry face. He'd give it to her straight. "Is it really that bad?"

Even through her tears, Jared's face—blue eyes grown soft and his head tilted to the side—gave her the answer she already knew.

...

*Shit.* He didn't want to make her cry. And he also didn't want to laugh at the fact she had red lipstick covering her front tooth. She might be a bit of a mess, but she looked so damn adorable he had a hard time not smiling. Besides the lipstick on her tooth, her color choices and the thick application would actually be comical, if he didn't know she hadn't meant any of this to be funny.

To see Allison out of her element sent his heart racing. She'd always been so professional, quiet, and confident—*even if she didn't think so*. At least when it came to work. To see this personal side of her, to know her deepest desire, softened his entire attitude toward her. He didn't feel sorry for her, because if he did she'd probably punch him in the gut, but he did want to see her happy. He'd watched his mother fight for years to get his father's attention, and although Allison didn't have a particular man in mind, he understood what she went through. She didn't deserve that type of pain. Hell, neither had his mother. Nobody did.

He lifted her chin with the crook of his finger. "It's not as bad as you think."

"That's not how you sounded a second ago."

"You took me by surprise. I'm not used to seeing you… look so different."

She studied him innocently. He caressed her chin with his thumb, hoping to stop that little tremor. As if that would erase the tears already drying on her cheek. Her skin was so soft, and she smelled like the cherry blossom trees in his grandma's garden. Her tiny whimper tugged at his chest, and all he wanted to do was take away her pain, hold her, and make her smile. He pulled her in for a tight hug. Whenever he'd gotten injured as a kid, his mom always said there were only two cures: chocolate—which he didn't have handy—or holding the hurt. If you held it, it'd feel better. If he held Allison, maybe she'd feel better, too.

He pulled her gently into his arms. She stiffened at first and then sagged into his chest.

"Don't cry, Al," he whispered against the side of her head.

Her soft scent surrounded him, and she sighed, even though her shoulders shook as she fought to control her tears.

"I'm sorry. I can't believe I'm being such a baby." She wiggled out of his grasp and took a big breath, giving him an unsteady smile. "I feel ridiculous."

"Don't."

"Time for an inspection of the damage. Maybe a little reevaluation."

"Al—"

She shook her head, independence filling her eyes as she pulled a round mirror from her purse with shaky fingers, fumbled, and watched it fall to the floor, her mouth slightly parted. As she stooped to pick it up, her shoe knocked it behind her and she bent, twisted around, and grabbed the mirror, crouching with her back toward him, staring at her face.

He held his breath as he watched her reflection in the mirror. Her wide-eyed inspection, the way the tilt of her chin lowered and then wobbled. How she delicately touched her lashes, traced her finger along her brow and down her cheek to outline her mouth.

He bent with the intention to pull her upright and offer

her some words of comfort, even though none came to mind at the moment. Something surely would. Any second. But before he took action another whimper escaped her lips, and she swiped her fingers across her eyes.

"You're going to smear your makeup." He regretted his words the moment she stiffened. *Real fucking comforting, Esterly.*

"It might be an improvement." She started to stand and, as he reached out to assist her, she lost her balance and landed on her butt. Her hands flew to her face, and her shoulders jerked.

His heart ached, and he kneeled beside her. It was only then that he realized she hadn't burst into tears. Her shoulders were shaking because she was laughing. A soft, tingly sound that picked up in intensity.

He couldn't help but smile as a small snort escaped from between her fingers.

"Could my day get any worse?" Her muffled voice was resigned, matter-of-fact, but strong.

He liked the sound of her laughter. Wanted to hear it again. "I probably shouldn't mention the lipstick on your tooth, then," he whispered cautiously.

She rewarded him with a wide-eyed smile, and then that smooth laughter filled the space between them. "Great, now I look like I ate a crayon." She rubbed her thumb against her tooth, turning the mirror in her hand so that she had the perfect angle. She lifted her face toward him and delivered a toothy grin. "Did I get it all?"

How come he'd never noticed how her laughter tinkled like wind chimes? Another remembrance from days spent in his grandma's garden. Peaceful days filled with no expectations or stress. Tension lifted off his shoulders, and he could breathe again, at least without that burning sensation filling his chest. He admired her spunk. Her ability to find some humor in an uncomfortable situation. Because surely she had to be uncomfortable. Allison wasn't one to lose control, or let her emotions get the better of her.

He melted at her bright-eyed, innocent gaze. The soft smile curving her lips that held a hint of shyness. The way she looked up at him—as if he could cure the world—made him want to protect her. Make her smile forever.

The awareness sent a jolt down his spine.

"You know, you don't need so much makeup. These changes you want to make..." She didn't need makeup or new clothes to be beautiful. All she had to do was open herself up. He held out his arms, palms up, as if that'd make her understand. "You're—"

"I appreciate that, Jared, but I need to do this for me. I know you don't get it, but I'm going to keep working on making changes until I get it right." Even though her smile wavered, she lifted her chin, exposing her neck. "First order of business is staying away from YouTube instructional videos, too much wine, and a drunk Colleen."

She choked out a laugh, then groaned, tucking a wayward strand of hair behind her ear.

"A drunk Colleen?"

"Long story." She waved her hand in front of her face.

"Maybe someday you'll share." His mind already put two and two together, but he imagined hearing the details firsthand would be a lot more interesting.

She still sat on the floor, her concentration centered on her little pocket mirror, playing with her hair, rubbing her lips together.

Damn. He shoved aside the voices inside his head—the ones telling him not to get involved—as she flipped her tiny mirror closed and tossed it into her purse.

He'd seen the strength and determination in her eyes last Friday, thought about her most of the weekend, and witnessed her heartbreak minutes ago. Through all that she hadn't given up. She might have faltered, but she returned full force.

Her persistence wrapped around him, and he wanted to help her make it happen. Allison was right. He did have contacts. There were several women in his life who'd like nothing better than to participate in a makeover. Shit, they thrived on stuff like that.

And if it made her happy…

"You're taking the day off." He'd barely finished his thoughts before he spoke the words aloud and pulled her to her feet.

She claimed her footing somewhat unsteadily and then shook her head, her smile growing in force. "It's not that catastrophic. I'll wash my face and get on with my day. I promise not to break out in random tears for the next forty-eight hours. Or more." A nervous chuckle complete with a short snort escaped her mouth. She released his hands.

The red creeping up from her neckline brought out another dose of his protective instinct, at the same time making her very appealing. He couldn't think of the last woman he'd met who'd blushed. Another unicorn?

"I should really have my snout looked at, you think?"

"Why? It's cute."

Her eyes widened. "Cute? You think a woman snorting is cute?"

He couldn't ignore her question, even though his focus lay more on his plan than her appealing—*yes, appealing*—little habit of snort-laughing. "It gives you personality. Enough about your snout and your snort. Let me rephrase what I said a minute ago." He gripped her by the shoulders, and she jerked to attention. "*We're* taking the day off."

"But I can't leave now. I have work to do. I haven't even—"

"Who's the boss here?"

"We both know the answer to that." A circle of pink filled

her cheeks.

"If you want this, Al, I'll help you."

"You will?" she squeaked. She tugged at her dangly penguin earrings as she scoured his face.

"Let me clarify. I'll help with your image, but that's as far as it goes. Deal?"

Sometime, but not right now, he'd have to ask her about her obsession with penguins. Plenty of women collected things, and he wondered why Al had chosen penguins. Most women seemed to concentrate on expensive jewelry. Travel. Clothes. At least the women he knew.

She squeezed his hand, drawing his attention back to her. "Okay, you're the boss."

"Damn straight."

He'd told her how beautiful she was before, but more as a form of comfort. Now, for the first time, he looked at her—really looked at her. Deeply. To the person without all the makeup who he'd known for years. How come he'd never bothered to see her?

How come they'd never really talked? Laughed? Become more than surface friends?

*Because she blended in with the wallpaper. Just like she'd said.*

But not anymore. Allison had beauty inside and out. He lost all ability to speak. Maybe even breathe. The way she looked at him—her lips softly parted, her eyes sparkly and full of anticipation—ate up the oxygen in his brain, depleted the air in his lungs.

He had the sudden urge to kiss her, and he didn't really understand why. This was Allison—Al. Nick's kid sister. Practically family.

Over the years he'd wanted to—and had—kissed many beautiful women, but no woman had ever affected him like this.

She kind of intimidated him. Actually, she scared the shit

out of him.

Was it because flirting with his best friend's—*hell, his business partner's*—sister carried a level of excitement like he'd never experienced?

Or did she really attract him that much? He grabbed her chin, and her tongue darted out to wet her lips. Before he went and did something crazy, he cleared his throat, turning her head from side to side. "Your application is flawless, but I think you could use a little help when it comes to color choices."

She glanced up at him, confusion settling across her forehead for a second before she recovered with a nervous laugh. "A tad overdone?"

Before he could answer—because all he could concentrate on was the way her lips moved, how the fluorescent lights made them shine, and if they'd be as soft underneath his lips as he imagined—her face sobered. "I thought you said you didn't know about makeup."

He forced his attention from her mouth back up to her eyes.

"I don't. Not really. But I know someone who does, and I'm calling in a favor." He turned her around and, with his hands on her shoulders, steered her toward the door. "We'll take my car."

Respect filled him for the way she'd handled herself. Her fortitude in planning to wash her face and get on with the day. Over and over again, Allison proved just how strong of a person she was. To him that equaled confidence. How come she couldn't see it?

And how come he'd never noticed the way her butt looked in a pair of slacks? The superb curve of her rear and the soft flare of her hips…

He tried to focus on the back of her head as he guided her out the door of the break room and down the hall, but he couldn't stop his eyes from continuously straying south.

# Chapter Four

Allison sat in stunned silence as Margarite's slim hands flew around her head and face with sure precision. They'd barely arrived at the salon—or as Margarite referred to her business: a specialty boutique of beauty—an hour ago, but the slender woman had wasted no time in pushing Allison into a seat and getting to work.

Her brow was a smooth line of concentration as she cut, plucked, dabbed, blended, brushed, and swirled. The hem of her bright, multicolored dress—which kind of resembled a cupcake—swooshed around her knees as she moved from Allison's left side to her right, then finally the middle. Over the course of the last twenty minutes, she'd pondered Allison with a stern stare, hands on hips, and a larger-than-life smile.

All the commotion had sent Allison's head spinning and her heart racing. She wanted to see what Margarite had accomplished in the worst way, but her back was to the mirror. Her gaze darted around the room, hoping to connect with some type of decoration where she could catch a glimpse of her reflection. No such luck.

Beneath the gown now littered with snippets of her hair, Allison twisted her sweaty hands into a tight knot. Margarite seemed to be a woman of few words—or maybe she needed to stay focused in order to get the job done—but a little chatter would soothe Allison's nerves in a big way.

"How long have you—"

"Shh. Shh. We'll talk after your reveal." Margarite's tone brokered no argument. Not that Allison planned to give her any.

She pressed her mouth closed and lifted one brow as she glanced at Jared. He stood a few feet behind Margarite's right shoulder. He offered her a quick nod of encouragement, although his face gave away nothing else.

She didn't know how much more she could take. The heels of her palms dug into her thighs as she swiped them over her slacks. If only she could read something in his expression, or maybe get a glimpse of what Margarite had accomplished in the reflection of her oversize, yellow-framed glasses. She moved her head to try to catch something—anything—but all she got for her effort was a temperamental grunt from Margarite as she grabbed Allison's chin and forced her to look straight ahead.

The tall woman had a unique look, but it suited her. Kind of a cross between Big Bird—with her shock of yellowish hair bouncing atop her head—and Katie Perry, with a wardrobe that would rival anything the singer wore onstage.

Finally, Margarite's lips curved into a beautiful smile that went straight to her big brown eyes. With hands on her slender waist, she stepped back, clicking one thumbnail with her pinkie finger. "Voilà. I do declare you a masterpiece."

Her gruff voice didn't match her wardrobe, or anything about her, actually. Anyone who dared dress like she did, along with her impressive personality, had to have an overabundance of confidence. She should bottle it and sell it along with the hair-care products she had on display in her salon—sorry, *boutique of beauty.*

But something about her reset Allison's pulse to normal. Maybe it was the way she took control, or the fact that her confidence level almost knocked Allison to the floor. Or that she'd finally finished, and Allison could get a gander at the results.

*So much for that normal heartbeat.*

Her gaze connected with the other woman's, and then she turned her attention toward Jared. Their smiles sent the pulse point in her wrist jumping, and she pulled her arm from beneath the gown to rub at the tickle on the tip of her nose. She could actually feel the pulse in her wrist pounding against her skin. Would she just spin the chair around toward the mirror already? *Before my heart explodes, please.*

The woman leaned forward and grabbed the sides of Allison's chair. Margarite blinked, causing her long lashes to brush against her lenses. That would have driven Allison nuts. "Are you ready to see perfection?"

"Are you sure you're talking about me?" Allison teased.

Margarite frowned. "There'll be no talk like that. You have the most beautiful skin, gorgeous eyes, to-kill-for honey-blond hair, and your smile fills your face. All that makeup you arrived in wasn't needed. Makeup is to be used as an enhancement, not a cover-up. Have you ever heard the saying 'a little goes a long way'?"

Allison nodded, mesmerized by Margarite's simple speech. Of course she'd heard the saying, it was one of many favored by Gramps.

"That's a makeup motto, my new friend. A little bit, the right colors, and it's magic." She kissed her fingertips with an eccentric flare.

"I love how you think, Margarite."

The woman waved her hand, a light rosy color highlighting

her cheeks. "Trust me, hon. I'm an original. I wasn't always the flamboyant woman you see before you. Years ago I was a quiet girl named Margaret from a small town in Kansas."

Allison had a hard time envisioning Margarite anything less than flamboyant. Or living in Kansas. And, Margaret? She definitely looked more like a Margarite than a Margaret.

Margarite laughed. "And that's why when Jared called me I told him I was in before he even got the entire story out. If I can make the changes I did to develop confidence in my appearance, I know you can do it, too. Tell yourself you're amazing every day, and you will be."

She spun the chair, and Allison locked eyes with her reflection in the mirror and gasped. Her heart slammed against her chest so hard and fast she knew for sure it filled the deafening silence in the room. She sat forward and squint-blinked as she touched her cheek and the soft layers of hair that framed her face. Margarite had tinted her hair in small sections with a deeper honey tone, and it brought out her blond. Of their own volition, her hands flew up to caress the wispy ends. So soft. She lifted a strand and smelled it, closing her eyes as the cherry scent filled her senses.

She stood, the gown dropping to the floor at her feet. Without looking, she stepped over it, leaning in toward her reflection. *Is that really me?*

She'd thought her look earlier knocked socks off, but nothing compared to what Margarite had done. She truly had worked a miracle.

"How? What?" She didn't even know where to begin. What to say. How to thank her.

Margarite smiled at their reflections. Jared took a few steps closer. His eyes darkened, and he tugged at his collar but remained quiet.

"I want to give you a little advice, along with this bag of goodies." Margarite grabbed a bag with her boutique name emblazoned on the front and shook it as if she were calling a herd of cats in for canned tuna. "This contains everything you need. Remember what I told you when I was doing your hair?"

"Blondes look best in softer tones."

Margarite nodded. "Stay away from reds and burgundy. Everyday makeup should be light and natural. Pink or beige eyeshadow. Avoid black mascara and go with brown. For your lips, stick with a rosy blush or a sheer gloss. That's really all you need, Allison. You're drop-dead gorgeous, and the little bit of makeup brings it out. All you need to do now is hold your head up high and be awesome."

"I don't feel right calling myself gorgeous—"

"You are, so you better get used to it."

Allison chuckled. She could hear her own discomfort in the tinny sound. She didn't like all the attention, but at the same time she savored it, letting the sensation roll through her until it smoothed across her body like a second skin. "I can't believe it's me." Silence echoed through the room as she turned her head from side to side, her hair caressing her cheeks, her smile growing larger with each passing second.

"You're beautiful." Jared's voice filled the silence.

She shifted beneath the weight of his stare. He'd told her the same thing a couple of times, but for the first time she allowed herself to believe him. She needed to let go of her insecurities and trust in Margarite and Jared. Her body warmed at the heated look in Jared's gaze. Was that really for her? She suddenly felt dehydrated. As if she could read her mind, Margarite handed her a cup of water from the nearby cooler. Allison downed it in one swallow and licked her lips, turning back toward the mirror. Not that she was conceited, but she couldn't stop staring at herself. Each time she looked, she discovered something new.

"I feel beautiful." She waved her hand in front of her face

to cool down her sudden burst of emotion. Colleen might have a freaking coronary when she saw her. "No, that's a lie. I felt beautiful this morning, but now. Well, now…"

"Just like Jared said a moment ago, you *are* beautiful, Allison." Margarite came to stand behind her. "And your hair. Do you like? I didn't take off a lot of the length or change up the color too drastically. Just gave you some layers and shaped it around the front so it'd frame your face, and the highlights bring out your skin tone. This should be an easy way for you to wear it. And you can still put it up or pull it back if you want."

"I love it." Allison smoothed down her hair, luxuriating in the feel yet again. She might never stop touching it. Whatever shampoo, conditioner, or spray that Margarite had used changed the entire texture. She could run her fingers through it all day. Never before had she looked more feminine—or felt more feminine—than she did now. A tiny giggle escaped, and she made a conscious effort to not bounce on the balls of her feet from the giddiness invading every inch of her body.

"Anything you'd change? Any questions?"

She spun around and hugged Margarite with such force they both lost their balance. "Sorry. Sorry." She released the other woman and stepped back. Her cheeks were starting to hurt from all the smiling. "And no. Nothing I'd change. I can't believe it's me."

"Oh, it's you. It's always been you. Now you know how to show yourself off using all your attributes." The woman shifted her weight to one hip. She fluffed the ends of her outrageous hair as she shot Jared a smile and a wink.

Allison couldn't keep her hands off her hair, or her eyes off her new look as she turned to face the mirror again. To think she'd always had the potential but didn't know how to make her eyes, hair, or full lips stand out amazed her. Anyone could be as beautiful once they learned a few tips and tricks.

She shook her head. "I don't know what to say except thank you."

The woman blushed, shaking her head. "You are very welcome."

Allison frowned, rubbing at her widow's peak. "I guess I do have one question. Is there any way to get rid of this?" Her entire life she'd hated her hairline. The main reason she'd preferred to wear her hair down had been because she could hide it to some extent, but the way Margarite had blown out her hair seemed to make it more noticeable than ever.

Margarite *tsk*ed gently. "We all have things about ourselves, inside as well as out, that we don't like. It's sad, really. We need to learn to embrace our differences and imperfections."

Her words were so simple but true. She'd have to remember that some of her insecurities were more in the way she looked at herself than how others looked at her.

Margarite slid her hands down the edges of Allison's hair, on either side of her face, stopping at her chin. "Your widow's peak is a bonus. It shapes your face and gives it definition. This makes Allison, *Allison*."

"Your face is a heart, Al," Jared whispered.

Butterflies spun around in her belly, and she swallowed them down.

Hers and Margarite's eyes widened at the same time as they regarded him in the mirror. He didn't seem to notice. All his concentration settled on Allison, and a little of her self-consciousness returned.

"A h-heart?" she stammered. His soft voice had sunk deep into her bones. But his eyes…

The way he stared sent her body on high alert. Her skin prickled, but at the same time a dizziness fogged her head. She closed her eyes, but when she opened them he still stood staring at her.

Is this what sexy felt like? She had an inner glow of empowerment, the warmth spreading through all the nerve endings in her body. The feeling was definitely new and thrilling. Although she expected her new look might get her some attention, and she would have to get used to it, she hadn't realized how much she'd like it. Devour it. Especially when it came from Jared.

She scrutinized her reflection and then darted her attention between Margarite and Jared before landing on her own image once again. She traced the shape of her face with her eyes, repeating Jared's words in her head. A heart described her perfectly. How come she'd never noticed that before? And for some reason the fact that Jared *had*, sent a chill down her backbone.

Margarite punctuated the excitement in the air with a solid peck on Allison's cheek. "Thank you for trusting me to make you over." She turned toward Jared and stepped up onto her tiptoes and kissed his cheek. "And you, Jared. Thank you for trusting me to help your friend. I'm so happy you called me."

"You were the first—the only—person I thought of." He squeezed the woman's hand and then smiled at Allison. "Do you believe me now?"

She couldn't speak, transfixed by his eyes. They shone so brightly and, along with his words, seemed to hypnotize her. At the moment, she'd believe or do anything he said or asked.

"I have one more tip for you, Allison."

She turned toward Margarite, although her peripheral vision lingered on Jared. "What's that?"

"Jared told me you are trying to find your confidence. He mentioned you plan on changing your look, your wardrobe, and your life. Are you doing this for you or a man?"

"For me. To improve myself. And if it leads to…" Did she really have to get into such personal terrain? She loved what

Margarite had done for her, but she didn't necessarily feel like she should bare her soul. "Why?"

"Just remember, always own who you are. Even if you think you're weird or different, if you own it, you'll have confidence." Her smile covered her face. "And if you ever need a lift to your confidence and are struggling, remember this one piece of advice."

"What's that?" Allison held her breath.

"Walk like you're being followed by three gorgeous men that you want to bed." Her husky laughter shook her shoulders, and both Allison and Jared laughed, too.

"Good advice." Allison's face heated as she released a stream of air.

But for some reason Jared's laugh sounded forced, and she didn't miss the flicker of something she couldn't quite identify in his eyes, although he'd quickly concealed it. Had it been unease, surprise, or her imagination?

...

Jared could barely peel his eyes off Allison. His best friend's sister. The thought should've brought him back down to earth with a thud, but it didn't even faze him. She had suddenly become something more than Nick's sister or his employee.

He rolled the words over and over in his mind. As if that would stop the attraction—*yes, attraction*—from awakening all his senses.

All this togetherness might not have been his best idea.

The more he revealed Allison's different layers—got to know her—the more he liked her. But that didn't mean he'd act on his attraction, so he didn't have to worry about betraying Nick's trust. Because he wouldn't.

No. Way. In. Hell.

He could control himself. *Then how come the unsteady*

*pounding of my heart and my body temperature tell another story?*

Fuck. He'd meant it when he'd told her earlier how beautiful she was, but standing back and watching her with Margarite blew that news right out of the ballpark. The anxiety mixed with excitement in her eyes, that damn adorable snort when she laughed that told him she was a ball of nerves, the way her hands flittered about—not to mention her stunning smile and sexy eyes—hit him over the head like a brick. She was one of a kind.

*Sexy? Hell yes, Allison Hall is sexy.* He regretted that he'd never taken the time to get to know her before. Shit. He regretted that she worked for him. That she was Nick's kid sister.

His skin crawled with self-accusation. His gut knotted. All his thoughts were so wrong. On so many levels.

She was beautiful, and now that she'd recognized that fact and her confidence could only go up, he feared the reactions she'd get from other men. Would they see her for more than the way she looked, or would they be surface dwellers only? The thought more than disturbed him. He balled his fists and then made a conscious effort to stretch his fingers several times to ease the cramp. For some reason he wanted to keep her all to himself. Just for a little while. But that wasn't fair. She wanted to change her life, and he wouldn't stand in her way. No matter how much he wanted to protect her.

*That's it. Everything I'm feeling isn't attraction. I just want to protect her. Because she's Nick's sister.*

He could tell himself that lie six ways to Sunday, but it didn't stop this new awareness from eating him up. He'd just have to learn to deal with it. He wouldn't muck up her chances of finding happiness because she suddenly appealed to him.

*But if I'm attracted, why can't I…*

*Because I can't. Don't even go there.*

She'd said it herself, they were polar opposites. And no matter that opposites attract, it didn't always make it right. He closed his eyes, and Nick's stern face appeared, warning him to keep his distance.

"I hate to push you two out the door, but I have an appointment with another client." Margarite turned her wrist and tapped the face of her gemstone-encrusted watch. "She'll be here in less than ten minutes, and she doesn't like to be kept waiting."

"I hope I can remember everything you showed me so I can duplicate the look." Allison hugged the other woman, her soft features glowing as Margarite squeezed her tightly in return.

"Thanks again, Mar." Jared pecked her cheek as she broke their hug. He turned toward Al, his thoughts still a jumbled mess. If he were smart he'd suggest they head back to the office. Work would get his mind off her. At the same time the idea of sharing Allison with everyone else made it difficult to breathe. What the hell was happening to him? "You ready?"

"Ready."

The moment they stepped outside onto the sidewalk, she turned and enveloped him in a bear hug. She squeezed him tight, digging her fingers into his back and making a little grunting noise as she rocked him back and forth. Her gesture took him by surprise, and her warmth wrapped around him like a snug blanket. A favorite blanket. He breathed in her scent with lungs that had shrunk to the size of kidney beans as he attempted to control his body's reaction. He stiffened in all the right places, and a few of the wrong ones. But that didn't stop him from gathering her closer, relishing the feel of her in his arms. He shut his eyes.

"Thank you, Jared. I love Margarite, but I have a hard time picturing you two together. You don't seem to fit."

She stepped out of his arms, and he instantly wanted to

tug her back but resisted the urge.

"Me and Margarite?" He laughed.

"You two dated, right? I mean, that's how you know her?"

He barked out another laugh. "You're more Margarite's type than I am."

"Are you saying—?"

"I'm saying Margarite lives in my old apartment complex with her partner Nicole."

"Oh. Well, that explains why I can't picture you two together. I was bamboozled at the thought." She winked.

"Bamboozled?" He grinned. Every once in a while she turned a cute word or phrase, and it knocked him sideways. "Where do you get some of your words?"

"Gramps. He kind of rubs off on you after a while."

He nodded. True, Grandpa Hall walked to the beat of his own drummer, but he'd never noticed that it was also Al's habit. Until now. Was it wrong to suddenly be attracted to a woman you'd known for years? Not because she'd changed her looks, but because she seemed to be coming alive. Blossoming.

He couldn't keep dwelling on these new feelings. After today they'd go back to the way things used to be. *Wouldn't they?*

He shrugged in answer to his own question, glad that Allison didn't seem to notice as they fell into step and made their way down the sidewalk toward the parking garage.

"Should we grab some lunch before we head back to the office?" he asked. Part of him wanted to get back to work, but another part—a more persistent part—wanted to prolong their time together.

Her footsteps slowed, and she licked her lips. "I thought we'd taken the entire day off."

"We finished early." *And I need to put some distance between us. Even though I don't want to.*

He caught her smile up at him from the corner of his eye.

"Do you feel good about helping me?"

"I do," he said, stretching each short word out as long as he could because the way she slowed down, and her inability to look at him longer than a couple of seconds, told him something more was coming.

"I was thinking," she said, lingering over each syllable as she gripped his fingers, swinging his arm with hers as they resumed their trek down the sidewalk, "after lunch we might as well go shopping. *Really* make a day of it. You can help me—"

"Our agreement didn't include shopping."

She stopped, frowning up at him as several passersby veered to either side of them. Then she smiled, and his heart stalled.

"I know, but you did say we'd take the day off, and my mind is already acclimated to not working." She giggled, resuming their walk and tugging him along beside her, because his feet had suddenly decided they didn't know how to work. She moved in closer to him, touching the side of his body with hers.

His throat went dry, and he attempted to swallow as a slow burn rippled across his left side. He took a step to the right, but she gravitated toward him. "Really? So, you get a new haircut and a few makeup tips and all of a sudden you're all flirty?"

Her little squeak sent shivers across his flesh. "Flirty? Am I really being flirty?"

"Yes." *Or maybe I'm only hoping. Wishing.*

She shrugged, raising her eyebrows and poking her tongue against the inside of her cheek. "Good to know. I'll have to file that away for later."

Not something he wanted to hear. Or know.

"Anyway, we should stick to the main plan. No work

today."

"Hmm."

"You're being very non-flirty." This time when she laughed she gave a soft snort, and her hand flew up to her face. She cleared her throat, then shot him a smile. Complete with the flick of her tongue wetting her lips. "You know how they say 'clothes make the man'?"

He nodded, too dumbfounded to speak by the effect of her smile and his own thoughts about kissing her.

"Well, they make a woman, too."

The sparkle in her eyes hadn't lessened since they'd left Margarite's. Even her walk seemed lighter, her hips swayed, her hair bounced. And he'd already wanted to slug a few guys who'd passed by and turned their heads to check her out from the rear.

And that was the deciding factor. He wasn't sure he wanted to let her out of his sight now—even though that voice in his head told him he was playing with fire and there wasn't an extinguisher nearby. He didn't care. Damn being cautious. And damn to all the attention she drew. Nick would want to kick his ass for helping her when he realized what type of reaction she'd be getting from the opposite sex, and at this rate he might let him.

"Fine." His voice sounded reluctant; he was anything but.

She tugged on his arm as she bounced up and down. "Shoes, too?"

Already pulled in, he couldn't have said no if he wanted to. And he didn't want to. Nothing else in the world compared to seeing her so animated as she chattered nonstop while they strolled down the sidewalk hand in hand. Excitement lit her eyes—her entire face—or maybe it wasn't excitement but her newfound confidence. Something inside him wanted, no needed, to be by her side as she continued to make changes.

# Chapter Five

Allison's stomach tightened. After all Jared had done for her, she didn't want to be mean, seem ungrateful, but…

"These aren't going to fit."

His lopsided smile disarmed her as his gaze ran the length of her. Her flesh tingled wherever his eyes lingered, curling her toes. For the hundredth, maybe the thousandth time today, whenever she looked at him her body grew warm. *Okay, maybe more inferno-ish.*

"Trust me. At this point I think I know what'll fit you better than you do."

"I highly doubt that." She rolled her eyes playfully. "So, you get me into a clothing store, think you know the score better than me, and the power makes you all flirty?" The urge to be reckless gave her a large dose of courage.

"Am I being flirty?" He touched his chin to his shoulder, batting his eyes.

She laughed. "Is that supposed to be an impression of me?"

"Apparently I pulled it off because you got it right on the

first try." He thrust the pile of clothes into her arms, nudging her toward the changing room. "Humor me."

"Fine, but I don't think there'll be any humor involved when you're eating crow."

"Gramps again?" This time *he* rolled his eyes, and she bit her lip in an unsuccessful attempt to control her smile.

"If I fit into half of these, I'll buy you a beer." The frisky words rolling off her tongue felt good—but she was thrilled more by the way his eyebrow shot up in surprise.

"Works for me. And if I'm wrong?"

*Then you owe me a kiss.*

Instead of speaking her thoughts aloud she licked her lips and stammered, "I-I don't know." Her belly flipped at the possibilities. At least all the possibilities that her awakening libido imagined.

If only she dared to be more brazen in reality instead of just in her mind.

A little makeup, a visit to a hair stylist, and a shopping trip had suddenly made her awareness of Jared grow tenfold. Or was it due in part to them spending the day together, getting to know each other?

Whatever the reason, it felt good. New. Thrilling and exciting.

A slow smile spread across his face. She rubbed her lips together as she imagined what his mouth would feel like on hers.

"Why don't you think about it while you're changing?" He tapped her temple, and she laughed, brushing away his hand. "But don't think too hard, because everything I handed you will fit."

"Whatever." She huffed in mock annoyance. "You're full of yourself."

"I'm confident."

"Me, too." She entered the dressing room, turning back

to look at him over her shoulder and batting her eyes. His smooth chuckle made her squirm, shooting goose bumps across her skin. For the last decade she'd worn the same size. She anticipated the moment when she'd peek out from behind the door to ask him to grab something larger. "Do you want dipping sauce for your crow?" she called through the door.

"I'm not hungry, but I am thirsty thinking about that cold brew you're going to buy me."

His words kept the smile on her lips as she hung her sweater on the nearby hook and unbuttoned her blouse, hanging it over her sweater. She thrust her hand into her sweater pocket and nabbed a piece of chocolate, popping it into her mouth.

Of course he was drop-dead gorgeous. It's not like she hadn't noticed before, but why did she become so over-the-top giddy when he looked, complimented, or smiled at her? Not to mention this little back and forth flirting competition.

She toed off her shoes, fighting the urge to dance in a circle and squeal. Yes. Squeal. She looked at the ceiling and closed her eyes, hugging her middle, pressing her heels together, and bending at the knees.

"How's it going in there?"

"It's going." She wiggled out of the rest of her clothes as she worked the piece of candy with her tongue, swallowing more of the melting chocolate. After their hug in the break room had sent all her lady parts on high alert, she'd told herself to keep some distance. But hot heck, every word he uttered, every look he shot her way, sent tingles across her flesh.

And when they touched…

She snapped the last bit of chocolate in half with her teeth. The sensation of heat mixed with pulsating chills and heart-stopping tingles was something she wanted to feel over and over again. The main reason she'd grabbed his hand after they'd left Margarite's was to relive the thrill.

"Come on. I'm getting thirsty."

She jumped as she tugged a pair of jeans off the hanger. "Give a girl a minute."

"A minute?" he teased. "It's been close to five. Not that I'm clock watching."

She pictured him looking at his watch. Heck, she pictured him just standing outside that little wooden door, hands in his pockets, rocking on his heels. Probably attracting all kinds of attention. She'd gone geek-girl giddy, like she had in high school over Brock Davis, star athlete and God's gift to women everywhere—at least those still in high school. The only time he'd ever talked to her was when he wanted to cheat off her math test. Not that she'd minded. Their mini conversations had given her enough material for a few daydreams, and a few night dreams, too.

But she wasn't in high school any longer, even though at times she feared her emotions had never graduated. She'd catch up in that area as soon as she got out there socially and went on a few dates. Experience would be key.

The moment she slid the jeans up her legs and over her rear, then buttoned them, she spun around.

*They fit?*

"Are you stalling because you're buying me a beer?"

"I'm stalling because I'm thinking about what type of dipping sauce I want with my crow."

His laughter soothed the sting of being wrong. She checked the view from the back, front, and side, pressing her hand to her middle and sucking in her gut and then pushing it out. They fit well, not tight in the least. As a matter of fact, not even one little piece of flesh puckered at the waistline.

How'd he know?

No matter. She wiggled her way into the casual tee and pulled it down to her waist. It snapped back a little and bared a teeny-tiny patch of her belly. The light blue, cottony material made her skin glow. And it fit so snugly around her boobs she wasn't sure she'd ever be able to wear it in public.

"Come out and let me see how right I am."

"Don't let it go to your head," she teased. "Unless, of course, this is your first time."

"Yeah, right," he said around his laughter. "My first—"

She opened the dressing room door, ready for his snarky retort. His eyes grew wide, and his mouth hung open as if he'd forgotten what he was about to say. His darkened gaze covered her like honey dripping over the edges of a biscuit. All slow, sweet, and mouthwatering. He licked his lips. And for some reason watching his Adam's apple work so hard when he swallowed turned her on.

Decision made. *Apparently I'll be wearing this tee and jeans everywhere I go.*

She liked his reaction. Definitely a confidence booster.

"I-I told you they'd fit." He raked his fingers through his hair.

How come his attention seemed so focused on her chest? More importantly, why was she taking advantage of the situation and thrusting her shoulders back.

Allison rubbed her lips together. "Looks like I owe you a beer." Feeling reckless, she slid her fingers down her waist and over her hip, reveling in the way his eyes followed her every movement.

"I could definitely use a drink about now." He laughed. A husky, sexy sound that came from deep inside his chest.

The sound rolled over her like a warm spring rain and made her knees wobble. There was something about a man's laugh that had always attracted her. Jared had one of the best. It'd been the first thing she'd noticed about him when Nick had brought him home all those years ago, but it'd never affected her so much until today. This moment to be exact.

He blinked several times, as if he couldn't focus. *Was he nervous?*

If not, she was nervous enough for the both of them but excited, too.

"What I want to know is how you knew these would fit." She pulled the hem of the tee again, but it didn't seem to do much good. Except that it drew his attention to the swell of her breasts. Was it wrong to like the attention? *Who cares about right and wrong—especially now?*

He shrugged. "I have an eye for a woman's shape."

"Oh, I'm sure." She shifted her weight to one leg.

"I'm not being a pervert." But that didn't stop another flush from creeping up his neck as he concentrated on her fingers tugging at her shirt. Just to test him—and maybe tease him a little bit with her newfound power—she rubbed her hand over the skin of her belly, lifting the fabric of her shirt by mere millimeters to reveal more skin. Her reward was the way his hand shook when he rubbed the side of his neck as his olive complexion grew a shade darker.

Her heart swelled. *The confidence king embarrassed?*

"Your story," she teased.

"You said yourself you didn't know what the hell you were doing when it came to clothes and makeup. I always assumed you preferred baggy clothes, but since you're all about taking chances and switching things up, it's time to start tailoring your wardrobe."

"Not only are you speaking pretty fast, you're mighty long-winded." She flipped her hair over her shoulder, enjoying the fact that he didn't seem to be able to deliver a comeback. "Either way, you were right. I can't hide behind my clothes and hair any longer. Part of being confident means attracting attention—and another part means I can't let it faze me. I have to learn to take things in stride."

"Now you got it."

"But right now this doesn't feel very natural." She pulled at her shirt again. Doubt had a way of creeping in, even though she tried to fight it. She turned slowly on the heel of her sock, pulling her shoulder in under her chin as she tried to get a glimpse of her backside again in the mirrors lining the wall. "You sure it's not too tight back there?"

From beneath her lashes she checked out her own image and then Jared's. All the color that had overpowered his face moments ago slipped away.

His eyes bore right through her, and he licked his lips again. Whatever danced in the air between them had to be sexual tension. It went nicely with the swoop of heat filling her core. She'd read about it, liked the feel of it between them, and wanted it to last.

He came up behind her and laid his hands on her shoulders, massaging her gently. "Don't let that confidence-eating bug back in, Al. Your clothes look great; you look great. Trust me."

"I do." His touch sent an array of shivers along her skin, and her body seemed to sway toward him of its own accord. He leaned in to her, the heat from his body wrapping around her. Owning her. She closed her eyes, her head bumped his chin, breaking her trance.

He cleared his throat, taking a step back. "Try on the rest. I'm going to pick out a few outfits suitable for work."

He turned abruptly, and she followed him with her eyes, pulling at her lower lip with her teeth. What the heck were they doing? More importantly, why the heck did she keep egging him on?

• • •

Jared couldn't wait for this day to end. Not that he wasn't enjoying his time with Allison. Actually, he might be enjoying it too much. What he didn't like was the constant threat of a boner every time she smiled at him, touched him, or tested out her newfound flirting skills.

She was a natural-born flirt—even if she didn't know it—and it scared the shit out of him. For himself and for any other man within the zip code. The most attractive part about her new skill was that he didn't think she even realized her effect. Her pouty lips, the way her lashes flickered over her cheeks, and how her eyes darkened whenever she said something a little bit out of her comfort zone.

For someone so new to the game, she'd mastered the art, plus some.

Although they'd left the store almost half an hour ago, his mind still lingered on the way her ass looked in those jeans—even though her nonstop chatter should've cut through his thoughts on the car ride to her apartment and the promised beer. The beer he wasn't sure he should accept since it meant being alone with her. In her apartment.

But hell, he liked to live on the edge. Test himself. Didn't he? And his mouth was definitely dry.

He came back to the present as he shifted a bag higher up his arm, his gaze honing in on the same ass in the same damn jeans he'd been fantasizing about seconds ago. In real time. Shit, he wished she hadn't decided to wear them home. How could a man concentrate with a view like that walking down the corridor in front of him?

The weight of all the bags draped over his arms didn't distract him enough from the way her hips swayed gently from side to side—calling his name, teasing him until his mouth had grown so dry he couldn't even work up a good swallow—as she led the way, carrying her own armful of purchases.

She looked over her shoulder and gave him a smile. "You've never been here before."

"It's a day of firsts." What would her place look like?

Would he discover something new about her he didn't know?

The idea of uncovering another layer had him stepping up his pace, even though he still kept tight focus on her perfect ass. Those jeans were made for her.

She balanced a box against her hip as she inserted her key into the lock, smiling at him. "Are you coming? I can't imagine I wore you out. We were only at the mall for a few hours."

"Long enough."

"You sound like a man who doesn't shop." She kicked the door open with her foot, and he followed her inside.

"My tailor has my measurements. I can shop with a phone call."

She nodded. "Nice. I guess. After today, I kind of like doing it in person."

"I'm sure." He unloaded her goods onto the couch and the floor beside it, taking in her apartment. His eyes immediately locked onto the *Kama Sutra* book on the dining table. Although it was closed, several pieces of paper stuck out at the top where she'd marked pages. He picked it up. "Whatcha got here?"

The sight of her blushing would never get old. She grabbed the book from his hands and hugged it to her chest. "That's for my eyes only."

His gaze strayed to where the book had laid on the table, hiding several printouts. He skimmed his hands over the pages. "What's all this?"

"More none-of-your-business stuff." She shooed his hand away, gathered the pages, and turned them over so he couldn't read what they said. But she hadn't been fast enough. She'd obviously been researching aphrodisiacs.

"I'll give you credit, Al. You haven't even met the guy you want to date, and you're already researching the next step." He'd laugh at her thoroughness if it didn't worry him so much.

Damn Lance, he'd really done a number on her.

"I like to be prepared."

"Like we discussed before, don't rush it. Meet someone, get to know him, and the rest will follow. It's not a race." *Fuck. Sometimes you sound like a girl.* The closeness he shared with his mother, their late-into-the-night talks and confidences, might have made him too soft. Too understanding when it came to women. Even though he played the field, he'd never slept with a woman without there being something more than sex between them. And he never would.

"I appreciate your opinion." She blew out a breath. "I've no plans to jump into bed with the first guy I date, but I'd like to have some experience when I do. Even if I get it from a book."

He held up his palms, as if preparing to argue his point. But what could he really say? It wasn't like she was a kid, or that she wasn't taking the time to prepare. Too bad that didn't stop the punch to his gut at the thought of her with another man.

She twisted the ends of her hair before tucking the length behind her ear. "I call change of subject. How about that beer I owe you?"

"Good idea. I'm in." He followed the line of her back until he reached the delectable curve of her rear as she made her way to the kitchen. He heard her twist off two caps, and then she returned to the living room, holding out a longneck.

He took a long swig as she grabbed a quick sip of hers and then scrunched her nose.

"Not a beer fan?"

"I keep it around for Nick. Wine is more my thing, but Colleen and I used up my reserves over the weekend."

He nodded, finishing his tour of her apartment with a quick appraisal. "How is Coll? She hasn't been to Sunday dinner in a long time."

"She's good. Busy with Jerry and work." She set her nearly full beer on the dining room table, leaning against the edge.

He nodded. Allison favored traditional furniture. Heavy wood with a few nice art pieces and family pictures filling the wall. A penguin pillow lay haphazardly on the couch as if she'd curled up with it recently, and penguin slippers sat on the floor in front of the couch. As his gaze circled back around toward her, he noticed the large curio cabinet filled with more penguins. Hundreds. Maybe more. She followed his gaze and grinned, walking over to the cabinet. "My addiction."

"I see that. What's the attraction?"

"For one, my mom collected them." Her voice went soft, and so did her eyes. "I took over her collection, and got a little carried away the more I learned. Besides the fact they're the cutest little birds on the planet, there's something that's..." She paused dramatically, spreading her arms out at her side as she studied him. "They're romantic."

He barked out a laugh, wiping with the back of his hand at the spray of beer that hit his chin. "Romantic?"

"Yes, romantic." She rolled her eyes, but that didn't lessen the obvious adoration she had for the subject. "If you ever have the time, you should take a minute and Google them. They really are amazing."

"Hmm." He took another pull of his beer. "Maybe I will." *More than likely I won't.*

"Did you know there are seventeen species of penguins?" She opened the door, gently picking out a black and white penguin with a red-orange beak from the back. "This is probably the most recognizable species."

"Which one is it?" He turned the figurine over in his hands, taking in the delicate contours, trying to understand what attracted Allison to this little bird.

"This is the gentoo." Her eyes sparkled, and his eyes dropped to her mouth. Shit. He wanted to kiss her. Maybe penguins *were* fucking romantic.

She grinned and took the figurine he offered, then traced her finger along the bird's beak. She propped the curio door open with her hip and, biting her bottom lip and holding her breath, snaked her hand around several other figurines until she put the penguin back in its place.

"What about you? Do you collect anything, or have some hidden addiction we don't know about besides motorcycles?" Humor tugged at the corner of her mouth.

*I might have an Allison addiction.* He cleared his throat. "Nope. I collect bikes like my oldest brother collects cars."

Her brow furrowed. "Roth, right?"

"Omar. I don't think Roth collects anything. Well, at the moment he might be collecting baby clothes."

"Oh, you're going to be an uncle?"

"Looks that way. I'm a little nervous about what type of obligations that entails." He grinned. Not nervous in the least.

"You'll be a natural, I'm sure." She locked the cabinet and dropped the key into the penguin bowl on top. "So, bikes are probably a lot cheaper to collect than cars?"

He shook his head. "Unfortunately for me, I have expensive tastes. I prefer the Harley and have one from the late forties, a couple from the seventies, and—" He laughed at her wide-eyed expression. She looked at him as if she'd never met him before. "Maybe I should tell you to search Google if you really want to know more."

She slugged him in the arm, and he almost choked on his beer.

"There you go getting all flirty again," she teased. "You get as excited about your Harleys as I do about my penguins. I almost feel guilty I know nothing about bikes."

"Is this the part where I'm supposed to confess the same and tell you that I'm sorry I don't know much about penguins, either?"

Her laughter filled the room. "Only if you mean it, and I'm pretty sure you don't."

"You're intuitive." He swallowed the last of his beer. "I'll have to take you out on one of my bikes sometime. I can teach you a few things." What the hell had possessed him to bring that up? And how come it sounded dirty, even to his own ears? Did he really want to get involved any deeper than he already was?

*Yes.*

*No!*

"Bikes are your only passion?"

"And penguins are yours?"

She tilted her head to the side and grinned. "After today I might have found a new addiction."

He held his breath as he waited to hear what it was.

"Shopping."

His shoulders sagged.

"Your turn. Drop some dirt," she teased.

He opened his mouth and then closed it—on the verge of confessing his little secret, the one nobody knew, because he'd taken a shitload of ribbing from his brothers as a teen.

When he and Roth were younger, one of the many classes his mother had signed them up for had been dancing. Ballroom dancing, to be exact. Over time, Jared found he liked the way he got out of his head when he danced.

It had always sounded crazy when he tried to explain it, and although he trusted Al, he wasn't sure he wanted to bare that part of himself. And right now, his emotions were already raw after their day together. He'd stick to the old college standby.

"I can make my pecs dance."

"Your pecs dance?" She busted out laughing, and the sound easily had him joining in.

"It was a fraternity party favorite."

"I bet. You'll have to show me sometime."

Now that'd be trouble. No shirt—around Allison—might be more than either of them bargained for. "At this point in my life, my pec dancing days are few and far between. I'd have to have one too many beers in me."

She eyed the empty beer bottle he tapped against his thigh. "Are you ready for another, then?"

"I'm easy, Al, but not that easy."

Her eyes sparkled, and she chewed her lip. The little bit of shyness mixed with her humor drew him to her. Maybe once they got to know each other better…

*Whoa. Whoa. Whoa. Don't start thinking like that. There's no need to get to know each other any better than this right here.*

She snapped her fingers as if she'd missed out. "Maybe another time."

"You're not going to try to get rid of me now, are you?"

"Why would you think that?"

"Because I shot down the pec dance?" But part of him wished she did. He'd be safer. He followed the flick of her tongue over her lips. Hell, she'd be safer.

She shook her head, her hair brushing against her cheeks, making his fingers itch to reach out and touch the silky-looking strands.

"Nah, I'm sure I'll eventually see the pec dance firsthand. Somewhere down the line you'll have a few too many, and I'll pop out of the shadows and persuade you to show me your moves."

A tinge of red crept over her cheeks, and she lowered her lashes. Desire shot through him with the force of a rocket launch. How the hell could she do that? Look so innocent but seductive at the same time?

After he regained his good sense, he laughed. A bit shakily. "I'm not too sure about that." Those days ended when

Nick and he had decided to get serious with their business. "Anyway, you were about to kick me out and—"

She playfully punched him in the arm, hitting him in the same spot she had earlier—her aim uncanny. "I was not."

He rubbed his arm, exaggerating the motion when she gave him a lopsided grin and shook her head.

"Then I better kick myself out." *Before I do something we'll both regret. Like take you in my arms and kiss you until neither of us can see straight.*

"Thanks for playing hooky with me today and for everything you did." She trailed her fingers against the wall as she led him down the short hallway toward the door.

"My pleasure. See you in the morning?" He stepped past her and turned, one eyebrow raised.

She nodded. "I'll be the one dressed for success."

"You're already a success." Unable to stop himself, he leaned in and grazed her cheek with his knuckles. Her quick breath drew his attention to the rise and fall of her chest. A mesmerizing sight against her tight T-shirt.

He lifted her chin and touched his mouth to hers in a featherlight kiss. Her lips moved against his, pliant and sweet like he knew she'd taste. He broke away, even though he wanted so much more. He'd have to settle for this as a good-bye before hello had even started. "Sweet dreams."

# Chapter Six

Allison's nerves were shot. Today would be ten times harder than yesterday. She had no choice but to paste on a smile and get through it for a couple reasons. One, she couldn't miss two days in a row or the guys would give her crap for the next month. And two, she couldn't let Jared down after all he'd done. With head held high and shoulders back, she strode the last several feet to the revolving doors of her office building as sprinkles of rain hit the cement. She repeated Margarite's mantra "awesome" in her head as she entered the lobby. It also didn't hurt that Colleen had drummed another dose of bestie pep talk into her head last night. Allison owed her big for her encouragement and support.

After Jared left, she had put away all her purchases while spilling her day to her bestie. She'd shared everything… except her feelings for Jared. Although she loved Colleen to pieces, the unexpected feelings she'd developed for Jared weren't something she wanted to talk about. Why get herself all worked up about how he made her feel when he smiled at her, looked at her, or paid her a compliment when that was just his nature? Nothing would come of it, and she couldn't let it go to her head. If she mentioned it to Colleen, it'd go to her head, too, and she'd start asking questions certain to consume both their thoughts with silly wishes. She might not have much experience, and sometimes her romantic fantasies even drove *her* crazy, but she never let her imagination float so high into the clouds that she lost touch with reality. She and Jared would never, ever happen.

Period.

She tugged at the waistline of her embroidered blazer, the one Jared had paired with the silver midi dress that hugged her every curve. He had assured her it picked up the lighter, brighter shades of her hair.

His words had left her openmouthed and speechless, but she trusted what he said and put the outfit in the buy pile. But now, out in the real world, she questioned her impulsiveness. If she wanted to survive the day, she best concentrate on something other than what she wore.

Jared's voice echoed in her head: *you'll get used to it.*

Her fingers pulled on the tiny pearl-like buttons of her jacket as the elevator raced—at least that's how it felt—up to the twenty-third floor and the offices of Firstline Security.

The people she shared the elevator with didn't know her from Eve, and it gave her a reprieve. Nobody had stared at her or given her the looks she'd earned twenty-four hours ago. So that had to be a good sign.

In order to not bare herself to the same extreme as yesterday, she'd worn her glasses. Kind of a shield of protection. A comfortable habit. Maybe tomorrow, or in a few more days, she'd try the contacts again.

The moment the elevator stopped, she sucked in a breath, which earned her a quick glance and smile from the woman beside her. She was about Allison's age and seemed nervous as she kept straightening her skirt and rubbing her hands up and down her side seams. If anyone could recognize a kindred spirit, Allison could.

The door opened, and she turned to give the woman a smile before stepping off. "Have a good day."

The brunette's eyes widened in surprise and then she smiled. "You, too."

Allison hoped both their days would live up to that one word—*good*. She turned the corner and entered the empty reception area. It paid to be early. Maybe she could make her way through the office to her own space and avoid all contact.

Not that she didn't think she looked good. Not that she didn't feel good. But after yesterday…

*Yesterday is long gone. I've got this.*

In order to boost her confidence she pasted on the smile she'd let go lax. She walked down the corridor—the silky swish of the hem of her dress brushing her lower thighs and urging her on—toward the break room, just as Jared emerged. He carried a travel mug, and the strap of his laptop case was slung over one shoulder.

"Morning, Al. Looking good." He winked playfully, and she lifted her chin, greeting him with a warm smile.

"Thanks. I feel good."

"You got this?"

She nodded, loving his support. It almost calmed her more than Colleen's encouragement. "Where you off to?" She motioned to his laptop.

"Nick and I are tag teaming it. He couldn't quite close the deal with Bricket Engineering, so I'm flying out to Denver. We'll have everything settled by the end of the week."

"Good luck." Another example of why she'd chosen to ask Jared for his help. And definitely another reason she was glad he'd changed his mind. He hadn't even considered he wouldn't get the contract with Bricket, it was only a matter of *when*. Never *if*.

"See you at dinner Sunday?" he asked.

Even though she'd just reminded herself Jared was off-limits, she couldn't stop the wave of anticipation that rippled through her.

"I'll be there."

"The one dressed for success?" His lopsided smile, mixed with his amazing voice, sent another wave of chills over her skin.

"I'll just be basic Allison. Sundays are my day off," she teased. How she managed to sound so normal blew her mind. Especially since her skin throbbed with excitement from the sound of his voice alone.

"Even though you'll never be basic, I'll try to follow your lead."

His words sent her mind spinning. She wanted to say something but had no clue what. He'd given her the best compliment, and he probably had no idea how his words made her day. *You'll never be basic.*

He cleared his throat, saluting her with his coffee mug as he continued down the hall. "By Sunday I'll be ready for a day off, too. See you then."

"See you."

She counted to ten slowly before she dared look over her shoulder in hopes of catching a secret glimpse of him before he left. The way his suit jacket hugged his shoulders; she could only imagine how his trousers wrapped around his rear. She almost lost her footing when she turned and caught him looking at her.

He gave her a mischievous smile, and heat invaded every inch of her body as she abruptly turned back around, but not before she misjudged the distance to the break room door and bumped into the wall.

"Smooth as silk, Al," she said under her breath as she pressed her hands to the wall. She snuck another glance over her shoulder to see if he'd witnessed her geek attack. He'd already disappeared from view, so hopefully he'd missed the show.

With a small sigh, she pushed her glasses back into place and continued to the break room, inhaling a large dose of coffee-scented air. Her heart squeezed when she noticed Glenda and Andrea talking with Kenny across the room. He looked out of his element. His eyes went back and forth between the women as if he watched a tennis match. Whatever they were saying, he appeared lost. His shoulders hunched, and his focus kept returning to the floor, looking like he wanted to curl into a ball and get out of sight.

And then he spotted Allison. His smile revealed his gapped front teeth as he gave her a slow appraisal.

The grin spreading across his face as he took in her appearance shot another dose of confidence through her. It was nice to see someone recognized her effort. That a guy sat up and took notice, even if it was Kenny.

Her confidence urged her to come to his rescue. All she had to do was get their attention, and then he could escape. Easy. Peasy.

She hummed as if she didn't have a care in the world and made her way toward the coffee station, only a few feet from where they stood.

"Allison?" Andrea's mouth fell open.

"Good morning, Andrea. Glenda, Kenny." She nodded as she looked each one of them square in the eye; all the while her mind was racing with a nonstop pep talk. Kenny mumbled something and broke away, poured decaf into his Marvel Comics mug, and left the room as if the soles of his shoes were on fire.

Allison grabbed a Styrofoam cup from the counter and poured her own coffee, adding a splash of cream and two sugars, trying to ignore the way Andrea poked Glenda in the ribs and her mouth hung open.

Did she really leave them speechless? The idea almost made her laugh. Now that would be a confidence booster.

She turned toward the two women, and their expressions—a little awe mixed with something else that she couldn't label—made her relax. A sudden bit of brazen sass spiked up her backbone. "Cute dress, Glenda. Did you get that at Bloomies?" She abbreviated Bloomingdales in hopes they'd think she was a regular. Why? She had no clue, but for some reason it made her feel better.

Glenda nodded, her mouth still open. She licked her lips, swallowing hard. "I'm surprised you'd know that—"

Allison waved her words away. "I saw it in their flyer a couple weeks ago. I thought about it, but got this one instead." She straightened the wrinkle-free fabric of her dress. At least she hadn't fibbed on that account. She had seen Glenda's dress in an ad and loved it, but after she'd tried it on she decided it was best left on the hanger.

She took a sip of her coffee, as if she didn't mind being in their presence this long. But in all honesty her entire body screamed at her to make an exit. Confidence was one thing, but she was in no way ready to play with these girls.

"What happened to you? Yesterday..." Andrea's hand dropped to her side, and the coffee she'd been holding, and apparently forgotten about, spilled over onto her hand, and tiny droplets splattered on her white skirt.

Allison lowered her own cup with deliberate slowness. No way would she make Andrea's mistake. A surge of pride rippled through her. Apparently today she'd passed the test, and her makeup enhanced instead of strangled. "What do you mean?"

That little bit of cockiness Margarite warned her about spiked. It might be fun to kind of drag it out. At least for a minute or so.

"Your hair, make—"

"Oh. That." She waved away their words with the flick of her wrist. "Nothing. The clowns all got together for a burning of the midnight oil and decided to shake things up. From now on we'll be using brushes instead of dipping our faces."

She gave each of them another smile that basically said *suck it* and walked toward the door. The click of her heels as she crossed the silent room matched the quick rhythm of her heart. She used all her control to hold on to her cup as her palms grew sweaty. At least she'd sounded surer of herself than she felt.

As soon as she cleared the break room door and turned the corner, she sagged against the wall and took a gulp of air, pressing her cup to her chest until the Styrofoam creaked.

She'd survived the office bullies. Confidence felt good.

Allison whipped the royal blue dress up and over her head and threw it onto the ever-growing pile of rejects that lay spread across her bed. She'd wanted to wear that dress so badly—she'd picked it out herself, mainly for the scalloped scoop neckline—but she didn't want everyone in her family to freak out at her new look. They'd need little spurts of change to get used to things. Nick had been out of the office all week so even he didn't know anything about her transformation.

She also didn't want to come off too cocky with Jared, especially after she told him she didn't dress for success on Sundays.

A smile fluttered across her lips at the idea of seeing him. She looked forward to it much more than she should. She pulled a pair of stretch jeans and a coral pink polo from the shelf in her closet. Couldn't get much more casual than that.

For some reason she felt on the cusp of hyperventilating.

"It's just Sunday dinner." *With Jared.*

Not like he'd never been there before. But in the past she hadn't ever cared. Despite knowing nothing would come of it, she'd liked his attention and wanted him to keep noticing her.

Maybe that she'd been so starved for male attention over the last decade had something to do with the nervous flutter in her belly. Or maybe that little voice in her head that told her she'd allowed a secret crush to develop for a man so out of her realm they might as well live on different planets could be blamed for her case of nerves.

But heck. She liked his attention, and what was the harm in enjoying it? Cultivating it? It would be great practice for when she finally did start to date.

Right?

*Right. It's my story.*

She wanted to look good—and her attention strayed back to that little blue dress on top of the pile. No. Casual was the word of the day. They never dressed up for Sunday dinner. Her father and Nick would give her the third degree if she showed up in a number like that—and embarrass her in front of Jared. She ran her hand over her polo and frowned.

The wooden dowel in her closet sagged and groaned as she flung hanger after hanger along its surface. Then she spotted it: the cute little tee she'd tried on first at the department store. The one that had caused Jared's eyes to bug out, and maybe had been responsible for that little bead of sweat that formed on his forehead.

Excitement built in her gut, and she hugged her middle.

She pulled if from the closet so quickly the hanger swung back and forth and fell to the floor. Within seconds her arms flailed overhead as she worked her way into the tee, and then pulled on a new pair of jeans—the ones that hugged her ass—jumping up as she pulled them over her hips. A little tighter than the last pair, but they made her feel…

*Sexy.*

*Do I really want to be sexy for Sunday dinner?* She did today.

She spun around as she buttoned the waistband and ironed out imaginary wrinkles with her palms. Looking in the mirror, she studied her reflection and smiled, touching the skin beneath her eyes—happy to see how wearing her contacts really brought the focus to her face instead of allowing her to hide. Margarite had been right, she did have nice eyes. She stepped back and put her hands on her hips.

"Awesome," she whispered. "Thanks, Margarite."

Even though she wanted to meet a special man, she couldn't ignore the way her breath caught in her chest at the thought of flirting with Jared. All in the name of honing her skills.

*Sure. It's still my story.*

She had to think of him as an excellent sparring partner. Nothing more. She wouldn't allow herself to take their exchanges seriously.

She would just have to keep reminding herself of that.

•••

The kink that had developed in Jared's neck from looking nonstop at Al as she sat to his left was worth it. He'd been unable to take his eyes off her, and in order to prolong his inspection without drawing too much attention, he kept spooning food onto his plate and then into his mouth.

She stood, reaching for her plate, more than likely ready to start clearing the table, because everyone had finished eating a while ago.

"Pass me the green beans, will ya, Al?" He didn't want her to leave yet. He wasn't done staring.

"Aren't you about ready to burst?"

"Never."

She shrugged. "I respect a man who goes in for seconds. And thirds, or even fourths."

"And today it looks like Jared is all about earning your respect." Nick's dry tone hit him between the eyes, but he pushed away his friend's obvious annoyance by ignoring him.

Allison lifted the bowl of green beans and, instead of passing it to him, spooned out a good-size serving and dropped it on his plate. Their shoulders bumped as she leaned over him, and they laughed, an uneasy sound that magnified the tension crackling between them. Because he knew, sure as hell, she felt the draw as much as he did. It'd been evident in the way she peeked at him from the side of her eyes when she didn't think he noticed, and how her voice got all wispy and soft when she leaned close to make a funny comment while everyone else talked around them.

She touched his shoulder, her fingers pressing into his skin. "Do you think that'll hold you over?"

He nodded, staring into her perfect brown eyes. Without her glasses they had endless depth and seemed more pronounced. Bigger. Softer. Mesmerizing. He shook off his thoughts, trying to control the unsteady rhythm of his heart. What the hell was happening to him?

From the corner of his eye he caught Nick's gaze narrowing as he pushed away his plate with more force than necessary, scrunching the tablecloth into the vase.

"I'm glad you decided to buy some new clothes, Al, but isn't the shirt a little small?" Nick asked.

Jared felt the unease roll off Allison as her free hand fell to her side.

"It's the style, Nick. I'm just trying to fit in."

"Hmm, I still think—"

"I think you look great, hon," Allison's dad, Neal, cut in as he leaned forward in his chair, rolling his coffee cup between his palms. His smile was indulgent and reminiscent at the same time. "You remind me more and more of your mom every day."

"Mom didn't wear shirts like that," Nick grumbled.

"I'm not talking about her shirt or her clothes in general. I'm talking about her attitude." Neal frowned at his son before turning toward Allison with a smile. "You look happy."

"I am, Dad." Her eyes softened. She glanced back at Nick, opening her mouth as if she were about to speak, and then changing her mind.

Gramps stood and grabbed his plate, planting a little kiss on Allison's cheek. "Just remember, Allygirl, all the flowers of tomorrow are in the seeds of yesterday."

Allison closed her eyes briefly as Gramps patted her cheek, and then she shared a smile with Jared. Gramps's little saying wasn't lost on him, either.

Allison cleared her throat. "Okay, I'm clearing the table, so everyone speak now or forever hold your peace." She turned her attention back to Jared. "I'm mainly speaking to you. Do you want more potatoes?"

"I'm good," he said around a mouthful of green beans. He swallowed quickly. "How about I give you a hand?" It'd give them a chance to be alone—and more of a chance to stalk her with his eyes.

Before Allison could answer, Gramps motioned for him to stay seated. "You take your time finishing. I'll partner up with Allygirl. This will be the first time in a week I've gotten to talk to my lovely granddaughter alone." He loaded his arms with dishes.

"You sure, Gramps? I thought you wanted to take your time with your coffee." Allison took some of his burden, adding to her own stack. "And didn't the doctor tell you that you're not supposed to be lifting so much with that shoulder?"

"I'm coffee'd out, and doctors don't know everything."

He grabbed a few more dishes off the table as soon as she turned her back before following her into the kitchen.

Minutes later their laughter and muted conversation floated from the kitchen into the dining room. Jared speared his fork through a few more green beans. Over the years, Sunday dinners at the Halls had been something he'd looked forward to. Endless conversation, laughs, good food, all mixed in with a touch of hominess. He'd never gotten that as a kid, except from a few sitcoms on television, but in the Hall household it really existed.

Too bad the glare accosting him from across the table soured his mood. A current of tension snapped between him and Nick, even though nobody else seemed to notice.

A sudden crash from the kitchen made everyone at the table jump. Gramps's voice erupted in a steady stream of apologies, followed by Allison's soothing tones. Neal was on his feet in a flash.

"I better give them a hand."

The silence became deafening when Jared and Nick were alone. Their friendship had never demanded constant conversation, but this silence had become unbearable, and Jared shifted in his seat as he pushed the last of his green beans around his plate.

Guilt ate away at him as all thoughts centered on Allison and how she looked in her tight jeans. Her ass. The way the denim pulled when she bent, or how it lay smooth over her thighs. How he'd watched her legs bounce beneath the table as they'd eaten. The thoughts of calming her nerves by placing his palm on her thigh. If only he had dared.

He ran his hands through his hair, cupping the back of his head as he leaned into his chair with a sigh. He couldn't even bring himself to meet Nick's eyes, even though he could feel his friend's gaze burning a hole right through him.

Jared closed his eyes, only to see Al's soft face, her

dreamy smile, silky hair. He'd rode over on his latest buy—a '48 Harley Panhead—and she'd look great on the back. She'd look even better pressed up against him as they soared down the highway. His body ached with wanting to touch her all during dinner, and the stress in his muscles from restraining himself burned.

Too bad the bike was built for one. The seat barely fit his ass, let alone two. Next time…

Nick shoved himself back from the table, the legs of his chair scraping along the wood floor. "So what's the fucking deal with you and my sister?"

And here it was. The conversation he'd known was coming. He'd hoped to avoid this talk for a while, preferably altogether. But not all wishes come true.

Nick's tone put him on the defensive. "Nothing's up." *At least nothing you need to know about.*

He thought he had controlled himself enough so that his oldest friend—who knew him better than most—wouldn't pick up on the fact that he couldn't take his eyes off Al.

He'd been dead wrong. Of course Nick had noticed. A room of blind men would've noticed.

"Bullshit. You've been staring at her all night. And she's been staring right back. All your little glances and whispered exchanges are enough to…" Nick leaned forward, thrust his elbows on table, and steeped his hands as he regarded Jared through narrowed eyes. They stared at each other for several seconds as Nick forced himself to calm down by taking controlled breaths. "I'm gone for a few days, and I come home to a sister I don't even recognize. Makeup, clothes—shit, even her personality's changed. I can't help but wonder if you had something to do with this since it seems more than apparent you two are now best friends."

"Don't tell me you're jealous of my friendship with your sister?" Jared couldn't help his cocky question. He also couldn't help his shit-ass grin. He'd always been one to use humor when things got tense. Blame it on his childhood.

Nick grimaced. "You're a real fucking comedian. I don't care if you and Allison are friends, I just don't like the way you're looking at her." He forked his fingers through his hair. "Or the way she's looking back."

Tension pinged across the table for several seconds before Nick took a breath. "Listen, man. I know you're a good guy, you're my best friend, my partner, but you have to stay away from Allison."

"Because nobody's good enough for her in your eyes?" Jared challenged. "Someday she's going to meet someone, and you better learn to accept it. She's a grown woman, with wants, needs, desires."

Nick's eyes sparked anger. "What the hell do you know about her wants and needs?" He growled from deep within his throat, standing to tower over the table.

Jared stood, too. No way in hell would he let Nick think he could intimidate him. "Al asked for my help. At first, out of respect for you, I turned her down flat, but circumstances changed, and I— "

"Should've kept your fucking nose out of our business. Allison didn't need to change. She's fine— "

"Wake up. She wasn't happy. She was going to make changes with or without me. With or without you. If you didn't want her seeking help somewhere else, you should've helped her yourself when she asked."

Nick pounded the table with his fist. "Okay. You helped her. I can deal with that shit, but not with the way you look at her. What the fuck is going on with you two? Did something more happen than a little shopping spree?"

Jared shrugged, trying to play it casual so things didn't get any more out of control. Hell, he couldn't even explain what was happening between him and Allison to himself, let alone try to clue Nick in. "Quit treating her like a kid. Why don't you fucking listen to her?" *And there goes casual.*

"What the hell does that mean?"

"It means you disregard everything she says so you get your way. Why don't you take the time to get to know her by listening? You might learn something, like the fact that she's funny, interesting, smart…" His chest constricted, and he stopped himself. If he wanted to convince Nick nothing was going on, he better shut the fuck up.

Nick's glare turned to ice. "Bullshit. I listen."

"No, you don't." Jared's focus shifted to the door that led to the tiny hallway and then into the kitchen, lowering his voice as he continued. "You bulldozed over her when she wanted to move; you practically chose her apartment." He leaned forward, matching Nick's steady glare. He'd had enough, and maybe he needed to hit the truth home. Allison was too softhearted and kind to lay it on the line with her brother, but Jared wasn't. "Oh yeah, you didn't *practically* choose her apartment, you *did* choose it. Along with her car, where she went to school, and the list goes on." It was about time Nick took a hard look at himself and how he treated Allison. "She's a grown woman, Nick. Why don't you let her make her own decisions? She's fully capable. Quit treating her like she isn't."

"I'm just helping her. It's not like she can't make up her own mind."

"Then you aren't paying attention. She wants so much to make you happy that whenever you 'suggest'"—he air quoted—"she makes concessions so you won't be disappointed. Or maybe because she doesn't want to argue with you."

Nick's eyes narrowed. "Don't try to tell me what's best between me and my sister. You're not in a position to give advice. At least my sibling and I have never broken communication for any length of time."

His chest tightened another notch. Not only because of Nick's words but because they'd never argued on this level before. And Nick had never used Jared's family against him. He knew the sordid details, the hardships Jared had been through being alienated from his father and his oldest brother Omar. "Don't even go there, Nick. You might not like the outcome."

The air crackled between them. Nick scrubbed his face and then folded his arms. "I love you like a brother, man, but I won't have you chasing after my sister. You're on totally different playing fields. She isn't going to be another one of your flings. She's off-limits."

"You're crossing the line. We're only friends." The sound of blood rushing through his ears became deafening. Their eyes dueled across the width of the table. But was Nick really crossing the line? Maybe the one crossing the line here was Jared. He'd crossed the line of friendship with both Allison and Nick. The steel band around his chest tightened further, making it hard to breathe.

"Don't bullshit me. I've seen the way you look at each other. I respect you, love you, man, but I won't have her getting hurt. And you, my friend, have the power to hurt her. Even if that's not your intention. Al is steady, true, loyal—"

"And you're saying I'm not?" Jared's blood boiled.

"I'm saying you're the quintessential serial dater. I'm saying I've seen you with one woman at dinner, and then another at dessert—on the same night. I'm telling you that Al is the type of woman who deserves someone who wants to be attached—to her alone, loves her from the depths of his soul, puts her above all else. Man, that's not what you want." Nick shook his head, his eyes pleading for Jared to see reason. "Don't let your dick lead you astray. Leave my sister alone. She's not as experienced or worldly as you and I. You'll end up hurting her, and I won't have it. You understand?" His voice grew dangerously lower with each word. "Allison. Is. Off. Limits."

Nick's words crashed in around Jared. Confusion closed his throat and made it difficult to swallow. He rubbed his neck with such force his fingers ached. "I'd never hurt Al."

"Maybe not intentionally." Nick's shoulders sagged, and he pinched the bridge of his nose, jumping slightly when the dining room door opened and Allison appeared.

Her smile wavered as her glance darted between Jared and Nick. "Everything okay? It feels a little thick with testosterone in here." Her attempt at laughter came out tinny and unsure.

"We're good." Nick moved forward and turned her back toward the kitchen. "Come on, we'll team up on dishes like the old days."

The tinkle of her laughter filled Jared's ears, and she shot him a concerned look over her shoulder as she walked out of view. He nodded and did his best to deliver what he hoped was an encouraging smile. As soon as they were out of view he fell back into his chair.

*Holy fuck.* His heated words with Nick grated on him. Mainly because what he said was true. He couldn't keep his eyes off Al, and he didn't want to. He'd like nothing better than to see where things would go, but at the same time he didn't want to hurt her.

And his track record left a lot to be desired. But maybe things with Al would be different. He wanted what she wanted. Why couldn't they have it together?

For some reason, he could picture things with Allison turning out differently than with the women in his past. She was different. She made him feel different. Whenever they were together, he was more relaxed, more himself.

He liked how she made him feel about himself.

He didn't want to hurt Nick, and he definitely didn't want to hurt Allison. But did that mean they couldn't take a chance? Allison had taken him by surprise tonight, and the full magnitude hadn't hit him until now. Until Nick confronted him. He wanted Nick to see his sister for who she was, but instead Jared had seen her as someone he could—would like to—have in his future. She wasn't just fucking cute, but was sexy, smart, and had a little sass. He loved the way her big eyes sparkled when she spoke. The animated way she used her hands when she talked, how her laughter bubbled over when she heard or said something funny. The excitement tinged with mischief in her eyes. She was the complete package like he'd never seen it presented before.

He rubbed his forehead, closing his eyes. But it was more than all of those things. More than the way she laughed or smiled. More than how her fucking jeans formed to her ass. More than the way she looked at him as if every word he uttered was a brushstroke of genius.

He enjoyed talking to her. He respected that even when she found something difficult to say, she looked him in the eye. *Fuck.* He might be a little nuts, but she made him feel special. And sexy. *When was the last time someone made me feel sexy?*

All he wanted was to continue getting to know her—on this new level. She'd surpassed being Nick's little sister. She'd become a vibrant woman who grabbed his attention and made him want to learn more.

All week long he'd talked himself out of what he'd been feeling. But the moment she opened the door tonight, he'd almost swallowed his tongue. He hadn't planned to be so transparent, but he'd been unable to control himself. She flirted, and he'd flirted right back. And enjoyed every minute of it—until Nick.

As much as he didn't want anything to come between

him and Nick, he wasn't sure he wanted to let go of what was happening between him and Al.

...

Allison kicked off her shoes and slipped into her penguin slippers as she tossed her purse onto the kitchen counter with a thud. Dinner at Dad's had been perfect right up until she'd heard the raised voices coming from the dining room. Dad and Gramps hadn't seemed to notice, but then again, they'd been busy cleaning up the broken plate and cup Gramps had dropped on the floor. And Gramps hadn't been able to stop apologizing as Dad kept reassuring him over and over again that everything would be okay.

Although the night had been good up until that point, it'd also been filled with tension. Anxiety about her new look, sexual tension between her and Jared that had gotten out of hand, and finally strain between Nick and herself, and then Nick and Jared. And that bothered her most of all. She'd only planned on a few flirty glances, maybe a cute comment here and there, but instead…instead Nick had noticed, and words between her brother and Jared had turned hostile. Not that she'd heard much of the exchange except for a few loudly spoken words here and there—like her name—but when she'd entered the dining room, she could've popped the pressure-filled air with a pin. If she hadn't arrived when she had, she feared fists might have started to fly.

Because of her.

She didn't want to cause a rift between them. They'd been tight for too many years. They ran a business together, were more brothers than some related by blood, and their friendship had never faltered. Never. She should know better than to flirt with her brother's best friend. It wasn't like Nick's protectiveness was something new.

She sank onto the sofa and pulled the little triangle pillow filled with penguin faces across her lap and sat back, playing with the corner tassel as she stared at her ceiling. A dull throb settled in the back of her head.

The love she had for her brother trumped her little dalliance with Jared. If she had to leave Jared alone, stop the flirting, and push aside the effect he had on her, she'd do it. Although she didn't want to, she'd make the effort to return things to where they'd been a week ago. Polite. Courteous. Distant.

But heck, she didn't want to.

She liked Jared, she truly did. *But I love my brother more.*

If she concentrated on the next step in her quest for change, that'd help get thoughts of Jared out of her head.

*Right?*

*Right.*

She needed to start dating.

# Chapter Seven

Allison bit into the center of her turkey sandwich—avoiding the dreaded crust—and frowned as she slid the cursor down the page. The remainder of her lunch fell onto the plate between her monitor and keyboard. She plopped her chin into her palm as she chewed slowly, reading the words and ogling the pictures of all the different bars in her neighborhood.

She wished she had a sidekick for this new venture. Someone to bounce ideas off. Colleen and Jerry were going away for a long-overdue vacation, so they were out. She'd been chatting with a few girls in the office but didn't really feel comfortable with letting them know of her quest for a date, and no chance in hell would she even think about asking her brother. There really wasn't anyone else she trusted. Besides Jared. But…

"Don't tell me you're surfing the web on company time?" Jared's teasing tone surprised her, and she spun in her chair, wiping crumbs from her blouse.

With gargantuan force she managed a friendly smile. "You caught me."

She'd planned to sound noncommittal and distant, but even to her own ears her words came out breathy and inviting. She cleared her throat when he tilted his head, confusion marring his gorgeous eyes.

"I didn't hear you come in." Her mind had been far away. Researching a spot to meet potential guys wasn't as easy as she'd imagined. There were too many choices.

"That's the point. You aren't supposed to hear me when I'm looking for on-the-job slackers."

She clasped her hands together, batting her lashes. "Please don't fire me. I need this gig."

He pursed his lips, but she honed in on the way the edges of his mouth tugged to form a smile. "I guess I can let you off with a warning."

She bit her lip, soaking in his smile. "I'll work late."

"You always do." His voice deepened and sent a shiver across her skin.

The room heated, and the playful atmosphere changed to one that snapped with tension. Or maybe she imagined the shift in the air between them.

Her gaze skimmed over him, and she tried hard not to linger on the way his biceps flexed when he ran his hand through his hair, or how his thighs pressed against the material of his trousers. Heck, he looked as good as he had four days ago at Sunday dinner. Maybe better. His eyes seemed bluer, his shoulders broader, and his smile sexier.

*And my attraction hasn't diminished one iota.*

She licked her lips with the cotton ball she used to call a tongue. In her attempt to avoid him the last few days, she'd resorted to eating lunch at her desk, except for yesterday when Megan had asked her to join her and two others at the coffee shop in the main lobby downstairs. She hadn't thought about what would happen if he sought her out in her tiny office. When nobody was around. Her leg bounced beneath the desk, and she stilled it by pressing her palm on her knee.

"You okay?" he asked.

She nodded. Her situation sunk in as she glanced around and swallowed. Her work cohorts had left early for the seminar she'd attended last month. She and Jared were alone.

Truly alone.

And they weren't supposed to be, not if she wanted to keep her head. Because, suddenly, being in a dimly lit room with Jared and his hypnotizing cologne threw her out of her comfort zone. The walls she'd been erecting since Sunday to keep him at arm's length swayed.

She forced a polite smile, pushing aside her playfulness from seconds ago. That'd been a mistake. A surefire way to get all giddy and silly by flirting, which would turn to cutesy words, touching, attraction… "Is there something I can help you with?"

"I wanted to see if you'd finished the report for… Are you looking up bars?"

His eyebrows rose in that sexy way that made her stomach dip, and then a tiny line formed between his brows. Her fingers ached to reach out and smooth it over. She clasped her hands together in her lap.

"Best bars in Chicago, if you want to be exact." Her smile hurt her face.

"Really?"

She nodded, then spun in her chair and gave him her back. Kind of late to minimize the screen now, but she didn't want him to read what she'd typed into the search bar: "best bars in Chicago to meet men." Before her finger could click, he'd rested his palms on either side of her chair, effectively blocking her in. They might not be face to face, but her flesh became ultra-sensitive. His breath tickled her neck and sent waves of awareness down her back. All thoughts of suppressing her attraction crashed, and she closed her eyes briefly and took a shallow breath. Her plan of resetting their friendship back to more than a week ago burned to ashes.

She'd thought he smelled good before. One large gulp of air later—then another for good measure—and her head swam with thoughts of him bare-chested and teasing her with his dancing pecs. She'd already played that fantasy over and over in her mind, and at this point she had every line of his chest memorized, even though she'd never actually seen it.

"I didn't think bars were your scene." His words warmed the shell of her ear.

"They're not, but after having lunch with Megan yesterday—"

"From accounting or reception?"

"Accounting." She breathed the word more than spoke it.

"Hmm."

Allison forced her lips to form words. "She's a total party girl."

From the corner of her eye, she watched as he shifted his attention to the pad of paper beside her keyboard. "Barhopping is the next thing on your list?"

"Hardly. Dating is."

"Are you sure you're ready?"

She squinted at him from the side. "No time like the present. I know Nick thinks I should wait until I'm forty, but—"

"I didn't mean it like that."

She nodded, biting her lip. "I know. It's a sensitive subject with me."

They didn't say anything for a couple of beats, and Allison figured she'd been honest to a fault up to this point, so why stop now? She tapped the notepad he'd inspected seconds ago. "Megan gave me a list of places to meet men. I looked them up, but I'm doing my own research, too."

"You can Google that shit?"

She grinned, a tiny laugh escaping from between her lips. "You can Google anything."

"Like penguins?" His breath blew a wisp of her hair across her cheek, and she tucked it behind her ear with shaky fingers.

"Especially penguins. And motorcycles…and so much more," she whispered. She swiveled slightly in her chair, catching him off guard so that his mouth actually brushed her cheek.

They each sucked in a quick breath, and he stepped back, straightening then folding his arms. Suddenly his stance reminded her of Nick. His authoritative posture told her before a word left his mouth that she'd lose any argument she might attempt. Her shoulders stiffened. Nick wouldn't intimidate her any longer, and she wouldn't let Jared start. She wanted changes, and that meant she had to stand up for herself.

"I don't think the bar is a good idea. Not for meeting men."

"Where do you suggest? The frozen food aisle, through a friend, a dating service?" She folded her arms in an attempt at her own intimidation. Although it didn't seem to have much of an effect since she still sat and had to look up at him.

She tilted her head to the side, tapping her chin with her finger. "I think Colleen can set me up with Jerry's little brother. I mean, he's barely a teen, but he did think I was cute, and I know I'd be safe with him. Of course I'd have to drive, and…"

He shook his head, his eyes hardening. "As a matter of fact, the entire idea's wrong."

She laughed. "Really? That seems an odd comment coming from a guy who's dated so many women he's gone through the alphabet at least ten times."

"A slight exaggeration." His lopsided smile disarmed her.

"I'm only saying you're moving pretty fast. What's the hurry? You're barely a week into your makeover."

"Don't even try it. Did Nick enlist your help or something?"

"Listen, Al—"

She waved his words away, already regretting what she'd said. "Never mind. We'll have to agree to disagree on this one. I'm ready to start dating, and a bar is a good enough place to start as anywhere."

He nodded his head slowly, and his eyes bored into her until she squirmed. He would never understand, but that didn't stop that little niggle inside of her that always attempted to be a people pleaser. She shoved it aside.

He rocked on his heels, his eyes scouring her face. She shifted in her seat and clicked the window closed. "This isn't a subject I want to talk about with you. You're not going to change my mind, and I'm not going to try to make you understand my reasoning." She shuffled a few papers on her desk, trying to dismiss him without actually coming out and asking him to leave. "What report do you need? I can print it out."

"Sander's Machinery." But his tone let her know he wasn't done spewing his opinion quite yet, he'd just taken a reprieve. More than likely to choose his words.

"It's not ready. I'll have it for you before the end of the day."

"Good, but that doesn't mean I'm letting this go. I don't agree with what you're doing."

"And now all you need to do is find the right words to get me to change my mind? Good luck," she said under her breath.

He might be amazing to look at, weaken her knees, and send chills across her flesh whenever he spoke, but that didn't stop the ball of annoyance from growing in her belly. Before she thought it through, she blurted, "Are you more bothered by the idea of me dating, or my determination to eventually break in my Posturepedic?" She laughed at her own raunchy humor, biting her lip at the stormy look marring his eyes and spreading to his brow with a tight scowl. So much for being reckless. She might have some confidence, but apparently she didn't know how to relieve stress with humor quite yet.

"Not funny." He cupped the crown of his head and sighed. "Since you won't see reason, how about I tag along?"

Surprise bit her in the stomach. "Why would you want to do that?"

"Because some of these bars are in rough neighborhoods." He opened the screen back up and tapped it.

She sighed. "How can I meet a guy if you're with me? Nobody will approach me."

"You can approach them. Or I'll sit off to the side."

"A silent protector?" She frowned. "Should we invite Nick along, too? Maybe you both can have a few drinks, some laughs, or conduct interviews with my prospective dates? Heck, why not all of the above?"

"Good idea."

Her stomach hit the floor, but before she could argue her point he cleared his throat.

"Then maybe we'll play a few rounds of darts or shuffleboard, and order a bottle of Dom so we can celebrate the greatness of your plan."

Allison groaned. "I told you I prefer wine. Plus, I'd rather go alone. I'll avoid the bad neighborhoods. I think I can figure out what parts of town are off-limits since I've lived here my entire life." She shook her head, but at the same time smiled up at him, hoping she looked more saucy than starstruck. She liked his protectiveness—to an extent—but she didn't need a babysitter.

He shrugged as if what they talked about really didn't

matter, but the way his shirt stretched tight over his shoulders and chest as his muscles tensed told another story. He should always be required to wear a jacket. Exposing that chest to the world—even covered by a pinstriped shirt—should be illegal.

"I've already gone this far in your makeover, I might as well give you some advice when it comes to finding your—"

"Man." She leaned back in her chair. Kind of enjoying his discomfort. Would he seriously go to the bar with her? All in the name of protection? She wasn't sure she bought that excuse. But then why was he offering? And more importantly, why did she kind of want to say yes? "I don't think so."

"Come on, Al. It'd make me feel better if someone—"

"Namely you." She rocked in her chair.

"Namely me, was there to make sure you're okay."

"I'm not thirteen, you know?"

"I know you're of age, but even you have to admit that you're not familiar with Chicago's nightlife. There are all kinds of creeps out there. Someone could buy you a drink and toss in a roofie."

"Oh, please. I'll buy my own drink."

One eyebrow shot up. "What would happen if some guy came on to you and you couldn't fight him off? At least I'd be there to make sure nothing happened."

He had a point. She could feel her mind softening. Surrendering. And she had wanted someone to go with her…

"You promise you won't invade my space, poke your nose in where it's not wanted?"

"So you're telling me to sit in the corner and keep my mouth shut?"

She grinned. "Except when you're opening it to take a drink of your beer."

"I can do that."

The resignation in his voice broke down her final barrier.

"Are you sure?" She dragged out each word as if that would give them both time to rethink where this was headed. "I don't want to make any more trouble between you and Nick. I've noticed that you're both keeping your distance, hardly talking. And at the meeting Monday morning, you couldn't even stand to be in the room at the same—"

"Don't worry about Nick and me."

The butterflies that had been sleeping in her belly came to life and spread their wings. She did worry about him and Nick. It shredded her heart knowing she was the cause of the rift between them.

Nick needed to butt out and quit worrying about her and Jared. The only place either of them were scoring any action was in her head.

She snuck a peek at Jared from beneath her lashes. The idea he'd be at her side—or at a nearby table tucked in the corner—thrilled her more than it should.

"Okay. We'll go together. Just remember the rules."

His shoulders relaxed. "Perfect. When are we going?"

He actually checked his watch, and she grinned. As if they could just pick up and leave work anytime they wanted. Well, okay, he could leave whenever he wanted because he owned the place, but that wasn't an option for her.

"Friday. After work." The butterflies fluttered, and she pressed her hand to her middle.

He acknowledged her with a nod. "I'll meet you here at five."

Her gaze followed his back as he headed toward the door. At the same time he grabbed the handle, he turned, and she averted her eyes, twisting the penguin charm on her necklace until the chain dug into her skin. She feigned reading the papers on the edge of her desk. The ones that were flipped over, blank side up.

She groaned inwardly.

"And bring me those spreadsheets on Sanders as soon as they're ready."

"Yes, boss." She snapped to attention and gave him a mock salute. Too bad the word "boss" didn't remind her of one more reason she shouldn't be thinking of him in any other manner than friend.

Friday would get here too quickly—and not quickly enough.

•••

The heavy-metal band in the bar rocked out another song, and Allison swallowed some wine, feeling more out of place than ever. This wasn't the type of club where people sipped wine with little white napkins to set their glasses on. It was a beer in the bottle and peanut shells on the floor type of place. Not that that was a bad thing, but just not *her* thing. The website hadn't mentioned this bar would be filled with men wearing chains, faux hawks, and makeup. And the women…

She'd reneged on her threat of having Jared stay out of sight in a corner. Her comfort level hovered around normal only when he sat by her side. The idea of being approached or approaching someone on her own—in this establishment—sent her pulse pounding. Jared commanded respect, and no chance in heck would anyone mess with him, or her, when they sat together.

"No way. Not that guy. You're kidding me, right?" Jared nudged her in the shoulder and laughed, nodding with his chin to the guy she had added to her list of potentials.

Although she didn't know his name, she'd penned him in as eyeliner guy.

"I'm serious." Out of all the men in this place, he ranked numero uno. "He's kind of cute, and I love his eyeliner. We could get ready in the morning and share makeup. You can't beat that." The wannabe rock star across the room had potential, too—in a bad boy kind of way—but so far nobody had really lived up to her expectations. Or apparently Jared's. But she'd grown tired of staring at her blank sheet of paper.

He took a slug of his beer. "I say we give this up."

"We've only been to three bars."

"Three bars too many."

"What about that guy over there?" She nodded toward a guy dressed in a gray suit tossing darts with two other guys wearing low-on-the-hip jeans and faded concert T-shirts. The suit guy had nice shoulders. One of the other men had so many piercings on his face he reminded her of the metal head that Gramps had given her for her tenth birthday that held all her earrings. She still had that holder in the back of her closet. The businessman seemed more out of place than she felt, but something about him reminded her of Jared, but on a smaller scale. *Must be the hair.*

Jared looked at her as if she'd grown two heads with horns and had purple skin. "Are you kidding me? He's the definition of uptight."

She bumped her shoulder against his. "You can get that from glancing at him from across the room? Give me a break. You don't know the first thing about that guy."

"I know his type."

"Like you know women's bodies?"

"Exactly." He finished off his drink and let out a satisfied sigh, sliding his empty bottle across the tiny table they shared in the corner. "Come on, let's get out of here."

She shook her head, staring him down. "I'm not ready to leave. We've only been here a few minutes, and I still have my wine." She lifted her glass. "Plus, I want to talk to at least one guy, and all this on and off your motorcycle is killing my hair."

Even though she'd loved every second they spent on the bike, mainly because she got to sit up tight and personal with her hands pressed against his abs, she wanted her list of potentials to include more than eyeliner guy. Not that she expected to meet any date candidates tonight—because the odds were dwindling as each minute ticked by—but she could use the practice when it came to talking to men she didn't know.

But then again, if they hopped on the bike, she… His muscles did amazing things on that bike, and she wiggled in her seat just thinking about it.

He rolled his eyes and dropped back down into his chair. "If you're trying to get me to nix my own personal helmet law, you can forget it."

Although she understood his concern, helmets were hell on a girl's hair. "But we don't need to wear them in Illinois."

"And I have had one too many buddies get hurt because they weren't wearing one."

She sobered for a moment, remembering two years ago when one of Nick and Jared's fraternity brothers died in a motorcycle accident. If he'd worn a helmet, the outcome would've been different.

"Good point." She left it at that, not wanting to get off topic with helmet laws. Her focus was a man.

Her gaze skimmed the room and landed on a buxom, peroxide blonde dressed in a leather mini. The woman gave Jared the once-, then twice-over as she strutted by with a tray of drinks.

Jared gave her the universal hand motion requesting another beer. Her smile brightened, and her lips moved as she said something, but the music drowned out her words. For some reason the way she looked at him annoyed Allison, and it annoyed her more when Jared flashed his smile and winked. Of course that's how Jared rolled. He probably didn't even realize the effect he had on most women.

With elbows on the table, he steepled his fingers, checking out the crowd with a grimace. "I don't think the bar is any place to find a"—he shrugged, ignoring the women one table over who were shooting him looks and laughing loud in hopes of getting his attention—"I don't know what you want to call it."

"I might be old-fashioned, but I call it a date." She smiled, eyeing him from beneath her lashes. "But my saucy side refers to him as my Posturepedic pal."

He stiffened, and then laughter rolled off him and on to her with smooth precision.

"If I think about that too much, it's kind of gross, but funny at the same time."

"Does it make you feel dirty?" she teased, taking a small sip of her drink.

"Extremely."

"Mission accomplished."

"You're so bad." He shook his head, letting his gaze travel around the room. "I knew you wanted to change but didn't realize you wanted to be the bad girl."

"Spank me now." She laughed, looking away as heat roared across her face. "Sorry, I think this atmosphere is bringing out my rough edges."

"Edges you probably didn't even know existed."

"Exactly." But she kind of liked them and the way she shocked Jared. At least in the playful way she shared with him. Even though she hadn't met anyone who perked her interest, the night hadn't been a total bust. She'd had a great time. She'd always loved people watching, and Jared did, too. Her cheeks were sore from smiling, and her ribs even sorer from laughing.

He took the beer from the waitress before she could put it on the table. He gave her a nod and another killer smile, and she added oomph to her wiggle as she walked back toward the bar. Too bad that the only one at their table who noticed was Allison, and it did nothing for her.

She leaned close so that Jared could hear her better. "You do realize all the attention you're attracting, don't you? I feel like I'm your wingman instead of the other way around."

He turned to face her head on. "I'm your wingman?"

"You've probably never been one before," she teased, her tone dry.

He leaned so close his breath moved several wisps of her hair. "As your wingman, I'm telling you this place is dead. If you're so determined to go through with this, let's try another spot."

"You're just not looking at anyone's potential." She grasped at straws, but in all truthfulness she was having so much fun chatting with Jared, she didn't want to interrupt their good time by getting up to leave.

"Because there isn't any. Not here." His breath tickled her ear, and she squirmed as tingles raced across her flesh, specifically to the vee between her legs.

*If only Jared…*

Things between them could so easily heat up, but she couldn't let it. And he obviously didn't want it, or he'd have made a move by now. She might not be an expert, but wasn't she sending off some kind of I'm-all-yours-for-the-taking signal? She scooted in her chair to put some much needed distance between them. That plan backfired when he scooted closer to her.

"Come on, Al. You might feel like you need to do this in a hurry, but there's nobody here good enough for you."

"Now you're making me sound like a snob." She knocked his shoulder with hers and turned away, studying the crowd. He might be right. Not that she was too good for anyone, but nobody really sparked her interest. Well, one person did, but even with all the signals she tossed out—and knew she shouldn't—he didn't take the bait.

Allison downed the remaining liquid in her glass with one

swallow. "Whenever you're ready."

His eyes flecked with humor as he pulled on his beer, drinking more than half in one gulp.

She eyed him playfully as she stood. "Should I expect a little pec dancing later?"

*I wish!*

"Sorry to disappoint, but the last three beers I've had were nonalcoholic."

"How responsible."

"I told you I don't party like I used to. One of us has to be able to drive and keep your bad-girl self in line." He rolled his eyes, taking another long draw on his nonalcoholic brew.

"You're kind of like an old man now." She bit her lip to quash her smile. Not that it worked.

"I'll show you an old man."

...

She laughed, a wispy, delicate sound that ended with a tiny gasp as he stood, pushed her up against the wall, and claimed her mouth.

He'd wanted to do this ever since he'd gone into her office Thursday on the pretense of needing that damn report. The report he could've sent Maureen to collect. Hell, he could've just called or shot her an email. But he'd been unable to stay away. He didn't want to stay away. What he wanted was to see where this attraction between them went. Even if he did have to hit a few bars with her all in the name of finding her some guy good enough to date her.

Couldn't he be her date?

His body pressed into her softness, and she curled her fingers around his neck, lifting her chin so he had better access to her lips.

He shouldn't be doing this, but he'd wanted nothing more

all night. *Hell, all week.* He didn't want to get involved, but he couldn't stay away. Every word she spoke drew his attention to the perfect lines of her lush lips. The way she talked with her hands only made him think about her hands on him.

*And those damn jeans…*

Her soft moan combined with the way her fingers tangled in his hair sent chills down his spine and inspired an erection that pressed against his zipper with such force he had to shift his weight to get relief.

He broke away, his breath heavy. Not because he wanted to, but because he could feel himself going over the edge, and he didn't want to grope Allison in the middle of a crowded bar. She was too good for that.

But damn, she tasted better than she had the other night when he'd sampled her sweet mouth.

"How's that for an old man?"

"Old man who?" She leaned her forehead against his chin, then tilted her head back, parting her lips and inviting him in for another kiss.

And he wanted seconds. More than he'd ever imagined. The soft blush creeping over her face, the way her breasts strained against her blouse as she tried to regain her breathing only encouraged him. *Holy. Fuck.* With her it'd be too easy to forget where the hell they were.

And he didn't like an audience. Not now. With Allison, not ever.

But that didn't stop him from running his thumb over her bottom lip. For a second he lost sense of where they were when her eyes grew dark and her lashes fluttered gently over her skin. She looked so beautiful, and that protective urge—or maybe he should just call it what it is…*lust*—overtook him.

He couldn't picture her with anyone but him. *Fuck.* He didn't want her with anyone else. Screw Nick. He'd deal with him later.

If anyone would teach Allison how to please a man, let a real man do the job.

Him.

She was ready, so was he. He was willing, and so was she. And they were both adults.

"Al, I don't want you with any of these men."

She sighed, sagging against him. "Are we really going to have this conversation again? I— "

He took her mouth in a hard kiss, parting the seam of her lips with his tongue and thrusting inside, swallowing her gasp. She melted against him. He slid his hands down her throat, past her shoulders, and lower still until he curved his arm around her back and squeezed her rear.

She smiled into their kiss, and this time *he* melted.

"Do I need to rephrase?" he whispered against her mouth.

She shook her head, their mouths still touching. "I really only wanted one man in this room, but I didn't think he wanted— "

"You better be talking about me." He leaned back just far enough so he could watch the way her emotions flickered across her eyes. Excitement. Uncertainty. Acceptance.

She nodded, her lips parted and moist. "Are you telling me—?"

"I'm telling you I've come to my senses. Or lost them completely."

Her body stiffened, and then a whisper of a smile curved her lips. "How about I rephrase? Just to clarify we're on the same page."

"I have a feeling we're more than on the same page. We're in the same sentence."

Her giggle pierced him with another shot of desire. She had no idea.

"You've not only helped me with my makeover, but you're willing to show me the dating ropes, and now you're going to help me learn how to drive a man crazy?" One delicate eyebrow shot up in challenge.

*Shit.* "You don't need to be taught. You're already driving me crazy."

"You're making me feel all flirty again." She bit playfully at his thumb as it ran the length of her bottom lip.

"For someone with no experience, you sure know how to blue-ball a guy."

Her seductive laugh wrapped around him and held on tight. But he didn't mind. She felt warm, soft, and perfect in his arms.

"Blue-ball?"

He wasn't sure if she were teasing or serious. For some reason his nonalcoholic beers made him feel drunk, or having her in his arms and tasting her mouth did. "Don't you know what blue—?"

Her lopsided smile sent him over the edge. "I'm a virgin, Jared. Not an idiot." With that she touched her mouth to his, testing, tasting, teasing, and he came unglued, pulling her close and pushing his tongue against hers.

She arched her back until her breasts crushed against his chest. Then she reversed their positions in one fluid movement so that she had him pressed tight to the wall. She traced his jaw with one finger, a delicate touch that made him forget his name. He couldn't take much more as anticipation built to the point his head ached—both of them—but at the same time he didn't want what was happening between them to become a bar show.

Her eyes, full of promise, feasted on him. He'd never been so excited about the thought of being with a woman, and it scared him.

"So, now that we're on the same page…I mean, in the same sentence"—she licked her lips slowly as he followed her tongue with his eyes—"your place or mine?"

# Chapter Eight

Allison sat with her front pressed up to Jared's back as he maneuvered his bike through the city streets toward his condo. She'd only been there once, when she'd gone with Nick to drop something off, and she'd barely caught a quick glimpse from the hallway. The thought of stepping inside, being in his personal space, sent a shiver through her.

The Hershey's Kiss she'd popped into her mouth before Jared slid on her helmet melted quicker than normal. Probably because her body temperature soared to new heights. Anticipation, mixed with a good dose of nervous energy, had her wiggling against his back, trying to get closer to ease the throb between her legs.

She parted the opening of his jacket and pressed her hand across his abs, loving the way his muscles flexed against his shirt with each twist and turn of their bodies on the bike. Soon enough she'd get to feel his skin. She rested her head on his shoulder—as much as she could with the bulky helmet—and he pressed his hand over hers as they moved down a straight patch of road.

Could they get there any faster? She was on fire, and the stiffness of his back and arms told her he was, too. How much more could either of them take? If she'd been more experienced, she'd have slid her hand down between his thighs, but uncertainty held her back. Not to mention the fact she didn't want to cause an accident.

She closed her eyes to gather herself and settle her heart rate, but it didn't work. If anything, her heart raced faster, her pulse pounded in her veins, and every nerve ending in her body throbbed.

Now that they'd made their decision, time couldn't move fast enough.

He seemed more than ready. And she definitely was.

All the hours she'd spent pouring over the *Kama Sutra* book, taking notes from various websites on sexual positions and how to please your partner, as well as every romantic movie she could get her hands on, had left her body aching for release. Real release, with a real man. She could only hope things would develop naturally. That she wouldn't freeze up, or let her doubts hold her back.

He squeezed her fingers as if assuring her it wouldn't be long now.

Lately the man in her dreams that would take her over the edge had been Jared. And now her fantasies were about to become reality.

He pulled into the underground garage of his building and circled down a few floors, taking them deeper beneath the streets of Chicago. He pulled up to a single door, hit a button in his pocket, and the garage door opened to reveal several of his other bikes and his car. Even though the bike still idled, he maneuvered it into the space using his legs.

Jared removed her helmet, then his. He pulled her into his arms, his mouth millimeters from hers.

"You're sure?" he asked at the last second.

"More sure than I've ever been of anything."

They crashed into each other in a jumbled mass of arms, legs, and lips. She couldn't touch him fast enough, and he couldn't seem to decide where he wanted to touch first. They banged against the cement wall as his mouth devoured hers and then tripped entering the elevator when she pulled him up close and gripped his rear.

The ride up to his floor was a blur. Somehow they managed to get off the elevator. Linked at the mouth, he hoisted her up, and she wrapped her legs around his waist as they moved down a wide hallway. The next instant they were in a room with polished wood floors and a bank of windows that glowed with the city's skyline. Maybe later she'd have time to check it out, but none of that mattered now.

Knowing they finally had privacy sent an explosion of heat to her every nerve ending. She slid down his body as they stood in the center of the room and kissed his neck, licking his salty flesh as her tongue found his pulse point.

He pulled her chin up so he could reclaim her lips.

"You taste so good." She ran her tongue over his lips. His soft groan and shudder gave her the courage to thrust her tongue into his mouth. "I can't wait to make love to you."

His body stiffened, but she kept kissing him, running her hands over his body, pressing up tight. So excited with the way he felt beneath her fingers, it took her several minutes to notice that his lips had become cool and unyielding. So had his body. He tasted different. Moved differently. As if his passion had been replaced by the not so sexy moves of a robot. His hands found all the right places, but his fingers felt rigid, as if he were following an instruction manual in his head. And she hated instruction manuals.

She wanted this to be perfect, but perfection had started to slip away. Had she done something wrong? Touched him in a way that made him lose the heat of the moment?

Or could he be just as nervous as her? After all, it wasn't just *her* first time, but it was *their* first time being together, too. To be naked and vulnerable with anyone new had to be a bit frightening.

*It definitely is.*

Allison pressed against him, running her hands down his back, sucking in air and trying to slow down. She hoped to alleviate the bunched muscles between his shoulder blades. With palms flat, she snaked them around to his front and slid her fingers between the folds of his shirt. They both stiffened when he grabbed her hand and pressed it against his chest, squeezing her fingers.

"Am I moving too fast?" she asked as she pulled back, her heart pounding out of control. Her chest ached as she held her breath. "What happened? What did—?"

•••

*Fuck.* He wanted her so badly he'd frozen up. When she'd told him she wanted to make love to him, he crashed back to earth. "Nothing, babe. I-I… This is your first time and I… Shit, Al. I can't get Nick out of my head." Or that this was Allison. He'd never looked at her the way he had lately. It not only scared him shitless, but the guilt had started to consume him. He ran his hand through his hair, gripped the length at his nape, and gave it a small tug—as if punishing himself with a dose of pain would ease his conscience. Once he crossed this line he could never go back. They could never go back.

She leaned her forehead against his chin and sucked in a breath of air. "I thought I'd done something wrong."

"Hell no. I'm sorry. You are perfect, it was going perfect, and then… I can't get it out of my head that you're Nick's little sister."

"Way to kill the moment."

"Tell me about it."

Her lips pressed together tightly before she gave him a weak smile. The disappointment in her eyes matched the feeling soaring through his entire body.

The heat that had boiled between them dropped to a low simmer, and he wanted every ounce of the fire back that had burned between them moments ago. She drove him crazy with her touch, the way she moaned into his mouth, how she melted into his arms.

She grabbed him by the collar. "I'm more than Nick's sister, you know. I'm a confident woman. I go for what I want. No ifs, ands, or buts."

Adrenaline coursed through him at the strength of her words. The fire in her eyes stoked the fire in his blood. Her grip on his collar tightened and she shook him playfully, but with enough force so that he knew she meant business. His heartbeat went into a mad gallop at the way she took control.

She pulled him toward her until their eyes locked. "You need to knock it off. Forget this is my first time. And, for God's sake, forget about Nick. Can't you just close your eyes and pretend you're making love to the most beautiful woman in the world? Or keep your eyes open, but concentrate on this." She shoved him back with the thrust of her wrist and unbuttoned her blouse, peeling the material off one shoulder to bare her creamy white skin.

Suddenly her cherry blossom scent filled the air, intoxicating him. She teased him with a soft smile as she pressed her shoulder to his chest.

"Go ahead. Kiss me."

He couldn't do anything but obey. His lips touched her skin, and then he moved his attention to the hollow at her neck, sucking at the pulse point pounding there until she shivered and her head fell back, lips parted. The movement shot a thrill through him. He loved the way she came to life when he touched her, and he continued to trail his mouth over the soft skin of her neck, pushing her shirt farther down her arm and creating a path with his tongue over her warm flesh.

She gasped. He cradled her head in his palm, pulling her body closer to his. Electricity zipped between them, and she thrust her hands into his hair, pulling him in as he sucked, licked, kissed, and nipped her skin.

God. She felt good. Tasted good. Smelled good. All his pent-up sexual desire surged through him, and he walked her backward until they hit the window. She shivered as the coolness of the glass penetrated her skin. He broke away to look into her sultry dark eyes, and she parted her lips, giving him the invitation he needed to reclaim her mouth.

She opened, and their tongues danced. So lost in their kiss, he didn't put up a fight when she reversed their position and thrust his back against the window, yanking his shirt from the waistband of his jeans. As her hands reached for the button at his waist, he spun her around until she was up against the window again, and he plunged his tongue into her, catching her surprised gasp in his mouth.

He pressed her hard against the windowpane, pulling her blouse from her pants. At the same time she undid the top few buttons of his shirt, sliding her hands down to the hem and fisting the material. A satisfied sigh rose from the back of her throat as his fingers moved along the goose bumps flecking across her skin. Not bothering with the remaining buttons, she lifted his shirt over his head and let it fall to the floor. Her hands pressed hungrily into his shoulders, down his biceps and back, and around his waist.

He needed to feel her skin so badly. To taste every inch. Learn every inch. But he didn't intend to allow himself to get out of control and go too fast. This was her first time, and it had to be special. Perfect. She deserved perfect. She deserved beautiful memories. That's all he wanted for her.

But shit, she drove him mad.

He lifted her in his arms, banging his shoulder against the wall, sucking in the pain as their mouths collided again and they fell onto the couch. Allison's knee bounced up and hit him in the groin, and he swore in pain, doubling over. The sound of his voice made her jump at the same time he came back up to a sitting position, and they bumped heads. The next thing he knew, he'd fallen to the floor, hit his chin on the metal coffee table, and a new round of pain surged through him. This one sharp and intense.

"Mother fuck!" His stomach quivered as he bit back another curse. He gripped his chin and pinched, applying as much pressure as he dared to stop the bleeding. At the same time he pressed his knees tight to ease the shooting pain spearing his nuts.

He rocked back and forth, biting his tongue. A warm liquid filled his hands, and he looked down to see blood dripping off his chin, even with his hand covering it. The searing pain between his legs was quickly forgotten.

"Shit. Damn. Fuck." The words flew from Allison's mouth in rapid-fire succession. If he didn't hurt so much he'd laugh. She didn't swear often, and although pain zapped his brain, the concern in her eyes kind of soothed him.

She knelt down, parting his fingers to check out the damage. Her eyes grew wide and bright with tears, and then she ran for the kitchen. Cupboard doors crashed open, and several drawers banged shut, and then the faucet kicked on. Soon she was back, a dishcloth in her hand, as she skidded to a stop in front of him and fell to her knees with a thud.

"Oh my God. Oh my God. I'm so sorry." She pressed the wet cloth to his chin, tilting his head back as if he had a nosebleed and she could stop the bleeding.

He clenched his jaw from the pain, pressing his lips together to stop from cussing again. From the watery concern in her eyes, she already felt bad enough. Moisture spiked her lashes, and he folded his hand over hers in hopes he'd ease some of her tears. She managed to hold the dishcloth in place, but her hand shook.

"It's okay, babe."

"No, it's not. My God. I kneed you, we knocked heads, and now you're bleeding. And it's not letting up." She pulled the cloth away to take a peek and grimaced.

"It looks worse than it is. I'll be fine." But it sure hurt like a bitch.

"I'm going to get another towel. It's not slowing down." She moved toward the kitchen, and he heard the cupboard door open and bang shut again.

Jared leaned his head back against the sofa cushion and pulled the cloth away. He'd never minded the sight of blood before, but this time all the red filling the white towel made him a bit nauseous. He pressed the towel to his chin again as Allison practically ran across the room a second time. She switched out the towel, balling up the other one and glancing around.

"I was going to ask about your laundry, but I think this towel is a lost cause."

"Trash is under the kitchen sink." He nodded toward the kitchen as if she didn't have a clue where it was, and she gave him a shaky grin. At this point any grin was better than none. "Could you grab my shirt on your way back?"

Ten minutes and two more towels later, Jared stood. Allison grabbed him by the elbow as if he needed to be steadied. He liked that she wanted to help him, take care of him. It felt good. "I think I need to go to the hospital."

"You need stitches." She ran her fingers through her hair, then buttoned her blouse, tucking in the hem. "I'm so sorry. This is all my fault. I'm such a klutz..."

His heart ached at the thickness invading her voice, the

tears brightening her eyes after she'd just gotten them under control. She turned away, and he pulled her back around with his free hand and cupped her cheek. When she pressed into his palm and closed her eyes, a little piece of him became hers. How could someone be so sweet and caring? He'd never seen a woman go so soft—over concern for him.

"This isn't your fault, Al. And you're not a klutz."

"None of this would've happened if I'd known what the heck I was doing." A sob escaped, and she snorted, then she pressed her face into her hands.

With his free arm, he gathered her against his chest, an easy feat since she didn't put up a fight but instead sagged against him, rubbing her hands down his back. "We both got carried away. That's all. You might claim you didn't know what you were doing, but believe me, you were doing all the right things."

Her soft chuckle came out muffled as she buried the side of her face into his shirt.

She stepped out of his arms and brushed her hands across his shoulders, smoothing his shirt down his arms. "And now I'm letting you bleed to death while I cry like a baby." Her lower lip quivered as she fought to gain control.

He lifted her chin and held her gaze. "I'm going to live."

"Well, we better make sure. I'll drive. Where are your keys?"

Not only did she have a soft side—which he couldn't help but adore—he also liked how she took control. Hell, he liked everything about her.

*Especially her kisses. Fuck. Especially her ass in those damn jeans.*

She gave him a liquid smile, removing her hand from her pocket and opening her fist. "I have a few chocolates. Hershey's Kisses can get you through anything."

"Even stitches?"

"Especially stitches." She unwrapped one, and he opened his mouth so she could drop it in.

He pressed the chocolate to the roof of his mouth with his tongue. "You're a girl after my own heart. Chocolate is one of my weaknesses, too. Especially Hershey's Kisses."

Her eyebrow shot up.

"What, you don't think men like chocolate?"

"I'm more surprised we share a Hershey's Kiss addiction. How come I never knew that until now?"

"I have a couple secrets." He waggled his brows, and her smile filled her face. He preferred that face over the one filled with tears any day.

"You mean besides the dancing pecs?" she said beneath her breath as he offered up his car keys.

"Dancing pecs barely scratch the surface."

"You're a man of mystery." She guided him toward the door with one hand around his waist as if he were unstable on his feet. He didn't fight her. He could definitely get used to being taken care of.

More than three hours later, Jared grimaced and sucked in a breath as the emergency room doctor stitched him up. The last piece of chocolate Allison had shoved into his hand before he'd been brought back to an examination room lay in a puddle on his tongue.

He'd had worse injuries as a kid—one required twelve stitches on the top of his head after Roth shoved him into a wall and a picture fell, the corner of the frame cutting his scalp. And another time they'd been wrestling by the screen door and Jared had crashed through it, requiring more stitches. Over the years he'd lost count when it came to accidents that involved horseplay between him and Roth. But he'd never had to have stitches because of a woman.

"Almost done. How you holding up?" the doctor asked.

"I'm good." But he wasn't. He felt like a fucking shit.

He hated the fact that Allison felt inadequate, and he'd been the one to put her there. He'd wanted her first time to be special. The best. Something she'd look back on years from now and smile about.

Instead he'd let his nerves paralyze him. When she'd told him to close his eyes and pretend he made love to the most beautiful woman in the world, he'd gotten a little carried away. Hell, a lot carried away. The image tattooed into his eyelids had been of a very beautiful woman.

Allison.

Her smile encompassed her face and made his mind numb, her sexy eyes hypnotized him to the point he could barely speak, and her touch made his entire body ache for more.

He couldn't get her out of his head. Even now with the pinch of the needle piercing his skin. Where had all his good sense gone the last week?

Since when had he become attracted to a nerdy girl who could weave a spell around him with just a few words or looks? Not to mention she kissed like she fucking did it for a living. He might be a good teacher, but he hadn't taught her any of that. Her sex appeal was all natural, and it drove him fucking over the edge.

"All set." The doctor slapped him on the knee and stood. "I'm going to prescribe something for the pain if you want it. Otherwise you should be good to go."

Jared hopped off the hospital bed. "Thanks, doc."

"And watch out for those coffee tables, hmm?" The doctor gave him a knowing grin.

...

Allison shut her apartment door with a thud, leaned her back against it, and sank down to the floor. She kicked off her shoes, not caring where they landed as she leaned forward to grab her slippers. It didn't matter that she'd put them on the wrong feet. Nothing mattered. Not even the continuous sinking feeling of her gut. She flung her arm over her eyes as she slid down the rest of the way until she lay flat on the floor. She wiggled her legs in frustration and groaned as she stared up at the tiny crack that ran the width of her ceiling. She'd have to call the super to have him fix that.

She closed her eyes for a second in an attempt to put some moisture back into them that contacts and lack of sleep had sucked out of her. If she were more experienced with the stupid things, she'd take them out right there on the entry room floor.

She and Jared had sat in the crowded emergency room for hours. By the time they'd left the hospital, found a twenty-four–hour pharmacy, and gotten his prescription filled, the sun had already started to peek over the horizon.

Even if she wanted to try to pick up from where they left off, her bones ached with fatigue. Not to mention Jared needed some rest, too. Of course, those pain pills looked like they were well on their way to knocking him out when she'd left him tucked in bed so she could catch an E train home. He'd tried to talk her into staying over at his place, but she wanted to be alone.

She felt like the world's biggest loser. Her first attempt with Lance still left his laughter ringing in her ears after all these years, and now she had the added guilt of practically maiming Jared.

Maybe she wasn't supposed to have sex. Ever.

Would Jared even want to try again? He'd made no mention of it, and she hadn't felt right bringing it up. It would have come across a bit self-serving if she questioned him about when they could get together again for another wrestling match. Especially since he'd come out with the most damage on round one.

She brushed her hands over her face and snort-laughed, folding her arms behind her head. Maybe next time he should wear some type of protective gear or they'd need to find a padded room.

*If there is a next time.*

*Oh, there'll be a next time.* She sat up and wiped the back of her hand over her eyes.

Maybe tomorrow, or actually later today, she'd make that trip to the department store like she'd promised herself and buy something smexy—as Colleen liked to say. Super smexy, that would have Jared pulsating with desire. He'd forget all about his stitches and the visit to the ER.

She'd take the initiative. Not that she knew what she was doing, but she'd read enough to have some type of idea. After he'd gotten over that huge hurdle of forgetting about Nick, their attraction had gone ahead full force. She'd lost all sense of time and space as she had succumbed to the pleasures of his mouth, hands, and body.

Shivers raced across her arms, then shot down her back. She hugged her middle.

They just had to watch out for knees, banging heads, and coffee tables.

Her snort-laugh filled the silence of her apartment and made her feel a lot better.

Next time they'd take things slow. Let the tension build instead of climbing all over each other in haste. He'd been right. They'd gotten carried away.

# Chapter Nine

Allison hesitated, her knuckles millimeters from Jared's door before she dropped her arm to her side. She looked up at the stark white ceiling and went over her mental checklist for the millionth time.

Sexy perfume—*check.* Super smexy dress that would hopefully tease Jared to distraction and make him beg for release—*check.* Sexier still bra and panties that'd push him over the edge and lead to a night of mad, passionate lovemaking—*check, check.*

A giggle-snort escaped, and she pressed the back of her hand to her mouth as she looked from left to right. Not that anyone was in the hallway to see or hear. Jared's condo was one of two that filled this floor.

She shook her head to clear away any imaginary hair that might be in her face, thrust back her shoulders, glided her tongue over her freshly brushed teeth, and finally wiggled her hips as she smoothed her palms over the light jacket she'd put on to cover her cling-to-me-everywhere dress. Her knuckles barely hit the door before it swung open, and Jared stood before her. His automatic smile teetered, but he quickly covered his surprise.

The nervous excitement swirling through her evaporated, and she lost her gung ho.

"I'm sorry. I probably should've called, but I—"

"No. You're okay. I just thought you were someone else."

"Like your date?"

He was dressed from head to toe in a tux. White starched shirt and blacker than black vest, jacket, and trousers. All topped off with a black bowtie that lay at his throat slightly askew and unclasped.

"You look like a penguin," she said. Her face heated. Had she really said that aloud?

"A gentoo?" His eyebrow lifted ever so slightly. The look only made him sexier.

Heck. He looked good. But then when didn't he? He'd be that guy who looked good in whatever he threw on, or threw off.

She shook her head. "Definitely an emperor penguin. You have the height."

He laughed, and the tiny bit of tension squeezing the air from her lungs vaporized.

"I'll take that as a compliment." He pulled her through the door, his warm hands sending frissons of heat up her arm, followed by goose bumps. "And there's no date."

Her gaze swept the room. "But I must've interrupted something." *Thank God it wasn't a date.*

"My guests just left."

She expected to see the remnants of a party, at least a few plates with hors d'oeuvres, a smattering of empty champagne bottles. Something party-like. Instead the only difference from yesterday was that the baby grand had been pushed nearer to the windows, and all the furniture—which had been sparse to begin with—sat up against the walls. The middle of the floor lay exposed, the wood gleaming.

Her gaze landed on Jared, a frown creasing her brow. “First off, how’s the chin? Secondly, what’s going on?”

“Chin is fine, and what’s going on? Well, it’s one of my secrets.” He sighed, rubbing his chin gingerly as he avoided the stitches.

That wiggly feeling invaded her stomach. “Are you about to tell me that besides dancing pecs you like to wax your floors in a tux in front of company? And if so, are you available for hire?” She bit her lip to hide her smile. Not that she had wood floors, but maybe he’d clean her tub. In a tux, or without.

When he laughed, she did, too. But at the same time she could see the discomfort in the way he rolled his shoulders.

“Do you promise not to laugh?”

“As someone who knows what it feels like to be laughed at, I’d never do that to you.”

He licked his lips and glanced down at his shiny black shoes before meeting her gaze with a boyish look of mischief. “And you’ll keep my secret?”

She nodded and jammed her hand into her jacket pocket, rolling the tinfoil ball between her fingers. They were sharing another secret, and according to the color creeping up from his neckline, this one would be a doozy. The closeness between them only ignited her attraction and anticipation.

He walked across the room and flipped a switch on the stereo. The light tinkling of piano music filled the room, and she turned on her heel, following the music as it pinged off one wall, then another, and another. He stood in front of her.

“Do you trust me?”

“I do.” She had no idea where this was going, but she wanted to find out.

Without another word, he helped her out of her jacket and tossed it on a nearby chair. His eyes raked over her slowly, and the way his throat worked as he swallowed gave her confidence a boost.

"You look beyond stunning."

"Thank you." She licked her lips slowly, savoring the way his eyes followed. He held out his hand, and she placed her palm in his.

With gentle force—or maybe it was more authoritative—he yanked her up tight to his front. They melded together, and he spun her around easily in his arms, and then stopped as the music changed tempo. Now they swayed lazily to the soft beat as his gaze smoldered. She relaxed, her backbone turning to mush as she conformed to his will.

Her body lit on fire, and every inch of her flesh that connected with him came to life with anticipation. He rested his face against the side of her head as they swung around the floor. His breath warmed the shell of her ear. "One of the main reasons I bought this condo was because of this room."

"Because you're a closet dancer?"

His chuckle melted her heart. He really did have a boyish quality at times.

"You could say that."

Before she could speak again, his arms tightened around her. The rhythm of his hard chest matched hers as their breaths rose in tempo with the music and they floated across the dance floor in tiny circles.

When he loosened his grip, she looked down at his feet, and he lifted her chin. "Don't watch my feet, watch my eyes."

Her body throbbed from the tone of his voice. "Isn't that a line from *Dirty Dancing*?" she whispered.

He shrugged, his smile filling his eyes. "We'll save the dirty for later."

"Promises, promises." Even to her own ears her voice sounded breathless.

He steered her across the floor with such speed and grace, she couldn't believe she hadn't tripped over her own feet. Of course, if she had, he held her so close and tight, she'd never have fallen.

When the music ended, he dipped her low and pressed his mouth to her throat, nipping the base of her neck where her pulse throbbed.

"I'm breathless. In more ways than one." She licked her lips, reveling in the sensation of his strong arms supporting her as he lifted her to a standing position once again.

Another song thrummed through the air, starting out soft and slow and then pounding out a quick tempo. Instead of torturing her—because at this point she'd been lucky to get through the slow dance—he pulled her toward the couch, and they sat.

"If you want to do a solo dance, I won't object."

The left side of his mouth lifted.

She brushed her hand down her lap. "Never mind. I'd probably have a coronary."

His mouth parted into a full-blown, sexy smile. "Maybe I'll dance for you later."

"Or maybe your pecs will?" she teased.

"You never know, but for now I want to tell you my secret."

"Spill."

He held up one finger. "Give me a second. I'm still trying to get my mind off images of dancing for you."

She laughed, the sound husky and rich. "That makes two of us."

He slid his finger down the side of her cheek, clearing his throat. "Let me start at the beginning. Like I said a minute ago, I bought this place because of this room. I belong to a ballroom dance club, and we meet here two Saturdays a month. We also compete from time to time around the state."

Her jaw relaxed, and her lips parted slightly. She thanked her lucky stars that her mouth didn't fall open and her eyes didn't bug out. To say she was surprised would be an understatement. She stared at him for what seemed like an eternity. She had no idea what his secret was, but she'd never have guessed ballroom dancing. "How'd you manage to keep that secret? You mean Nick doesn't know?"

He opened his mouth, shaking his head at the same time, but so many questions burst through her mind she didn't give him time to answer.

"Where do you compete? Can you do the same dances they do on *Dancing with the Stars*? How long have you been doing—?"

He covered her mouth with his. A light kiss that sent fireworks shooting through her blood. Jared would always be sexy, but for some reason the fact he danced added another layer of sensuality to him. She liked learning new things about him. Liked it even more that although he was confident, he wasn't so sure about revealing this part of himself. It gave him more appeal, because he had some of her own issues. He really did understand.

She peeked up at him with surprise when he sat back and put his finger over her lips.

"Can you give me a second to answer?"

"Or you could just kiss me again," she teased.

"That's a very generous offer. I thought you wanted to hear my story, though."

She nodded, afraid to open her mouth in case she shot more questions at him, or begged him to kiss her again already. With one hand she pretended to zip her lips closed, and he grinned, rewarding her with a quick, warm kiss.

"My mom wanted us boys to be well-rounded. She signed us up for so many classes and lessons I've lost count. Some stuck and some didn't. There were cooking lessons, swimming lessons, piano lessons, painting, and dance. Just to name a few."

"And dance stuck?" she asked in awe, forgetting her vow

of silence. "I've always wanted to learn to dance. I watch *Dancing with the Stars* every week."

"You just did dance. And if you hadn't done it before I'd have never known."

"I think I was too stunned to be nervous. I just followed your lead." She dried her palms on the lap of her dress. "Not to mention it felt amazing to be in your arms. You dance beautifully. Why do you keep this a secret?"

"Roth hated every minute of dance, so I played along. As a kid it was nice to commiserate. The more time that went by, the harder it was to say anything."

She grinned. "I get you."

"But truthfully, I loved the freedom of dancing. Ballroom especially. It helped me through a tough time as a kid. When I was dancing, and the music surrounded me, I could forget all the stresses from home. My parents' crazy marriage—the fighting, then the silent treatments—the way my father had no time for either Roth or me because he focused all his attention on Omar…" He rubbed the side of his neck so hard he left red marks that took a few seconds to vanish.

She took his hand and squeezed his fingers. "I'm sorry. I didn't know." Funny how she assumed Jared's life had been sunshine and rainbows. He might not have had confidence issues, might not have been shy, but from the brief glimpse he'd given her, his home life hadn't been as golden as she'd pictured. "Your family wasn't very close?"

But—now that she thought back—she already kind of knew the answer from little things Nick had said over the years. And why else would someone spend holidays and vacations with the Hall family when they had a family of their own? The idea poked at her brain that she'd never taken the time to realize that.

Frown lines marred his brow. "I've always been close with my mother and older brother Roth. Until recently, Omar wasn't in our life. My parents weren't together much, and Roth and I traveled with my mother. Omar stayed behind while my dad groomed him to be his mini-me." He made an attempt to laugh off his words, but the painful sound hurt Allison's heart.

"I thought both your brothers were visiting recently…"

"We've come a long way. Omar and I mended our relationship right away. As soon as he reached out, I was more than happy to have him in my life. He'd always wanted us to be brothers but didn't know how to go about getting us there." His lips thinned and then turned into a stiff smile. "Roth and Omar had a little bit of a rougher time, but it's all working out now."

She rubbed his leg. "I'm glad. Family is so important. And having a sibling you're close to is amazing. I love Nick, even though he can get a bit overprotective at times."

"He loves you."

"I think when Mom died, he tried to take on the role of parent because Dad was out of it for so long. Gramps tried to step in, too, but he had enough on his plate with my dad." Even now the pain in her dad's eyes when he talked about Allison's mom twisted her heart into a pretzel. After all these years he still loved her. Probably always would. Her father had become the role model of love for her. She wanted that all-consuming, lifelong love with someone. Of course, through the years she'd encouraged him to date, and he had from time to time, but nothing had developed.

"Enough about dance and family. Let's talk about that dress."

Allison stood and held out her hand. "Dance with me. Slow. Easy." She swayed to the music in her head, her hips moving back and forth as she peeked at him from beneath her lashes. Her nerves eased at the way his eyes feasted on her from north to south and back again. She might not be experienced, but even she couldn't mistake the look of desire in his smoldering eyes.

"Are you trying to make me pop my zipper?" he asked.

She couldn't stop her eyes from straying to his trousers as she grinned. The obvious effects of her words and little dance sent her pulse pounding. He pulled her into his arms, and she lost all ability to think as they moved slower than two leaves on a windless day. The only music the rhythm of their breathing.

Heat swirled around them as they pressed into each other, their feet never leaving the floor. Not much of a dance, but she didn't care. Mesmerized by eyes, touch, smell, and body, everything in the world stopped when his lips pressed into hers.

"I want you to teach me how to please you." Her breathy voice sounded foreign to her own ears.

"You already know." One of his hands skimmed down her side and cradled her hip.

She rose on her tiptoes, walking her fingers up his chest to pull him down and claim his lips, careful to avoid his chin. His groan fueled her fire, and she pressed closer—if that was even possible.

"Did you come here to seduce me?" He kissed the lobe of her ear, and flames shot through her veins.

"Is it working? Because I have no clue what I'm doing."

His chest rumbled against hers and a shiver skated down her backbone. "You're doing everything right. I'm the one who's nervous."

"You?" Her voice cracked.

He nodded, grazing her cheek with his knuckles, sending another ripple of awareness through her. His touch alone excited her. She'd fall to pieces when they made love. Flesh upon flesh. From head to toe. She had no doubt it'd happen, now it was only a matter of *when*, not *if*. Her body wanted to get right to the action, but her mind wanted to relish every moment and make it last.

"I have a lot to live up to. Your first time has to be perfect. Something to be remembered."

"I have a feeling you won't disappoint."

"I feel the same about you." His sexy voice resonated through her.

He had her right there. Not only with the timbre of his voice—so deep, sexy, and strong—but with his words. Those six words sent her confidence to new heights. She'd do anything he wanted. Whenever he wanted. However he wanted. Their feet came unglued as he led them into a sexy dance. Not really a dance, more of a press-into-me-everywhere move that required a few foot maneuvers to get closer. Heat circled around them; his hands slid down her back and settled into the small curve above her rear. They pressed in to her as he groaned from deep within his throat before smoothing over the flare of her hips and then back down to cup her butt. Her body became a live wire wherever he touched, and a few places he didn't.

His fingers found the zipper running the length of her spine, and he slid it down gently. The cool air kissed her skin and then was quickly warmed by his palms. His lips found her earlobe, and his ragged breaths sent a shot of promise mixed with impatience straight through her as he brushed the straps of her dress down her shoulders, past her breasts, and over her hips. She wiggled slightly until the material slid down her legs and pooled at her feet. For a second he held her at arm's length, devouring her with his darkened eyes, before taking her hand to walk toward what she hoped was the bedroom. A blanket of self-consciousness overwhelmed her as his gaze continued to rake over her, but the urge to cover herself didn't compare to the need to have him continue to touch every inch of her body with his eyes—as he did now—then his hands.

She felt beyond beautiful. And he looked more than mouthwatering. When they reached his large room, his personality stamped every surface. Modern metals and rich colors of brown and bold red filled the space. She got a case of nerves at the sight of the huge powder-coated wrought-iron bed. Its presence filled the room, and for a moment she broke out in a nervous sweat.

But the moment he brushed his mouth over hers, all fear evaporated. A tiny gasp escaped when he picked her up—his muscles bunching and flexing—and laid her gently on the bed. He trapped her in the circle of his muscular arms as he owned her mouth again. She opened, drawing him in, and grabbed him by the collar to pull him down. Somehow he still managed to wrestle his way out of his jacket, and it fell to the floor with a soft thud.

"You're sure?" he asked.

"Beyond sure."

His mouth abandoned hers to make a path of wet kisses down her neck to the pulse point at her throat, then around to nibble on her ear. She arched to give him better access.

The quickness with which she lost control compared to nothing she'd ever felt before. Her breaths came in short pants, her body ached with the desire to touch him, feel him, have him touch her. All the stupid magazines and internet searches hadn't prepared her for this onslaught of feeling.

She wiggled, pulling him down so that their skin made contact, but he smiled against her skin, holding back.

"Slow and easy. Isn't that what you said?"

"Yes," she panted. "But can't a woman change her mind?"

He nipped at the sensitive skin between her neck and shoulder and laughed. The low, husky sound throbbed against her flesh, and her belly quivered.

His hands cupped her breasts, pushing them up to give his mouth full access to her cleavage. She arched toward him, begging him with her body to ease her ache. The feeling new, overwhelming, smoldering.

He finally settled himself onto her, and she gave a nervous laugh as they stared into each other's eyes. But laughter quickly turned to soft moans as his hands explored her thighs, her legs automatically parting, her flesh shaking and trembling as his warm palms slid from her inner knees to her moist center. He cupped her sex, and she thrust against him, her body reacting on its own to his touch.

He lifted slightly and ran his hand over her hip and down her leg, taking her panties with him. He moved to stand at the side of the bed, bent over quickly, and pulled his pants and underwear off in one fluid movement. Unable to resist, she took in his manhood and her mouth watered, her body tingled, and the moistness between her legs had her squirming with anticipation. Even though she'd seen plenty of pictures—all in the name of research—nothing compared to seeing his cock live and in person.

All her nervousness flew out of the room. She could only think about how he'd feel on top of her, inside her. The excitement of her first time, so long overdue, gave her a burst of boldness.

"Come here." She panted as she helped him rip off his shirt. Her actions were clumsy, but she didn't care. And he didn't seem to mind, either. His shirt landed on the edge of the bed as he leaned to unclasp her bra and then flung it behind him before moving over her, lowering her farther back onto the mattress with the weight of his body.

He felt delicious. She squirmed against him, savoring his scent and heat. He reached across the bed toward the nightstand and pulled out a package, quickly tearing it open and slipping on protection.

Her sensitized body screamed for him. Blood pounded in her ears as his mouth found hers and explored every area, igniting a fire from deep within that consumed her inch by inch. He finally settled between her legs and the weight of him only increased her passion. Her body shook as his cock brushed against her folds. She pressed herself against him. And slowly he pushed into her, moving his hips from side to side as she whimpered in anticipation.

She wanted this, but at the same time she feared it. Would she satisfy him? Would she even know if she didn't?

His kiss deepened as he gathered her close, the soft moan coming from the back of his throat vibrated against her lips, and suddenly she had all the reassurance she needed. He wanted her. *Heck yeah, he did.* She didn't need experience to recognize that.

She grabbed his hips as she spread her legs farther, pressing into him, urging him forward as she gripped his rear. He entered her in small degrees, moving slowly, holding back. She stiffened at the pinch of pain for which no book in the world could prepare a woman. Then his hips pushed forward gently, and he caught her tiny gasps in his mouth as she grew accustomed to his feel. His length, width. His everything.

Even though uncomfortable at first, as her body relaxed, each millimeter became more delicious than the last—until he filled her, and she arched her neck, letting the tingles wash over her. Once his hips became flush with hers, they both stilled, their chests heaving. Her flesh quivered, and her body throbbed with need.

He smiled and touched his nose to hers, and she carefully kissed his chin, sliding her tongue lightly over the stitches. They didn't need to speak, they were in tune. She instinctively knew he waited for her to catch up. And he knew the moment she did.

He moved inside of her. Slowly.

Her walls quivered and gripped him as he withdrew at an even slower pace than he'd entered her, then she gasped as he pushed into her again. She arched, her body aching for release. He palmed her rear and lifted her. His growl fierce and primal as he pulled back then plunged deep, filling her with his length. Her body shook, and he stiffened, but she urged him to continue by biting his earlobe, her breaths coming short and fast as she lifted her pelvis.

Then he thrust into her again, and again, and her body soared. She closed her eyes, planting her feet firmly on the bed, and tried to match his thrusts with her own. She couldn't keep up, and he grabbed her legs, wrapping them around his middle. The shift of butt muscles as he pushed in and out of her became an entirely new aphrodisiac. She dug her nails into his back, raking her fingers down his backbone to grip his ass. He nibbled her shoulder gently, teasing her skin, and she bit her lip to stop from crying out as his pace quickened.

Her legs tightened around his middle, and she dug into his shoulders. She couldn't hold back any longer. Both of them cried out, but the noise became a buzz in the back of her head as she strove toward something. Something she couldn't identify but that her body craved.

She'd never felt such an overpowering sensation like this before. Every inch of her body tightened, fighting, with a greediness she didn't know she possessed, to reach that peak. That point of freedom. Release. At the same time, she didn't want the sensations to end. Shivers rode her flesh, pressure built inside her until her toes flexed and curled and almost clenched in pain. But a delicious pain that she wanted to feel again and again.

Tension swelled inside her at an alarming rate. She pressed to him, pulling him in closer. A desperate coil wound tight in her belly as they matched their bodies' rhythms.

Her breasts shook as Jared lifted himself slightly on his elbows, moving faster, pulling her legs up higher, and suddenly she yelled out his name in a voice that shook the room. She closed her eyes and got lost in the thick, heavy, hot lava filling her veins. Her body tensed, and as she moaned Jared arched his back and pushed into her one final time, pressing himself against her as beads of sweat slid down the side of his face, neck, and chest.

She'd never seen a man look so desirable before. Prickles of awareness overtook her as he collapsed onto her, holding her tightly as if he'd never let go. They lay still for several seconds, and then he lifted himself on his elbows and rested his brow against hers, their sweat mingling.

He brushed her lips with his as he rolled off to the side, taking her with him and tucking her into his shoulder. Her cheek lay pressed against his amazing pecs. Those pecs that she had yet to see dance. She smiled to herself. That would be a request she'd save for another time. Right now she hadn't quite come down from her high, and she was in no hurry.

The scent of their bodies and the aftermath of their sex filled her breath, and she gulped in another dose of air, not wanting to lose the smell. She rubbed her cheek against his chest, snuggling farther into the crook of his arm.

"Not only are you beautiful, but you're amazing." He kissed her temple.

"You're not so bad yourself."

His chest rumbled when he laughed, and the vibration in her ear calmed her heart. She hadn't been sure her heartbeat would ever go back to normal.

"You okay? You want anything? Water?"

His concern softened her already gooey heart, and she shook her head. "I'm fine."

Allison didn't want him to move. To get up and leave her. Even if she'd been to the point of shriveling up like a prune due to lack of moisture she'd have told him no.

She wanted to ask him if she'd done it right. If she'd pleased him as much as he had her, but she couldn't get the words to come out. Truth be told, she couldn't have spoken another word if the building were on fire. Her mind whirled with what had just happened. Her body hummed in all the right places, and she hoped it would never stop.

They lay in each other's arms on top of the covers. She wasn't embarrassed or cold. She could stay here for the rest of the night. Maybe the week.

Long after he fell asleep, she lay staring at the even rise and fall of his chest. Her smile didn't feel like it'd ever fade, and she touched her lips with her fingertip. Feeling him there. Tasting him. Wanting him again, so that she'd never forget how he smelled or tasted. This moment shouldn't end, but her body told her something different. Her eyelids became heavy, and she had a harder and harder time focusing on the tiny dusting of hair around his nipples and across his chest. The lazy happy trail that led to his length.

A throbbing ache filled her, overtaking parts of her body she didn't know existed.

She traced his nipple, and he mumbled and brushed his cheek against the top of her head. All the books she'd read about the first time, positions, and anything else she could get her hands on that involved lovemaking hadn't prepared her for the emotional journey she'd just experienced.

Fantastic was an understatement. Sex was spine-tingling. Orgasmic didn't even begin to describe what had happened between these four walls. Her body pulsed with the aftershocks, and she was ready for round two, three, and four.

*Well, maybe not quite yet.* She forced herself to open her eyes so that this moment wouldn't come to an end.

The thin dusting of hairs on his chest tickled her fingers. He shifted again in her arms, and she tilted her head to meet his hooded gaze.

"Don't tell me you're ready for seconds."

The place between her legs tingled with anticipation.

She could feel she would be sore, but right now all she could think about was tasting what Jared had to offer again. She'd deal with any discomfort tomorrow. A warm bath would do wonders.

"You had your seconds Sunday, I want mine today."

He turned to his side, and her head slid off his shoulder and on to the mattress. She tentatively touched his erection and shivered as it filled her hand. Hard. Amazing. Delicious.

"I've always respected a woman who could ask for seconds."

"What about thirds or fourths?"

His eyes sparked with mischief. "Are you trying to make up for lost time?"

"Something like that." She giggled, but only long enough for his mouth to claim hers.

...

Did she have *devirginated* stamped across her forehead?

Allison couldn't take much more. Sunday dinners at the Hall house were never this…*well, quiet*.

An uneasy swell filled her gut like a helium balloon as her gaze darted around the table. Gramps sat contentedly chewing his chicken, patting his mashed potatoes down with his fork. Dad actually had a book. He never read at the table but confessed before dinner he couldn't put this one down and if there were any earth-shattering conversations he'd try to pay attention.

As for Jared and Nick, they not only weren't speaking, but they barely made eye contact.

Dad lowered his book. "And I forgot to mention. Dinners might be put on hold until further notice. Gramps and I are doing a kitchen overhaul. New appliances, paint, floor. I'll keep you posted."

"The old girl needs a facelift," Gramps looked up long enough from his plate to pass a smile around the table.

"I can't wait to see what you come up with." Allison added a bit too much sparkle to her words, in an effort to erase some of the tension around the table. It failed miserably, and she slouched in her seat.

Nick grunted, and Jared continued to smear butter on his potatoes, although he did manage a slight nod toward Gramps.

Things had been tense last Sunday, but she couldn't help but think everyone knew what had happened between her and Jared last night.

She rubbed her forehead, just in case a neon sign had really attached itself to her with the pulsating words proclaiming innocence lost.

At that moment she met Jared's gaze from across the table. Her stomach swooped, and she could feel her whole body blush as they exchanged a smile. Unfortunately, it was the same second Nick glanced up from his plate.

His frown contorted his face.

She'd had enough. "I'm not very hungry." Could she feign illness and make an early departure?

Without another word she scooped up her plate and headed into the kitchen. The scraping of a chair grated across her backbone, and she spun around after she dumped her dinner into the trash.

"I tried to talk to Jared, now I'm coming to you." Nick's tone flooded her with another dose of unease. This time it strangled her chest.

"What's your problem, Nick?"

"My problem is you and Jared and all the little coy glances." He crossed his arms.

"And what difference does it make to you? We're friends. I think you're reading more into it." A rush of nausea invaded her throat. She felt like she might puke at how easily that lie had spilled from her lips.

Jared took that moment to come into the room. The smile on his face fell away when they both glared at him.

"Give us a moment," Nick growled.

Jared didn't move. Instead he turned his attention toward Allison. She smiled, any thought of hurling forgotten. His face relaxed as he mouthed a question, asking if she were okay.

"Fuck, man. I'm right here, and I'm not blind. Yes, she's okay." Nick ground the words out with such force Allison stepped back. Her family hadn't been immune to disputes over the years, but Nick had never used that tone. Never.

She pressed her fingers to her chest, reattaching the smile to her lips as she met Jared's eyes. "We'll be done in a minute."

"Sure?"

She nodded, the stress binding her chest returning the moment he vanished from view.

"Spill, Al."

"I'm pretty sure Jared already filled you in." She shot him a stern glare, but it didn't faze him. If anything, his anger kicked up a notch, and that large vein on the side of his neck bulged.

"Give it to me again in a nutshell."

She rested her weight on one leg. "I wanted help in making some changes. You said no. I approached Jared. He said no—"

"If he said no, what the hell—"

His voice fell away when she held up her hand. "You asked for a nutshell, let me give you the nutshell."

He nodded, crossing his arms over his chest, drumming the fingers of his left hand over the arm of his right.

"I tried on my own, well, with a little help from Colleen."

That earned her an eye roll. No surprise there.

"Things didn't work out as well as I'd hoped. Apparently I

had no clue what I was doing. People laughed at me, Nick…" Tears welled behind her eyes, and she swallowed in an attempt to stop from crying. "I've never felt worse in my life. Embarrassed."

"Al." Nick moved toward her, but she stepped back, her butt colliding with the counter as she waved him away.

The moment she had herself under control, she took a lungful of air and straightened her shoulders. She didn't want to break down in front of him. All that would do was prove she needed his big-brother protection.

"Jared not only came to my rescue, but he took me to see one of his friends. She helped me with my makeup, colored my hair, gave me some advice. Jared and I had lunch, took in the mall, and he's now giving me some dating advice." *Whew. That sounds a lot more innocent than the real-life version. Good thing.*

Her resolve filled her further, and she lifted her chin. "Anything else you need to know?" Even as she directed her query toward him, she questioned herself. Was Jared just helping her? Or was there something more between them? Did their moment of lust leave her wishing for more than there actually could be? After all, they were complete opposites. On so many levels. They might have an attraction, but could it—would it—last?

"I'm sorry you were hurt. But I didn't buy Jared's version, and I'm not buying yours, either."

"And why not?" She hated feeding Nick a line, but there were things in a girl's life that brothers shouldn't be privy to. If something did come of all this confusion, then she could share more detail, but until she could make sense of it all, how could she explain anything to her brother?

"Because there's something more going on than either of you are confessing."

She'd had enough of his attitude. Who did he think he

was? "Look, Nick. You're not our lord and master. We don't answer to you, and you have no right to interfere—"

"What the hell are you two bickering about now?" Dad strolled into the room, book-free, hands on his hips. "I can hear you in the other room. We can *all* hear you."

*Great.*

Dad turned on Nick. "Why are you so worried about what either Allison or Jared are up to? What busin—"

"The better question might be why *aren't you* worried about what's happening between them?"

"Jared's family, and Allison's a smart girl." Dad used his greater height to intimidate Nick as he stood over him.

"But everyone makes mistakes. I don't think Allison knows what the hell she's getting mixed up in tangling with Jared." Nick lowered his voice a few octaves.

"And you think you know better than her? You have no right trying to run your sister's life. Get over it, Nick."

Nick actually had the good sense to sink back against the counter, expelling a large breath of air. "But—"

"Thanks, Dad." She might be a chicken, but Allison took that opportunity to make a quick exit. From there she dropped a kiss on Gramps's head, mouthed an apology to Jared, and raced out the door.

She couldn't handle this. Not today. She hated coming between Jared and Nick. And now Dad was involved, but at least he was on her side. The right thing to do would be to put an end to things now. It was going to have to come to an end sometime anyway.

But could she do it? In such a short time, she'd already formed a sweet addiction to her brother's best friend. Her boss.

She slid behind the wheel of her car and dropped her face into her palms, squeezing her eyes tight.

Good thing there'd be no Sunday dinner next week or

she'd have opted out. Maybe renovations would take a few weeks, months. How about years? Heck, maybe she'd move across the state, across the country.

How had this become such a big mess?

Her passenger door squeaked open, and she peered sideways between her fingers as Gramps slid in beside her, patting her knee.

"Hi, Gramps. What are you doing here?" She sat upright, licking her lips and wiping a frustrated tear from her cheek.

"Checking on my Allygirl. I didn't like the way you left. I don't like seeing my girl caught between a rock and a hard place."

"I know I should be used to being at the bottom of the pecking order in our testosterone-laden household, but I can't take much more of Nick. I'm so angry at him I could burst." She flung her head back against her seat, pressing the heels of her hands against her eyelids to block out the tears.

Gramps squeezed her hand as he sighed. The leather of his seat moaned as he shifted his weight. "As far as Nick goes, he will always think you're a babe in the woods. He loves you."

"I understand that, but he has to let me live my life. Even if he thinks I might be making mistakes."

Gramps nodded. "Nobody can learn if they don't make their own mistakes."

Her heart stalled as she sat forward, twisting in her seat. "Are you saying I'm making a mistake?"

"Don't go getting a bee in your bonnet." He laughed. "Who are any of us to say that what's happening between you and Jared isn't the best thing since sliced bread?"

She huffed out a breath of air. "So we're that obvious. Or I'm that obvious?"

"We'd all have to be blind if we didn't pick up on the heat between you two."

"I like him, Gramps."

"And he likes you."

"You think?"

"I know."

"Nick is so pissed. And he's making me angry. I don't know what I'm doing when it comes to men, but I like how Jared makes me feel. Can't we just coast along the road we're on and see where it leads? Why does Nick have to get—"

Gramps laughed. "You gotta admit, Jared has a reputation when it comes to women."

She blinked. "You know—"

"I'm not hard of hearing, Allygirl. You know, years ago your dad went through something similar when he started dating your mom." His tone held a tinge of reminiscent humor. "Your mom's dad and brothers wanted her to have nothing to do with him. You know, your dad had quite the reputation as a ladies' man himself."

"Dad?" How come she'd never heard any of this before?

Gramps nodded, pushing his glasses back up the bridge of his nose. His smile lit up his face. "Over time, as Neal got to know them, showed how much he cared for Amanda, everyone calmed down. Maybe that's going to be the case here."

"But Nick—"

"Can't see his ass from his elbow. Give him time to get used to the situation."

She groaned in frustration. "That's the problem, Gramps. I don't even know if there is a situation."

# Chapter Ten

Monday morning had Jared clock watching.

Allison was amazing. His mind shifted back twenty-four hours to Sunday morning, after the night they'd made love. She was adventurous, he had to give her that. A grin crossed his face. She'd asked him to try a few positions she'd read about in her book. He'd loved how easily they'd tried new things, and her ability to laugh when a few of the positions hadn't worked out as expected.

Her sense of adventure had moved sex from serious to playful, and she'd shown him a new side to lovemaking he'd never imagined. To think he'd learned something from a novice made his smile widen.

*Shit.* What was happening to him? Nick wanted Al to have a man in her life who put her first, and Jared wanted to become that man. Would she be receptive?

He frowned and rolled his shoulders as his mind raced back again to Sunday morning and their lovemaking. So much changed in a few hours' time.

The day had gone south after the altercation between

Allison and Nick. The way Nick spoke to her had Jared clenching his fists. They had been so loud that their dad had been drawn to the kitchen to calm things down. And Al had stormed off without saying good-bye. She didn't pick up her phone when he'd called later that night. But who could blame her? No doubt she had a lot on her mind. Her top priority being how to get Nick to mind his own business. He didn't like coming between her and her brother, and he had no clue if he even had the right to intervene.

He loved Nick, but he had to let go of the picture in his mind that Al was a little girl who needed protection.

And now—Jared glanced at his watch again—he counted down the minutes to lunch. She might not have answered his calls last night, but the moment he'd shot her an email this morning asking her to lunch, she'd not only apologized for how she'd left the night before but agreed to try out that new sushi restaurant down the block. But at the end of the email she'd claimed having lunch would give her another chance to get her bearings in a social setting. What the heck was that about? Was she still considering dating someone else, after what they'd shared?

Or was he reading more into the situation than there was? Maybe her goal all along had been to lose her virginity, and he happened to be the handiest.

Even as the thought pinged through his brain, he hated himself for thinking she'd do that. But he'd certainly like to know what was on her mind. He could ask her, but part of him feared pissing her off—like Nick had. And then he'd be left with nothing.

Fuck, this was confusing. A mess.

He ran his hand through his hair as a light tap sounded on his office door, and Allison peeked in. "You ready?"

"And waiting." He'd drive himself crazy with his own thoughts later. For now, he'd enjoy an hour with Al. He slid into his jacket and made his way toward her. Excitement curled in his gut, and he couldn't resist leaning down to give her a soft kiss on the lips.

Her mouth parted when she gasped, and a tinge of color stained her cheeks. She quickly looked behind her. "We don't want gossip, do we?"

"Would I embarrass you?" *Damn, Esterly. Are you a girl now?* He cleared his throat. "Nobody's around. Don't worry."

Just to prove his point he boxed her against the wall and slowly claimed her mouth, parting the seam of her lips with his tongue and deepening the kiss until she moaned. He loved that sound.

"Jared." She snort-laughed as she pushed at his chest.

He grinned. He loved that sound, too. "Okay. Okay. It'll be a chore, but I'll try to keep myself under control. Just so you know, you don't make it easy. Especially with that dress. And those damn shoes. Your legs are a mile long."

The proud tilt of her chin and the sparkle in her brown eyes were reward enough, but that didn't mean he didn't enjoy the tiny kiss she pressed to his lips. "Thank you. This confidence thing is hard, and I'm not sure I'm always pulling it off. But your words make me feel a whole lot better."

"Well, if you were worried about what you chose to wear today, no need." He slapped her on the rear, and she made a small sound from the back of her throat—one that made it clear she liked how he teased her—as he put his palm on the small of her back to steer her out of the office.

"Behave yourself." She rubbed her behind.

"I'll try."

They both sobered the moment they stepped onto the elevator and turned, spotting Nick standing by the reception desk with his gaze locked on them. Allison stiffened, and a tightness filled Jared's chest. Thunder boomed across Nick's face, and his mouth thinned into a straight line.

Jared's gut clenched at the look on his friend's face. Part of him felt betrayed. Angry that his best friend didn't think he'd be good enough for his sister. Then that other part of him, the side of doubt, wondered if maybe Nick was right. What if he wasn't the best guy for Allison?

He shook off his doubt, but he couldn't lose the pain in his gut at his friend's cold eyes. The only other time he'd seen that arctic expression had been the time Allison had brought Lance home for the first time. For a second that internal struggle between friendship and being with Allison twisted through him. He didn't want to piss off his best friend, but he also didn't want to ruin his lunch date with Allison. He'd been looking forward to it since the second he opened her email.

He wouldn't let anything spoil it. Not even Nick. Jared gave him a solemn-faced nod as the elevator door slid closed. He might have hell to pay for that later, but right now he didn't give a shit. At some point Nick would have to adjust to the idea that men were going to notice Allison.

And Jared might have to get used to the idea that he might not be the one she'd want to be with.

He shook his head. All that mattered was for Al to be happy. If he had to swallow his own desire, help her find the type of guy she wanted, he'd do it. Even if it killed him.

...

"I'm going to burst." Allison patted her belly. "Now that you know another of my addictions is sushi, will you please remind me to stop next time so I don't overeat? I'm going to be worthless behind my desk this afternoon because all I want to do is take a nap."

She bit her lip. Next time? Presumptuous much?

But Jared didn't miss a beat. "I can think about ten other things we could do to pass away the afternoon hours besides a nap."

"Oh, I'm sure you can, but I'm afraid to ask for details in case we decide to skip out on the rest of our workday."

"Don't tease me, because as your boss I can make that happen."

They laughed as they stepped off the elevator and started down the hall.

"Even though I'm stuffed, we're still on for tonight, right?" She could tell herself all day long and six ways to Sunday that going out with Jared tonight was to help her get comfortable in social situations—just as their lunch had been—but she'd only be lying to herself. Not that she'd clue him in to that. If she did, they wouldn't have a reason for lunch dates or to make plans for after work. Not to mention the sex. Something that new and delicious shouldn't end so soon. Even though that little voice in the back of her mind reminded her again that this couldn't last, she wasn't ready to end things quite yet. Not even for Nick. For now she'd just push that voice of reason right out of her head.

"Drinks at Concords after work. And, in order to hone your social skills, I challenge you to go up to at least one guy and start a conversation."

"Alone?" How come his voice didn't ring with the same conviction as his words? Or had her wishful thinking kicked in again? If only this thing between them could…

He rubbed her shoulders. "You got this. All you have to do it ask someone to play a game of pool or darts, or just sit at the bar with them and make small talk. Once you do it a few times it'll get easier. You up for it?"

She nodded, squaring her shoulders in an attempt to feel more confident than she did. More excited. She'd prefer hanging with him, laughing with him, making small talk with him. But she also needed to distance herself a little. Already her heart had become too wrapped up in Jared. She couldn't quit cold turkey, but baby steps might be the smart route to take before she got too attached.

"I've been reading some current events online. I even looked up a few jokes, but I'm not sure I'm ready to break those out." She gave a shaky laugh. "But I'm game." Truth be known, even though Jared would be there and she was fine one on one, the idea of approaching someone to ask them to play a game of pool or darts did make her palms grow a teensy bit sweaty.

But she could do it.

She jumped when a weight settled across her shoulders and almost choked on her tongue as Nick fell into step beside her.

"Well, aren't you two cozy?" His stern gaze swept from her to Jared. "Lunch, now plans after work? But there's nothing going on, right?"

"Get a grip, Nick. You're acting like we eloped and didn't invite you. It's lunch. Drinks. Do you want to tag along?" Not that she wanted him to, but at this point if she didn't ask he'd be angrier than he already was.

Jared's jaw ticked as he looked at Nick. "I think we need to have a talk."

Nick shook his head. "Maybe later. My day is full."

Guilt gnawed at her ankles at the cool look Nick shot Jared. But when he turned his attention back toward her he smiled, although a little stiffly. "Can I see you in my office?"

"Now?" She practically choked on the word.

"Unless you have other plans?" Nick's arrogant eyebrow shot up in challenge.

"No. Sure. I'll be there in a few." She swallowed heavily as his arm fell off her shoulders, and he moved past them down the hall. All the confidence she'd gained fell to the wayside when it came to her brother. She needed to work on that. And fast.

She slowed her pace until she stopped dead center in the hallway. The weight settling over her chest had her fighting for air. "I don't think I'm looking forward to this conversation."

"This is more about me than you. How about I talk to Nick and— "

"Not on your life. Don't you start treating me the same way Nick does. If I'd spoken up years ago, Nick wouldn't be pushing me around now. It's time I start fighting my own wars. I just hadn't expected a battle today." She closed her eyes to collect her thoughts. "I'm sorry you got sucked into all of this. I know the tension between you two is because of me, because you helped me." She touched Jared's sleeve. "I really appreciate what you've done, and I'm going to try to make things right."

"Get ready for a fight. He doesn't like our friendship."

For some reason the term friendship hurt her feelings, but that's exactly what they had. She'd asked for his help. After he'd realized how much help she needed, he'd agreed. As a friend. He didn't want anything more. And, really, did she honestly think if he did he'd be interested in her?

Okay, they might have grown closer, shared some laughs and secrets—along with some great sex—but none of that meant he was interested in a relationship. Not the kind she wanted.

*Don't forget that.* No getting caught up in a fantasy about a good-looking guy who happens to be her brother's best friend. He was there to help her reach her goal. He didn't want to *be* that goal.

Jared put his hand on her shoulder and squeezed. "Let me talk to him first."

She waved away his words, forcing a smile. "He asked to see me, and it's me he'll see. If he needs to talk to you, believe me, he's not shy."

"I know, but— "

She pressed her finger to his mouth. "Plus, we have to look at this as another lesson in building my confidence. I just have to channel Margarite and tell myself that I'm awesome."

"That you are." His lopsided smile tugged at her heart. The chickenshit part of her wanted to take him up on his offer. But her chickenshit days were over.

She moved past him, but not before he swatted her gently on the rear. She jumped, looked around, and snort-giggled. She covered her face. "I hate when I do that."

"I love it. It's sexy."

"You're sick." She winked, and they parted ways at the break room. When this flingy-thingy was over, she'd miss him.

Heck, she'd more than miss him, and the thought tugged at her heart again, but this time in a more painful way.

She walked into the shared waiting area that separated Jared's and Nick's offices. Maureen was nowhere in sight, so she tapped on Nick's door and then pushed it open since he was expecting her. He stood with his back toward her, staring out the windows.

"What's up, Nick? I'd rather we didn't have a repeat of yesterday." Her voice came out duller than intended. Although she'd planned to stay upbeat, she dreaded this confrontation. His rigid posture foreshadowed what lay ahead.

"You mean the conversation we didn't finish?" He turned and pulled at his tie.

"Nothing is stopping me from walking out that door."

He blew out a breath. "Allison, you know I love you, right?"

She nodded, the rigidness in her back evaporating. She walked toward him and touched his sleeve. "I know, but—"

"And I love Jared like family, but I'm not happy. Not happy at all." He shook his head, plopping down on the edge of his desk. He grabbed her hand and absentmindedly rubbed her fingers as he studied her face. She remained standing. All her life she'd given in to Nick's demands, but she had to cut herself free at some point.

"I'm sorry you're not happy. I know you're upset about Jared and me, but you need to hear me out."

He shook his head. "Nothing you say will convince me that what you two are doing is good. Jared said he was helping you out, but I sense there's more to it than what either of you are saying. I love you. I don't want to see you get hurt, and Jared is the type of guy who'll hurt you."

Her temper bristled. "How can you say that about your best friend?"

"Because I know him. I know his rep. Not that he's a bad guy, but he's a ladies' man. He's not interested in anything long-term."

"You don't know that." Why was she even arguing the fact? What Nick said was true, but hearing it versus thinking it had her wanting to make it a great debate.

"And you do?"

"Who says *I* want anything long-term? At least with him." She ran her free hand through her hair. The idea of having something long-term with someone other than Jared didn't feel right, but more than likely it was nerves. She was comfortable with Jared. When she eventually met the man she could have a future with, she'd grow comfortable with him, too. Jared was just giving her the tools to get there.

Right? *Right.*

"I know you're both telling me you're working toward personal changes. And I remember what you said when you asked for my help. I know you want to build your confidence, social skills—I get that, Al. But I feel like you're setting yourself up for disaster. I can see it in your eyes. You're already past the friendship mark. If you keep walking this path, you're going to fall in deeper."

She smiled, tilting her head to the side. No doubt his

concerns were valid, but… "Can't you let me learn all of this on my own? I know Jared is a ladies' man. I know he doesn't want anything more. I haven't dated much, you know that. I'm certainly not in the market to settle down before I've had a chance to date around a bit. I want to have fun." But that partial lie tasted bitter. If Jared even gave her an inkling he might be interested, she'd definitely go for it. Who wouldn't? The man ticked all the boxes off almost every girl's wish list. But she wasn't stupid, and she also wasn't that naive. Not any longer, anyway.

"I don't want you to get hurt."

"I won't, but you need to understand I'm a big girl. Life is all about taking chances, and sometimes those chances lead to hurt." She shook her head as he opened his mouth to speak. "I'm saying that figuratively. I'm not saying Jared will hurt me, or that there's even a chance of that. I'm saying it's part of life. Truthfully, I love you, but I don't always want your protection or advice."

"But—"

"In the future, if I do, I'll ask for it. But this isn't up to you. You don't get a vote." She squared her shoulders, loving the strength in her voice. If nothing else, knowing she had finally stood up to Nick proved she'd grown.

His face darkened, but she wouldn't budge or be intimated. "Al, I want you to stay away from him. I really—"

She shushed him with her hand. "I don't want to argue with you. Like I said, I appreciate all the help you've given me through the years, but from now on, if I need your advice, I'll ask."

She turned on her heels and walked out his office door.

Maureen sat at her desk and gave Allison a wink as she walked past. For sure she'd caught every word of their conversation since the door hadn't been closed tightly, but she didn't care. She actually felt good that Maureen had heard and had shown her quiet support.

Telling Nick to stay out of her business had been easier than she thought. Hopefully he'd listen. She should have said it yesterday. Even so, the moment she made her way into the hall and rounded the corner, she leaned against the wall and shook out her limbs.

Confidence could accomplish a lot. Too bad she hadn't realized it years ago.

• • •

Jared clenched the neck of his beer bottle until his knuckles turned white. He'd switched over from nonalcoholic to alcohol with this last beer. He'd needed every damn drop to stop from getting up and pounding that guy twirling Allison around by the pool table.

They'd arrived only forty-five minutes ago, and she hadn't even bothered to sit down with him to work up her courage, instead marching straight over to the four men circling the pool table to strike up a conversation.

He admired her determination and the way she dove in headfirst, but at the same time he hated the reaction she'd received. The guys hadn't even hesitated, enveloping her into the folds of their group like they'd all been friends forever. And one in particular couldn't seem to keep his eyes—or hands—off her.

The sound of her laughter vibrated the air around him, and he sat taut on the edge of his seat. The clock behind the bar clicked onto the hour. He'd sat here, mouth shut, sweating through each second as Al cozied up with her new friends. He didn't like that another man made her laugh so easily. He also didn't like that the same man had whipped out his cell and was punching in numbers that Allison doled out. He'd have to school her about not giving her number to just anyone.

Especially some guy she'd just met. In a bar, no less.

He forced a smile onto his stiff lips as she made her way across the busy floor, weaving between tables with a little wiggle of her hips. She looked so damn cute and happy he couldn't stop staring, even though steam blew out his ears as he looked over her shoulder to the four guys she'd left by the pool table—all with their eyes glued to her backside.

She dropped into the chair beside him with a satisfied smile.

"Well, that was fun. And for the first time in my life some guy in a bar asked for my number." She practically bounced in her seat as she grabbed his hand.

"The first time?" Now he felt like even more of a heel for getting annoyed. She wasn't his property. The only reason he was here at all was to help her. And now that she'd found herself, could experience some of what she thought was missing from her life, he wanted to ruin it by getting jealous.

*Jealous?*

*Yes. I'm jealous.*

That hadn't been part of their deal. But then again, what did he expect? After all they'd gone through, wasn't it natural to develop these types of feelings?

He might be jealous, but that didn't mean he thought of her with long-term intentions. Did he? Well, sometimes his mind drifted to daydreams involving a future, and Allison's face was always part of those dreams. He shook off the thought quickly. Any guy would be jealous when the woman he slept with a few nights ago wanted to move on to someone else. Right?

"I know. I'm behind, aren't I?"

"Nothing wrong with that." Spoken like an overprotective jerk. Of course she wanted to have someone ask for her number. Hell, he fucking liked it when it happened to him, why wouldn't she? But that didn't mean he liked it happening right in his face.

She sobered, and the light filling her eyes dimmed as she leaned in. "Can I tell you a secret? But you have to promise you won't judge."

"Never." He sat forward, more than curious at what she wanted to share.

"I gave him a made-up number." She covered her face with her hand, her eyes full of mischief as she peered at him from over her thumb. "I know that's bad. I'd hate it if someone did it to me but, truthfully, he's not my type, but I didn't want to hurt his feelings by saying no. I wasn't sure what to do, I've never been in that situation and—"

He grabbed her hand and squeezed. "Forget it, Al. There are worse things that could happen, and I think he'll live." No denying that his heart galloped a little at her words. She hadn't liked the guy. Good. He hadn't, either. At least what he'd seen from across the room.

She dropped her hand, and her eyes grew wide. "Oh my God. Maybe I should go tell him. I really feel bad now that I think about it."

"Like I said, he'll live. Anyway, I'm starving. Let's go grab a burger or something." He stood, and she grabbed what was left of his beer on the table and chugged it down with a grimace.

She shook her head, her lip curled. "I still don't like beer. When we grab that burger, let's get a soda, too. I need something to wash that bitter taste out of my mouth."

He laughed and turned her toward the door.

She glanced back at him over her shoulder, her brown eyes soft. "Are you sure I shouldn't say—"

"Move." He pushed her forward with his hands on her shoulders. "I know the perfect burger place." He leaned forward to whisper in her ear, drinking in her cherry blossom scent. The perfect place where he could have her all to himself.

The perfect place where he could ask her the question that had been on his mind for a few days.

"Good. I'm starved."

He followed her out the door, his eyes instantly drawn to her ass. She'd worn those damn jeans again. They formed to her rear like they'd been tailor-made for her body. No wonder every guy in the place had checked her out.

He ran his hand through his hair. Bullshit. Every guy had checked her out because she'd been the most vibrant woman in the room. Full of life and fun. Her laughter still echoed in his ears. And his question hung on the tip of his tongue until his mouth grew dry. He'd never been nervous about asking a woman a question, but then again, he'd always known what her answer would be.

…

Allison turned the corner, loving the feel of Jared's arm hooked through hers. Now she understood why everyone who was part of a couple always walked around with a smile—well, for the most part. Human contact felt good. His touch uplifted her. Made her feel beautiful and special. And the fact that she'd actually had fun in a bar, talked to a few guys on her own—and had given out a number, although it hadn't been hers—didn't hurt, either.

"And here we are." They stopped outside a diner that had her feeling like they'd stepped back in time, circa 1940.

"Seriously?"

"You said you wanted to experience someplace different. And don't you want to be well-rounded in case the guy you start dating likes retro burger joints?"

"Who's ever heard of a retro burger joint?" She dropped her hands low on her hips.

He shrugged, but the corners of his mouth tugged with

humor. "Could be the next big thing. Either way, their burgers rule."

"I do want to try new things. But I'm not so sure if my stomach is up for the greasy-spoon challenge."

"Give me a break. You sound like you're sixty-three instead of twenty-three." His eyes twinkled. "You get some of your best eats at greasy spoons."

"I've heard that, but…"

"Didn't you experience any of these in college? In the middle of a late-night cram session, or after pulling an all-nighter, or walking home from the bar at three in the morning starving?"

She shook her head. All that he mentioned sounded fun, but she'd never done any of those things. "I was the girl who was home by ten. My late-night cram sessions were solo, and all-nighters wouldn't have involved more than ordering a pizza. And…" Her voice trailed off. She'd never walked home from a bar in the morning starving. For a moment her good mood waned.

He nudged her in the shoulder before she let herself sink low. "No matter. We're in the here and now. Pretend it's four in the morning and you've not only studied all night but you're drunk on top of it."

She laughed, rubbing her lips together and pinching the ball of tinfoil in her pocket.

"Now let's get in there and order a spoon loaded with grease."

She grimaced. "I'll pass."

"Then how about a burger?"

"I'm in."

…

Not only could Jared watch her all night, listen to her talk until the sun came up, and just be with her, but the way she ate a burger drained all the blood from his head and sent it down south.

Her tongue darted out at every opportunity to catch a drip of ketchup before it hit her chin or lick off a dollop of mustard on the corner of her lip. Her eyes sparkled as they talked, and the way she used her hands when she got excited about something mesmerized him. She might not even be aware of the way she teased him with every look, movement, and smile.

Or maybe she was, and he wasn't giving her enough credit.

Either way, he didn't care. All he knew was he wanted to be with her. Nick wasn't happy about it, but too bad. He'd have to deal with it.

His question hung in the air between them, even though she didn't have a clue he wanted to ask her something. She might be gaining confidence, but he'd started to doubt his. At least where she was concerned. "How do you think tonight went?"

"Really well. It wasn't as hard as I thought to walk up to those guys and ask to play pool. I didn't even need liquid courage to do it. Colleen will be so proud."

He cleared his throat and wiped his palms on his jeans. That jumpy feeling in his gut—the same one he'd gotten when he'd asked Sue Stevens to the seventh-grade dance—hit him full force. "Are you ready for a bigger event?"

The French fry she'd been pushing around her plate fell as she tilted her head to the left. "You're making me nervous."

*That makes two of us.* "Are you in the mood for a wedding?"

"A wedding?" she whispered, as if she'd never heard the word before. "Who's getting married?"

"Omar."

"Your brother." Her full-on smile returned.

He liked that she remembered his brother.

"I think I remember Nick mentioning him getting married. Are you sure you want to take me?"

"I'm positive. It'll be fun." He'd originally planned to ask her to boost her confidence, but that was no longer the case. Now he didn't want to bring anyone else.

"That means I'd meet your family." She squeaked out the last word.

"They don't bite."

She sat forward in her seat, her eyes widening and taking on a faraway look. "That'd be a perfect place to test out my conversation skills. I've been scouring through current event magazines and surfing the internet for trending topics."

"As in Twitter?" For some reason her response deflated his mood. But what had he expected. They weren't dating—as in real dating. This wasn't a relationship.

"I mean, tonight was awesome, but those guys weren't interested in discussing anything but beer and pool."

"And phone numbers." *Did that sound bitter?*

"If you're sure, I'd love to go. But I'll have to go shopping." She pushed away her plate.

"I know you're looking forward to that."

"Now that I know a little more about what colors look best on me, and what cuts are most flattering for my body type, it is kind of fun."

He smiled at her words. The day they'd shopped, he'd helped her pick out several outfits, but one of the saleswomen had taken a special interest in Allison and had offered her lots of advice. "I haven't even had to call in any of my friends."

"Only Margarite. She's amazing."

"I can't argue with that."

She rubbed her lips together. "Where and when is the wedding?"

"North Carolina in a couple weeks. We'll fly in the night

before, the wedding is Saturday, and then we'll leave Sunday morning." He wanted Al to go with him, but the heaviness invading his gut warned him it'd only add more stress between him and Nick.

"Will we stay with your family?"

He shook his head as she took a sip of her soda, chewing on the straw. "Omar and Devi booked several rooms at the hotel where the reception will be held. We can either share a room or you can have your own. Up to you…"

"Well…" She licked her lips, and the sweet look she gave him made his desire hit him again full force. "I think I have some parts down about pleasing a man—"

"I can vouch for that."

She giggled, and that soft blush covered her face. She was beautiful. He'd never known a woman like her. Her innocence and sweetness had become a huge attraction.

"But practice makes perfect."

Just the words he wanted to hear.

He cleared his throat and fought the urge to dive across the table and kiss her. "We'll have fun. I don't mean sharing a room—I mean that'll be fun, too—but you'll like the wedding." Since when had he lost his ability to flirt with a woman? For some reason—at least with Allison—he wanted so much to say and do the right thing he tripped over his own damn tongue.

She covered his hand with hers. "You're more nervous than I am."

"I think you're right."

"I like it. Thank you."

He laughed. "You're welcome. Why do you make me so nervous?"

"Must be I'm rubbing off on you."

"I like the sound of that."

"You're a tease."

“I like to tease you. You turn all pink, your eyes grow wide, and you get flustered.”

“I was thinking the same thing about you.” She grinned and squeezed his fingers.

And he wanted to drown in her eyes.

“I’m excited about the wedding, even though I’m sure there will be hundreds of people. I hope I don’t embarrass you.”

“Never. You might surprise yourself at how ready you are for this.” The more he talked, the more the excitement of taking her to the wedding knotted his gut. Not that he’d changed his mind, but he wanted the weekend to be about them. He wanted it to be a real date, and the realization sucker punched him until he couldn’t breathe.

The idea that their little fling would come to an end and she’d move on froze his brain. He didn’t want her to move on to someone else. Would she consider anything with him? Did he really want anything more, or did he just not want anyone else with Allison?

# Chapter Eleven

Allison sat in the break room. Her table for five was now filled to capacity. Even though the conversation buzzed around her, she wasn't paying attention. Her thoughts circled on Jared and how she missed him—and not in the way you missed a friend but like you missed someone special—because they'd hardly seen each other the last couple of weeks.

He'd been out of town the last few days, and the week before that he'd been busy finalizing the contract with Sanders Machinery.

As for Sunday dinners, they remained on hiatus as Dad and Gramps ran into one problem after another. First the appliances had been delayed, and now the plumbing had to be redone, which caused an upheaval with the installation of the floor.

She'd put all her energy into work, and any extra time had been filled with thoughts about the upcoming wedding this weekend. She still hadn't found the perfect dress, which seemed to consume more of her time than it should.

All her begging Colleen to hit the mall with her had been

for nothing, because her friend was working on a deadline.

Allison wanted to be pretty. To look good on Jared's arm. Most of all, she hoped his family liked her, although she knew it was wrong to care so much, especially since this wedding didn't have anything to do with them as a couple—because they weren't a couple. It was just another testing ground for her social savvy.

That didn't stop her feelings, though. No matter how wrong, her friendship with Jared had grown and changed. He'd become so much more than a friend. Were they friends with benefits? Lovers?

She mentally shook her head. They weren't lovers. They'd only made love that one night—*but a couple of times.* She wiggled in her seat at the thought. After this weekend she'd have a higher tally. Warmth flooded through her. She couldn't wait to be with him again. On so many levels. Part of her wanted more, but the sane part of her warned that it would never happen.

Did her attraction have more to do with her liking the attention? Had he become that shiny new penny in her life? Or was it something else?

And what did it matter since they'd never have a future? He didn't want one.

Nick strolled into the break room and refilled his coffee mug. They made eye contact, and he gave her a cold nod. Her heart sank. He hadn't gotten over the way she'd stood up to him, but eventually they'd find common ground.

But would he and Jared?

She speared a leaf of lettuce with her fork and twirled it around her plate. Her appetite vanished.

Guilt consumed her on so many levels, but mostly for the way she'd come between two friends. As much as she knew she should pull back, she couldn't. Not yet.

"Oh. My. God." Megan shoved the latest department

store catalog at her, tapping the page with her finger. "Please tell me I just found you the perfect dress for that out-of-town wedding you're going to."

For a moment Allison froze, hoping against hope Nick hadn't overheard. She glanced at him again as he talked to the latest temp girl as he refilled his coffee, and her shoulders sagged in relief. Eventually he'd find out she'd gone with Jared to his brother's wedding, but she'd prefer it happened after the fact. She might have stood up to him, but that didn't mean she was ready to have it out with him again.

Allison pasted on a grin and pulled the magazine closer. She squealed—because there was just no way she could hold back her excitement. Several pairs of eyes in the room landed on her. She grinned, bouncing in her seat. "Megan, you're a lifesaver. You did find the perfect dress." A line of penguins circled the hem of the dress. Not overdone, but enough to add a touch of whimsy. She'd been having fun discovering her style. A month ago she'd have wanted that dress but wouldn't have dared to wear it outside her apartment, but now... Now a bubble of excitement filled her as she ticked off all the places she could wear it.

Mary, another new temp, leaned across the table. "Good price, too."

In her excitement, Allison hadn't looked at the price, and she released the breath she held. Right in her budget.

But...

"Is it really okay for a wedding?"

"Why not? It's perfect." Megan grabbed the magazine and held the picture of the dress beside Allison's face, as if that would be the deciding factor. "You look so good in blue."

"It's a little curve-hugging." Even though she'd asked Megan for her help in picking out something to wear, she hadn't given her much more detail other than it was for a wedding. Definitely not a wedding she'd be going to with

Jared—the buzz that would create was beyond anything she could handle.

Nick brushed past their table on his way out, offering a stiff smile to everyone seated. Normally he'd have stopped and chatted, and it killed her that if she hadn't been there he probably would have. At the same time a heavy dose of annoyance mixed with another round of anger bubbled up inside of her. He needed to get over himself. He thought she was immature and not ready to handle the world, but he was the one acting like a spoiled kid who didn't get his way.

A trickle of trepidation slithered down her spine at what he'd do once he found out she'd gone away with Jared for the weekend. All hell would break loose. She'd told Dad and Gramps, who both wished her well, and Gramps had even thrown in a saucy wink for good measure.

She tried to harden her heart and remind herself again that Nick was the one being difficult. She shouldn't even care what he thought or how he'd react. But she did. No matter how much she and Nick might fight, she'd never get over caring.

An avalanche of guilt crashed down and settled at her feet. Maybe after this wedding she should take Nick's advice. In the name of preserving his friendship with Jared, she should step aside. One more weekend. Then she'd let herself down easy. Move on. Let Jared move on.

Even though her heart ached at the thought. Sometimes doing the right thing wasn't necessarily the easiest. Or what you wanted to do.

Allison stood at the top of the stairs. Her heartbeat pounded in her ears. Gripping her hands together, she stared across the expansive tiled lobby and through the double doors of the crowded banquet room.

She and Jared had landed in North Carolina only a couple hours before. They'd been whisked off to the large oceanfront hotel and had gone directly to their room to get ready for the rehearsal dinner.

She'd made the mistake of telling Jared to head on down without her as she finished messing with her hair—sweeping it up, and then brushing it down, and finally sweeping it back up again—searching for the best look. The shaky confidence she'd owned while getting ready vanished the moment she found herself perched above all the activity.

Now here she stood, her stomach unsettled, wishing she could run away to hide in the shadows. If only she had a chocolate Kiss, but she hadn't brought a purse, and her cap-sleeve gray dress had no pockets. Hadn't she promised herself to always buy outfits with pockets?

She channeled Margarite. *Time to own your nerdiness.* She lifted her head and made her way down the stairs.

*Don't trip. Don't trip. Don't trip.* Her mantra tamped out a dull rhythm in her head. At least she'd been thinking straight when she bought the shoes, keeping the heel at a modest two inches instead of going for the stilettos Megan kept pushing at her. The closer she got to the bottom of the stairs, the more her mind whizzed with the knowledge she'd have to make a solo entrance. What had possessed her to think she could walk into a room full of strangers and not drop ten pounds in sweat?

But no, she needed to be tough. She might have more confidence than she did when she started, but there was still that little niggle of fear when it came to social situations. Not to mention that bigger nagging voice—the one reminding her that after this weekend she needed to break away from Jared so that he and Nick could make up.

She stepped off the last stair and stopped, pulling in a large lungful of air, pressing her hand to her chest and considering herself lucky that the pace of her heart hadn't landed her in the emergency room.

"There you are."

She jumped at the sound of Jared's voice as he came up beside her.

"Where did you come from?" She glanced around, her gaze settling on him. She'd never seen a more welcome sight in her life as the smile filling his face.

"Men's room."

She eyed the sign pointing to the restrooms on the other side of the lobby. He hadn't come from that direction. He didn't fool her. He'd waited for her to come down. All along he'd known she'd be nervous, and the fact that he stood in the shadows and didn't argue the point with her earlier made her go warm inside.

"Thank you."

"For what?"

"You know what. And we'll leave it at that." She smiled up at him.

He steered her toward the entrance to the banquet hall. The huge room was humming with conversation and laughter.

They were barely two steps inside when they were surrounded by a slender older woman with huge green eyes and gorgeous black hair, a cute pregnant blonde, and a man who could almost be Jared's twin. Definitely a brother, at least if the eyes were anything to judge by.

The older woman reached up and pulled Jared down for a quick kiss on the cheek. Her eyes glowed bright, the love on her face evident. "You look wonderful." She turned her attention to Allison, and her face softened even more. "And this must be Nick's little sister."

Allison held out her hand, and the woman laughed. "Not a chance. I'm all about the hugs. Especially tonight." She pulled her into her arms and squeezed, whispering in her ear, "By the way, I'm Gianna, Jared's mom."

"Nice to meet you." Allison swallowed, amazed that her voice sounded so normal.

As soon as Gianna released her, Allison's hand was swallowed up in the other man's grip. "I'm Roth, and this is my wife, Holly."

"Nice to meet you."

"I know we just met"—Holly already had her arms wrapped around her in a hug—"but my pregnancy hormones have made me all touchy-feely-huggy lately. So—"

"No worries. I'm a total hug advocate." Allison squeezed her tight, and when they parted Holly rubbed her arms. "Cute dress. I can't wait to wear real clothes again. I'm about done shopping in the tent section of the sporting goods store."

"Give me a break." Roth hugged her to his side. "You look beautiful as always."

"Wait a minute. Let's rewind. Did I hear the word wife?" Jared's eyes darted between the pair.

Holly nudged Roth in the side with her elbow and gave him a mock scowl. Allison liked her immediately.

"You didn't tell him?"

"We've been a little busy." Roth's sheepish expression endeared him to Allison in a second.

"Two of my boys married and my first grandbaby on the way. Life is looking good for the first time in a long time." Gianna's gaze took in the group, settling on Holly's cute little belly.

"Ohh, she's kicking." Holly grabbed Gianna's hand and pressed it to her middle. "Can you feel that? She's going to be a handful."

Roth grinned. "Like her mom."

"Her dad," Holly said, laughing.

Holly pushed out her belly, and Roth laid his hand across

the side, grabbing Jared's hand and putting it next to his. "Your first nephew."

Holly shook her head. "Niece."

"When did you get married?" Jared pulled Allison to his side, and she relaxed as his arm settled over her shoulders.

She couldn't believe how comfortable she felt. Of course the huge welcome hadn't hurt, but neither did their easy conversation and laughter. Jared's mom wasn't the intimidating shadow she'd built in her head, and neither was Roth, and definitely not Holly.

"I wanted to wait until after the baby, but Roth wanted to be traditional. Even though that goes against my nature." She rubbed her tummy.

"You're more traditional than you let on." It was clear Roth adored his wife as he smiled at her and then Jared. "Don't let her fool you. I didn't drag her to the justice of the peace kicking and screaming like she's trying to make you believe."

"That's great, man. Congrats." He pumped Roth's hand and leaned in to give Holly a peck on the cheek.

Gianna's face lit up. "Come on. Let's introduce Allison to Omar and Devi before we all sit down for dinner."

They made their way across the room, and Allison couldn't wipe the smile off her face. She'd had nothing to worry about. Jared's family was as easygoing as her own.

...

The door to their room had barely closed when Jared pulled Allison into his arms. Not that she'd fight him about it.

All through dinner she'd anticipated their being alone.

Every time they made eye contact her blood fizzed. When his hand brushed her shoulder her skin burned. It wasn't enough to have his eyes on her, or a fleeting touch, she needed to be with him in the most intimate way a man and woman could share.

"What is it about this ocean air?" she whispered against his mouth.

"It makes you think about sex, doesn't it?"

She smiled against his lips. "So it's not just me?"

He groaned, and the sound sent an array of shivers spiraling through her.

"God, I couldn't wait to get you alone." His words came out rough and ragged. Exactly the way she felt. Need shot through her. She wanted to rip off their clothes as quickly as possible, but she'd promised herself she'd try something new.

"Although I want nothing more than to have us both naked, I was reading an—"

"Are you trying to kill the moment?"

She shook her head, swallowing her laughter, as she stepped out of his arms just enough to lose some of his warmth. "Hardly. I think once you see what I have planned, you'll be all about my reading." With each word she undid one of his buttons. His brow quirked, and his smile got that mischievous lift at the edge.

"I might like where this is going."

"Oh, you'll definitely like." *At least that's what the article promised.* She unbuttoned the last button and slid his shirt, along with his suit jacket, off his shoulders and let them hit the floor. She tried to undo his pants, but she'd suddenly become all thumbs. When he came to her aid, she didn't argue. Instead she tugged his trousers down his legs as he stepped out of his shoes. "I want you to strip down to your skivvies—"

He laughed. "My skivvies?"

Allison grinned, her face growing warm. "Sorry, blame it on Gramps." She shoved him down on the bed before she walked to the dresser and removed the box of goodies she'd unpacked earlier when he'd been in the shower.

"Whatcha got there?"

"A box of fun just for you."

He sat tall to get a glimpse inside when she removed the lid.

"Ah, ah, ah. No peeking." She pushed aside the zebra-print handcuffs that she wasn't sure she could bring herself to use quite yet and pulled the fuzzy blindfold from the box. With a flick of her wrist she twirled it around her finger. "I want to make sure you don't cheat, so put these on and lay on your belly."

"You can trust me. I won't peek."

She shook her head, licking her lips. "Nope. I need a guarantee."

He gave her a slight nod, his eyes holding a tinge of challenge. "You put them on me, then."

She fought down the nervous ball forming in her stomach as she adjusted the blindfold over his eyes. "You have less than a minute to get comfortable while I get comfortable."

He did as she instructed.

Allison stepped out of her dress when it pooled on the floor at her feet. The soft *swoosh* of the fabric caught Jared's attention, and his smile widened. She held her breath as she slid her underwear down her legs and then unclasped her bra, letting it fall to the floor.

She placed the box on the edge of the bed as she slid up Jared's legs until she sat on his backside. She grabbed the glass bottle marked JASMINE from the box and poured a small amount into her palm.

Jared crinkled his nose. "What's that?"

"Jasmine. An aphrodisiac. Not that I need an aphrodisiac to be attracted to you, but it'll relax you while I give you an all-over body massage."

He groaned, and the muscles of his jaw relaxed when she slid her hands from his lower back up toward his shoulders.

"In my research I discovered that men consider massages a huge turn-on."

"Mmm. Definitely foreplay."

"Good. What's the best part of the massage for you?" She kneaded his shoulders as she bent over and flicked her tongue along the outer shell of his ear, rubbing her breasts into the center of his back.

He groaned again and his muscles bunched. "Are you naked?" he croaked.

"As a jaybird."

His laugh came out raw and throaty. The sound definitely turned her on.

"Do you like it when I kiss you here?" She nibbled on his earlobe. "Or what about when I do this?" She gyrated her hips over his butt in agonizing slowness, squeezing her legs on either side of him until he moaned and tried to rise up, but she pushed him back down. "Maybe you like this." She ran her tongue along the length of his spine, pressing tiny kisses on the nape of his neck. "Tell me what you like about massages so that I can please you."

In an instant she was yanked off his back until she lay front side up staring at the ceiling behind Jared's smiling face and hungry eyes. He somehow had managed to remove his blindfold, straddle her middle, and hold her arms above her head, with lightning speed.

"How the heck…" Her chest heaved from the quick exertion that was over in seconds, but she couldn't deny the thrill it gave her as his gaze circled her nakedness, lingering on her breasts.

"You know what pleases me?"

"Being on top," she teased.

He butted their noses, lightly pressing his mouth to hers. "Top, bottom, sideways, they're all good when I'm with you. But what pleases me the most is pleasing you."

"You please me when you teach me."

"Then let me lead the way."

"You were excellent in the training videos at work. I knew you'd be the perfect guy to get the job done."

"You're a tease, Al."

She shook her head, taking her time sliding her tongue across her bottom lip. "Little ol' me? A tease?"

"Definitely." Jared grabbed a bottle of oil from her box and placed one tiny drop on each breast. "But two can play at that game."

She arched toward him as he lowered his head, his breath fanning her face. "Does it please you when I touch you here?" With one finger he rubbed the tiny bit of oil around her nipple as it stiffened into a hard peak. His eyes grew dark, and she made a small moan that came from deep within her throat.

"Or do you prefer me to use my tongue?"

She cried out his name as his tongue flicked along her sensitized nipple.

"Have you been conducting your own research?" She could barely breathe enough to get the words out.

"When it comes to pleasing you, I just do what comes naturally."

"Good tactic." She wrapped her arms around his neck and dragged his lips to hers.

A desperate, frantic wave enveloped her. The desire pouring through her, too strong and overwhelming to quench.

His hands ran the length of her body as he lay beside her. She gripped the waistband of his boxers and worked them down his legs until they reached his knees, then used one foot to tug them the rest of the way off.

"You drive me crazy, woman."

"Anything to please you."

He laughed as he kissed her neck. "Anything to please *you.*"

"Is this turning into a competition?" She giggled.

"Let's call it a draw." His fingers lingered when they touched the edge of her breast. She arched into him as he lowered his mouth to her nipple.

Her brain became a fuzzy ball of gray matter. All she could concentrate on were the sensations of his mouth, hands, and body pressed against her. When he broke their connection she gave a soft moan and whimper.

"After this lesson, I say we take our training session into the bathroom so we can break in that Jacuzzi tub." He punctuated the last three words with tiny kisses around her ear.

"I'm all about more lessons."

He circled her waist in his strong grip and urged her body to his, claiming her mouth. His actions were sure and confident and kicked her desire up another notch. The moment his tongue parted her lips, she sank against him, luxuriating in the skin-on-skin connection.

She took her time exploring his flesh, reveling in the little sounds of pleasure that came from deep within his throat when she found the spots that turned him on. The lobe of his ear. When her tongue circled his belly button. That sensitive patch of skin on the inside of his upper thigh. The way his cock twitched when she ran her tongue lightly over the tip.

After he sheathed himself in protection, she rolled him until he lay beneath her and straddled his middle. She caressed her center against his length, dropping her head back as his palms kneaded her breasts. He bucked up, and she rubbed against him with more urgency, sliding over him before lowering her mouth to catch his in a needy, greedy kiss.

"You're killing me, Al."

"Don't die on me yet."

He choked out a laugh, followed by a guttural groan as she lifted off him and then slid her wet center over his engorged cock.

They both froze. His eyes widened, and then darkened. She squirmed, getting accustomed to his length inside her. The pleasure wasn't something she'd ever be able to put into words. Her world became focused, right, perfect.

She wanted tonight to last forever. She lifted slowly, rising up and then pushing down to meet his thrust.

Their breaths filled the room. Slow and soft, and then becoming quick pants as their bodies moved faster.

Jared cradled her hips with his strong hands. They locked eyes, and the passion and softness in his filled her to her very being. Warmth seeped through her body, tiny shards that grew in intensity until slight tremors overtook every inch of her flesh. Her toes tingled and curled, her heart gained rhythm, and her lungs burned in an effort to take in oxygen. As if he knew her struggle, he lifted himself and pulled her down to meet him halfway, claiming her mouth with his and sharing his breath.

•••

What a day. They'd all woken at the crack of dawn, enjoyed a pre-wedding breakfast, and then listened to Gianna bark out orders to the caterer and the wedding planner. Her preparations paid off. The wedding had gone off without a hitch and everyone seemed to be enjoying themselves.

Jared watched as Omar swung Devi around in a loose circle and then grabbed her in his arms, twirling her the last couple of feet toward them. Her unconventional wedding dress—layers of muted yellows that stopped mid-calf—floated around her legs, and she'd kicked off her shoes long ago in favor of going barefoot. The muted fairy lights sparkled overhead, and the band played a classic love song from the sixties.

Devi's laughter filled the air, and both her and Omar's faces were animated—with eyes only for each other. Their wedding day had been full of smiles and laughter, and although the reception had started to wind down, Jared hated to see the evening end.

Jealousy, mingled with happiness, gripped his chest. He was happy for his brother, but at the same time he wished he had someone special in his life.

*I kind of do…*

His gaze skimmed over Allison as she stood next to Holly. He'd never seen her look more beautiful than she did tonight.

Well, except for last night as she'd lain beneath him. His body tingled at the memory. Not that they'd shared endless hours of lovemaking, but for some reason the tenderness last night took his breath away.

Devi grabbed his arm and laughed, pulling him out of his thoughts.

"Time for a group dance." She gathered the family together, and they swayed in a tight circle, arms around shoulders and waists. "Thank you for being with O and me on our big day. It wouldn't have been the same without you." Her eyes brightened with tears as she met each of their gazes. "And, Holly, I know you've been a ball of emotion, but you really look absofricking adorable in that dress."

Holly laughed. "You lie so well. I look like a—"

"A beautiful woman about to have a baby." Roth dragged her very willing body against his and kissed her soundly on the mouth.

"You lie even better than Devi." Holly laughed, her face bright. "And if you don't all stop telling me how damn cute I am, I'm going to cry."

Everyone laughed.

"And you." Devi turned toward Allison and broke the circle as she pulled her arms out to her side to inspect her dress one more time. "I can't get over that cute little dress. I think I love penguins now, too." She glanced over at Holly. "That won't make you cry, will it, sis-in-law?"

"I can handle that." Holly winked.

Allison smiled. "Thanks, Devi, but your dress is the winner. You have the best style."

Jared had never seen Allison's face so bright, her smile so big. His family had gathered her into their arms the moment they'd arrived and hadn't let go.

"This old thing?" Devi laughed, pulling at the layers of yellow silk that floated down from her waist and spun around.

"Don't get her started," Omar teased.

"Get me started. Get me started." Devi's laughter flitted across the room and drew several guests' attention.

"I loved that you had everyone hum the wedding march instead of the traditional piano," Allison said.

"That was my favorite part, too." Holly nudged Allison on the shoulder playfully.

"I'm glad. Gianna wasn't too sure about it, but besides a yellow dress, I wanted something different and fun," Devi said.

Omar draped his arm over his bride's shoulders. "And she wanted to have something in common with Brangelina."

"Shh, don't share my secret." Devi silenced him with her finger, which he instantly tugged between his teeth in a gentle bite. She laughed. "No shark bites on our wedding day."

"Shark bites are for all year long, woman." He swooped her into his arms for a kiss.

"Get a room." Holly laughed, pressing her hand to her side. "This little girl is kicking like crazy this weekend."

"Like you said, he's going to be a handful." Roth winked.

"She." Holly lifted her chin.

Jared leaned back, enjoying the banter, but his eyes never left Allison for long.

He loved seeing her with his family this weekend. The way she dared to stretch her comfort zone and wear the clingy little navy blue dress. How she'd come out of her shell and talked nonstop—mostly with Holly.

The tight circle broke apart. Roth stood behind Holly with his arms wrapped around her middle, Omar tossed his arm casually over Devi's shoulders, and Jared tugged Allison to his side. Her body heat comforted him, but at the same time made him wish they were alone so he could take her in his arms and kiss her like he had last night.

She had it all: beauty, brains—and confidence that increased her sexiness tenfold. At least in his eyes.

"Come get a drink with me." Holly tugged Allison out of his arms, and they strolled off to the side to fill a cup with orange punch.

His eyes followed her, refusing to let go. Although he loved her new look, her changes, another part of him had a fascination with the woman who wore glasses, snort-laughed, and wore sneakers.

Roth moved beside him and bumped him with his shoulder. "She's great. But I don't need to tell you that. The way you feel about her is written all over your face."

"What do you mean?" Jared's heart pounded to a stop.

Roth gave him a shit-eating grin. "You'll figure it out."

"What—"

Holly stopped in front of them, thrusting a cup of punch in Roth's hand. "You might need this."

His brow furrowed. "And why's that?"

"Because you're going to need to stay hydrated in order to dance with me." She lifted on tiptoe and pecked his cheek. "While you can still get your arms around my waist."

He downed the drink and then kissed her full on the lips.

"Tell me I'm still sexy."

"You know you are, babe."

Allison came up beside them, her face glowing with a soft blush as she watched Roth and Holly. She smiled at Jared.

"Dance with me." He didn't give her time to answer, instead pulling her into his arms and circling the dance floor.

The music, combined with Allison's body pressed against his, took his breath away, along with his concentration as he tripped over his own two feet. She laughed, and the swell of her curves brushing against him, the smell of cherry blossoms, and her quick intakes of breath filled him with desire.

Her laughter died when he pulled her closer, and their steps slowed. She fit to him so perfectly. He closed his eyes and let the music consume him, wishing this night would never end.

At the same time he could hear the countdown of the clock that would signal the end of their time together. How much longer would she need his help?

From the looks of things, not long.

# Chapter Twelve

"Today was amazing." Allison spun in a circle down the hotel hallway and stopped at their door, leaning against the jamb.

"One of the best weddings I've ever been to." Jared brushed his finger down her cheek before he slid the key card into the lock.

Anticipation had coiled deep in her belly the entire day. After last night all she could think about was another night of passion, but something in the air between them had changed during the reception. Tonight would be even more fantastic. She could feel it, and her entire body had been on alert. With every touch, look, or word the spring had wound tighter. She refused to think about tomorrow or that their time together might be drawing to a close. Out of necessity more so than lack of desire.

She wouldn't think about that. Not tonight.

They'd spend the night together. Again. They'd make love. Again. She'd sleep in his arms. Again.

She could get used to this. Things between them could be so much more than their little fling.

Then reality poked through her happiness. Again. Maybe things could have been more than a fling, if he and Nick hadn't been such good friends. If she hadn't already decided that continuing the way they were would only lead to heartache.

Her heartache.

She didn't want to end things, but if she were smart she would. She wanted something Jared couldn't give. He was with her now, but that didn't mean he would be in a month. Or even in a week.

Maybe as soon as tomorrow.

She pushed her oppressive thoughts aside. No way would she ruin their beautiful day—and the amazing night about to happen—by thinking about a future that was a one-sided wish.

Jared pushed open the door and ushered her inside with his hand on her back.

"I had a bottle of champagne brought up earlier. Would you like a glass?"

"Sounds good. But not a full glass; I've had enough already." She didn't want her head fogged over. Their nights together were limited, and she wanted to remember every single moment.

She slid out of her heels and sighed.

"Feet sore?" He popped the cork, jumping back slightly as some liquid escaped.

"I'm not used to heels quite yet. And truthfully, I still prefer my sneakers." She grinned as he handed her a drink. "Actually, I prefer my slippers."

"One reason I'm glad I'm not a woman. I could never walk in those heels."

She took a sip, relishing the cool liquid as it slid down her throat. "Some women make it look easy, that's for sure."

"You make it look easy. From the way you danced with half the male population tonight, and mingled with the rest,

I'd have to say you have your confidence under control." He smiled around the rim of his flute, downing most of the glass in one swallow.

"I felt like Cinderella." And she had. Although she'd danced until her feet ached, her happiest moments had been when she'd twirled around the floor in Jared's arms.

She was in over her head, but she couldn't let go. She didn't want to. If only this thing between them could turn into the type of relationship she wanted.

A permanent one.

"I admit I didn't like all the attention you were getting."

His words sent a dash of hope into her chest, and she held her breath. Could he have realized he wanted something more? She pressed the heel of her hand to her chest, forcing the mouthful of liquid she'd just taken down her throat. "You didn't?"

"I'm just being protective. I know. I've always felt like I'm second in command next to Nick when it comes to you."

Her heart crashed into her gut as hope faded. *Well, that lasted all of five seconds.*

His words were not what she'd wanted to hear. She had enough men in her life who wanted to protect her, and that was all fine and dandy, but she wanted more than someone to look out for her. She wanted a lover, a partner of equal footing—someone who was as obsessed with her as she would be with him.

Her other half.

Obviously Jared didn't feel that way. At least not with her. And she should never have let that little seed of hope take root and allow herself to think that maybe over time he'd want more, too.

"My family loves you."

"They're great. Devi and Omar are perfect for each other, and so are Holly and Roth. And when you put your hand on

Holly's belly to feel her baby kick, I have to admit my heart turned to mush." That'd been the moment she'd known she was already halfway in love with him. Maybe three quarters. *Hell, who am I trying to kid. I'm in all the way.*

"You liked that, eh?" He set his glass on the table.

"I did. Seeing you like that… Your eyes… I can't even explain it. Full of wonder. I don't know if that's the right word. But when you and Roth put your hands on Holly's belly and looked at each other, I could see your bond. It was…"

"It was what?" He moved toward her, his brow drawn in question.

"You'll laugh." She laughed herself, waving away her words.

"I'd never laugh at you. And you'd never laugh at me. I thought we already had that established."

He grazed his knuckles down her cheek, and she shivered. Right now she might just reveal any secret he wanted to know.

"It was"—she swallowed her nerves—"sexy."

He circled her waist with his arms and nudged her closer without being forceful. "I love how the simplest things in life give you the most pleasure. Hershey's Kisses—"

"Your kisses."

He touched his lips to hers so softly that her skin tightened with anticipation. "Penguins," he whispered against her lips, his breath teasing her sensitive flesh.

She chuckled. "I love penguins. But maybe not as much as your kisses."

Her emotions swayed back and forth on a tightrope. God, she wanted him so much. He drove her crazy, but the sensible voice inside her head told her not to get carried away. Enjoy the moment, but when they got back home, she needed to end this thing between them. This thing that was destroying his friendship with Nick, this thing that would take her on a road to heartbreak.

She'd gotten what she wanted. He'd fulfilled all she'd asked of him—and then some—asking for nothing in return. It wasn't fair to keep monopolizing his time. And it wasn't fair to her, either. Her heart would require a lot of damage control.

•••

"I think we're done talking, Al. I want to make love to you."

A tiny tremble engulfed her body as she pressed in to him. He wanted her so much. He loved how she could be so sexy and bold one minute, and shy and blushing the next. The contradictions were a huge turn-on.

"And I want you to make love to me."

That was all he needed to hear. He claimed her mouth, sweeping his tongue inside to seek her warmth.

He led her to the bed, peeling off her clothes along the way, until she stood before him in nothing but her panties. The cutest fucking little pink lacey things he'd ever seen.

"God, you're fucking hot." He ran his finger from her lips and traced a path between her breasts, bending to kiss one pert nipple and then the other. He stepped back, drinking her in as she made quick work of removing his jacket, unbuttoning his shirt, and sliding his trousers down his legs. He fought his way out of his shirt as she kneeled to pull off his socks.

"You could be an underwear model." Her voice had grown husky as she peeked at him from beneath her lashes, that pink glow highlighting her cheeks.

"I was just thinking the same about you. But then I decided you look better without underwear." He lifted her and tossed her playfully on the bed. Her laughter tickled his ears, and her breasts gave a couple satisfying bounces before he leaned over and slid her panties down her smooth legs.

"You make my entire body ache with awareness and

come to life. Can you touch me all night long?" She grabbed his hand hesitantly before boldly pulling him down on top of her.

His lips found hers again, and he sank into her softness. Her fingers worked their way around to his back, pulling him in tight for a blood-boiling kiss. He grabbed one of the packets on the nightstand and quickly sheathed his cock.

"I don't need foreplay tonight, Jared. I need you."

He settled between her legs, swallowing her small gasps in his mouth as he pushed inside her. She swelled around his length, rocking her hips up to meet his slow thrusts, begging him with her body to give her more.

She arched and moaned as he trailed his mouth down her neck. Her fingers raked across the flesh of his back until she found his butt, gripping him tight. Then, before he could thrust inside her again, she rolled him over and straddled him, sliding over his length. Her head fell back, her hair cascading across her shoulders, as she balanced herself with her hands on his chest.

Her eyes widened the moment he filled her, and she stopped, moving tentatively, driving him over the edge with her parted lips and dark eyes. He ground his teeth in an attempt to let her find her own rhythm.

Slowly she slid up and down, her hand circling around to cup his balls and squeeze gently. He wanted to burst, but he clenched his toes in order to focus and keep some control. He thrust up as she slid down, her movements increasing as her breath came in short pants.

He arched his neck, and she grabbed his shoulders and rode him harder, faster, surer.

"Oh, Jared."

"Al. My. Fucking. God."

He didn't want to control himself any longer. He couldn't.

With one fluid movement, he grabbed her around the

waist, rolled her over, and sank deep inside her. She released a low growl, clutching his back as she matched each of his thrusts. Blood pounded in his ears along with her soft moans and gasps. He settled his mouth over hers, matching the thrust of his tongue with the thrust of his cock.

Every fiber in his body tightened. He could feel the sweat from her body mingling with his as her belly grew tense, her legs squeezed around his waist, and then she shattered in his arms. At the same moment, a flash of light and tiny silver specks flecked across his eyelids and he struggled to take a breath.

He collapsed on top of her, holding her in his arms, and he turned to the side, taking her with him.

"After I catch my breath, I want to do that again. And then again." She ran her finger along his jaw.

He laughed. "I think that can be arranged."

They lay in each other's arms, their breathing returning to normal and their chests rising and falling to a steady rhythm.

He twirled her hair between his fingers.

She lifted herself on one elbow, tracing his nipple with the tip of her finger. Goose bumps ate up his flesh.

"So, how many drinks did you have tonight?" She gave him a lopsided grin.

"Why?"

"I still haven't gotten to see these pecs dance." She ran her finger along his chest.

He touched his mouth to hers and then pulled back. "Okay, I'll give you a private show."

She scooted herself up to a sitting position.

Jared clasped his hands behind his head and moved one pec, then the next, and then both. Her snort-laugh made him grin, and she bent to kiss each of his pecs, then ran her tongue lightly over his nipples. Her warm tongue flicked up his chest, over his neck and chin, until she connected with his mouth.

"How can something so silly-looking be such a turn-on?" she whispered against his lips.

"Turn-on, eh?"

"Major." She lay beside him, pressing up against his side and wrapping her arms around his waist. He rested his chin on the top of her head.

"I-I—" *Shit.* What the hell was he thinking? He almost said he loved her. He cared for Allison, deeply, but he didn't love her. Not like she wanted, needed—deserved—to be loved.

He stiffened for a moment when she sighed and snuggled farther into his arms. She drew lazy circles on his biceps, each rotation slowing as her body relaxed. Within a few minutes her breathing leveled off, and he knew she'd fallen asleep. He pulled her closer, drawing in a lungful of her cherry blossom scent.

He'd allowed their lovemaking, her sweetness, vulnerability, and innocence—something he should never have taken—to cloud his head, blurring the line between lust and love.

And because he couldn't keep his fucking head on straight when she was around, he'd taken advantage of her in a way he shouldn't have allowed himself to.

In the process, their friendship changed, and it'd probably never be the same again. He'd also put his partnership and friendship with Nick on the line.

All because he'd let his ego convince him that nobody was good enough for Al.

Hell, *he* wasn't even good enough.

Because she deserved more, and guilt ate away at him for how he'd let himself become involved.

He didn't blame her. Hell no. He'd gone into this with eyes wide open, he just hadn't expected the surge of emotions: protectiveness, caring, respect—a good dose of guilt—and something more. But not love.

Definitely not love.

•••

Allison traced the beak of the tiny penguin figurine as she picked up her cell with her free hand and scrolled down to Jared's name. She pressed his number and held her breath as it rang.

"Hello." His deep voice shot a thrill through her, and she straightened from her slouch against the closet door in her bedroom as if he could see her.

"Guess what I'm doing?" she whispered.

"Are you going to talk dirty to me?"

She laughed. "The only dirt around here is my dirty laundry. I'm unpacking. And I wanted to call and say thank you." She grinned into the mouthpiece.

"I take it that means you found it. You like?"

"What I like best is that you know exactly what I'm talking about." She pressed the figurine against her chest, cradling it with the palm of her hand.

"I saw it in the hotel gift shop and thought of you."

Could her knees go any weaker? She moved across the room to sag onto her mattress, and then flung herself onto her back, pressing the phone against her ear as if that would bring him closer. But he'd never be close enough. Her hold on the figurine had turned into a death grip, and she loosened her fingers, lifting it over her head, making it dance back and forth.

"And you snuck it into my suitcase?"

"Not an easy feat since you seemed determined to wait until we could walk down to the lobby together."

She laughed, laying the penguin on the pillow beside her and gently rubbing her fingers over it. "It's beautiful."

"Not as beautiful as you."

His deep voice oozed sex appeal, and her body warmed—hell, went up in flames. She licked her lips, swearing she could taste the salt from his skin.

"So all that crap about having me check out at the front desk and you following me down with the cases was a huge ploy?"

"You didn't make it easy. How come you like to argue so much?" The smile in his voice made her grin.

"I'm not usually one to argue, but I wanted to walk down together." Heck, she wanted to spend every second together they could, because those seconds were limited. Her smile wavered.

"Next time don't question me when I'm trying to do something—"

*Special. Romantic.*

"—for my friend."

She cleared her throat, swallowing the tears forming. She was such a sap. Why did she keep letting herself get her hopes up when she already knew this was just temporary? He'd made it obvious. He wanted to protect her. He thought of her only in terms of Nick's kid sister.

It took all her effort to hold her tears in check. That'd be a lie. He desired her, but it ended there.

But, then again, what red-blooded male would continue to say no when he was offered mind-blowing sex? And he had felt sorry for her. She knew that. *Am I pity sex?* She shook her head, answering her own question silently. No. It's been more than that, but not quite what she wanted.

"Did you check your emails yet?"

His question sent her crashing into the moment. "No. I wanted to unpack before I came back to the real world."

"Looks like you'll get to test yourself again."

"What do you mean?"

"Seems the aquarium is having a vendor appreciation dinner next Sunday. Nick selected a handful from the company to represent Firstline, and your name is on the list."

"Yours, too?" Allison pushed herself up until she sat cross-legged. *There goes another Sunday dinner.* She hated to disappoint Dad and Gramps, but hopefully they would still be working on renovations.

She grabbed her laptop and flipped it open, quickly logging in to her work email. She skimmed through the subject lines until she found one titled *Vendor Appreciation.*

"We're both going."

"With how angry Nick's been at me, I'm surprised he wants me to go." She flicked the cursor back and forth with the tip of her finger on the pad.

"Mad or not, he knows how much work you've put in for the aquarium's software program. So do I."

For some stupid reason, his warm words sent a new round of tears burning behind her eyes.

"Why so quiet? Aren't you excited about the dinner?" His soft words tugged at her heart.

Her life felt at a crossroad. One she didn't like. She knew his name was on the list, that she'd see him there, but a part of her wanted him to suggest they go together.

*Like a date.*

"I'm okay. Tired from the long weekend," she lied. Maybe she should initiate? "Want to ride to the event together?" Her entire body stopped as she waited for his reply.

"I'm not sure I can make it that night."

She covered the mouthpiece as she let out her breath. "Why?"

"I'm heading out of town Wednesday. More talks with Sanders Machinery regarding their sister company. I don't know if I'll be back in time."

Did that mean if he'd been in town, he'd have suggested

they go together? She shouldn't hope, but she did.

*I need to get over this, break things off. I'm way too attached, and when we finally do go our separate ways I'm not sure I'll be able to handle it.*

She hated that Nick had been right. But she had been, too, when she told him that she had to learn on her own. Isn't that how Gramps said most life lessons were learned? And Gramps was no slouch when it came to common sense.

Shit. She had to talk to Jared. *Just not right now.*

"You've gone quiet again. Not nervous, are you?" His voice sounded playful but reassuring at the same time.

"I'm okay. Thinking about what to wear." Each lie came easier. She didn't care. Not really. In the big picture, her dress—heck, her own insecurities—didn't compare to the turmoil in her life when it came to her feelings for Jared.

Their breathing filled the phone lines for a moment, and then he cleared his throat.

"I'll let you get back to unpacking. Lunch tomorrow?"

"I'm not sure. I think I have a few projects that are on the brink of being finished. How about a rain check?" But deep inside she knew there'd be no more rain checks. They needed to go back to business first. Friends second. Anything else—never. But how could they return to the way it was after all they'd shared?

...

Jared's blood boiled, and he pulled at his tie that suddenly seemed to strangle him. He hadn't been sure he'd be able to make the vendor appreciation dinner, but he'd wanted to see Al. Badly.

Now, standing in the small group of five, which included Roy West—president and CEO of the aquarium for the last eight years—he wished he'd stayed home.

The man had always shown a fondness for Allison, relying on her as the point of contact for all his questions. But he'd assumed that'd been because of her brain. Now that didn't seem to be the case. The look in the other man's eyes held more than mere interest about her programming capabilities.

"One of these days I'm going to steal you away from your brother so that you can work for me." Roy grabbed another champagne flute from the passing waiter's tray and replaced the empty glass in Allison's hand, his hand lingering a little longer than necessary over her fingers.

"You'd be a great addition to our team," Perry White, Roy's right-hand man, chimed in.

"It's always nice to know I have options, but at the moment I'm happy where I am." Allison sipped her drink.

*Damn straight she's happy at Firstline.*

"You shouldn't try to steal my employee right out from under my nose, Roy." Jared slapped him on the back, proud of himself for not punching him in the jaw.

Roy nodded, frowning. "Unfortunately I've tried to steal Allison away numerous times, but she always gives me the same answer."

"Good to know." Jared gave Allison a tight-lipped smile.

"And if you won't let me steal you away from your brother and Jared, how about you take me up on the offer of dinner?" Roy placed his hand on her shoulder, and she actually leaned in toward him.

"Hmm." Allison blushed but didn't meet Roy's gaze. "Now that's something I can say yes to."

Jared clenched his fist. Their flirty conversation grated on his nerves. Could Allison really think this guy was attractive?

Obviously Roy couldn't help but notice Allison. Her flowing pink dress showed off her legs, and the way her hair cascaded down her back and bounced with every step or turn of her head made her stand out. Jared wouldn't let himself even think about the way her glossy lips attracted every beam of light in the room.

Shit. He'd always liked Roy, up until about fifteen minutes ago, but he didn't like the attention he was paying to Allison. Not that she was fighting him off. They'd exchanged several glances, her little giggles pinged his ears like needles poking his flesh, and her hand gestures always seemed to end up coming into contact with Roy's arm, chest, or cheek.

Jared couldn't fucking breathe.

"Did Nick discuss the new addition to the aquarium with you?" Roy turned toward Jared. "I can't wait to see what Firstline comes up with in the way of securing our latest project."

Jared nodded, pasting on his businessman smile. Nick had told him all right, via memo. He'd been happy at the news, but not so much any longer. "Congratulations. We're always happy to work with you and the aquarium."

"You guys are the best." Roy stepped closer to Allison. "Looks like I'll have to keep you on speed dial."

"I could think of worse things." Allison blushed.

Jared gritted his teeth. He had no say in how Allison lived her life, but that didn't mean he had to sit by and watch her make a mistake. Roy West wasn't for her. She could do better. And he should tell her before she led him on any further.

Because she was just honing her skills. Right?

*Hell no. She looks interested.*

All week long he'd managed to keep his distance. And she hadn't sought him out, either. Didn't she need him anymore?

*Doesn't look like it.*

But that didn't stop him from missing her. Seeing her here tonight only made that ache hit home.

He couldn't deny the whisper of relief that washed over him as Nick sauntered over to join the group. Now he didn't have to worry about talking to Al, butting into her business, and playing the overprotective friend—because there was no way in hell Nick would approve of her seeing Roy.

*Why not? Roy's an upstanding guy. He doesn't play the field. He has a great job. He's proven he has what it takes to be in a committed relationship. He'd probably still be married if he hadn't lost his wife to cancer several years back. Whereas you…*

*Fuck.*

Then Jared's stomach sank as Nick and Roy shook hands. "Did I just hear Allison agree to have dinner with you?"

"Finally." Roy grinned. "You know I've been after her all night to agree."

Nick nodded, his beaming smile traveling between Roy and Allison with a seal of approval. When his gaze landed on Jared, he merely lifted his brow.

*Fuck. Fuck.*

He needed a drink. More importantly, he needed to keep his distance before he made a fool of himself. He might not be in love with her, but his attraction—*protective instinct*—was totally out of control.

"Excuse me. I'm going to get a refill." He lifted his half full glass of whiskey, turned on his heel, and made a beeline for the bar.

Nick fell into step beside him and grabbed his upper arm. "Hold up, Jared."

He stopped, and they turned to face each other. "What? You can talk to me now? You don't want to send a memo?"

"I know you too damn well, man. I can see that the attention Roy is showing Al is pissing you off." His smile showed traces of compassion.

Jared couldn't fucking believe it.

"Was I wrong about you? What exactly are your intentions toward my sister?"

Jared couldn't answer. He didn't even open his mouth

to try. He had no damn clue what his intentions were. To go along on the same path they had been? To see where it took them? Hell, he didn't even know if what he felt for Allison was something real, or something in the moment. How would he know? He'd never been in love before.

*And I'm not in love now.*

The softness in Nick's face hardened in an instant. "I should've known better. Fuck." He swiped his hand down his face. "I thought I saw something there, but apparently not."

"Nick—"

Nick shook his head, holding up his hand. "I recommend you take the advice I'm dishing out."

Jared lifted his chin, the air between them stretched taut. "What's that?"

"For the last time, stay away from her. She needs a man in her life who will be there for her. For. Her. You got that? Whatever game you're playing with my sister stops now."

"I'm not playing any fucking games." He didn't want to stand in the way of Al's happiness. If she wanted Roy, he'd look the other way, even if it killed him. But he didn't appreciate Nick going all caveman on him.

"Bullshit. You can't even answer my simple question. You're not the guy for Al. She's a one-man woman, and you're not a one-woman man."

"You don't even fucking—"

Nick grabbed him by the shoulder and squeezed. "I've known you long enough to feel confident in what I'm saying. Stay away from Allison. I can see the way you're watching her. Roy's a nice guy. He told me that he'd like to get to know her better, and from the looks of things she feels the same. Leave her alone."

"And if I don't?" He didn't even know why he asked. Did he like pushing Nick's buttons? Or did he want his friend to punch him in the face to ease some of the pain in his heart?

"If you don't you can consider our partnership dissolved. I've already talked to our lawyer. I'll either buy your ass out, or take leave myself, start up my own company, and run you into the dirt." Nick poked him in the chest, his eyes gleaming steel. "Friendship is one thing, but family is another. Got me?"

Jared shoved his hand off his chest and thumped his knuckles on Nick's chest. "Oh, I got you, bud. Don't worry about that. Now you listen to me. I'll leave Allison alone, if that's what she wants, and if you dissolve our partnership that's your choice, but I will not just shrivel up and blow away. I'll give you the biggest fucking run for your money, and if anyone will be eating dirt, it'll be you."

# Chapter Thirteen

From the corner of her eye, Allison saw the exchange between Nick and Jared, and it didn't look pretty. What she wouldn't give for a pocket with at least one chocolate Kiss.

"Will you excuse me a minute, Roy?"

"Sure. Sure." But he didn't sound sure. He sounded deflated.

She liked Roy. They had everything in common. He was just the type of guy she was looking for—at least he should be. But she couldn't get Jared out of her head.

And now an urgency filled her. What the heck had just happened between him and her brother? She had to find out.

She hurried across the floor as Jared grabbed a longneck from the bartender and made his way through one of the doors to the outdoor balcony.

Allison pushed her way outside and glanced from right to left, spotting him in the deep shadows, a sliver of moonlight illuminating his profile.

As she approached, she could almost feel the tension rolling off the straight lines of his shoulders and the stiff posture of his back. She touched his arm, and he jumped, spinning around to face her.

"Hey. You okay?"

"Never better." His words came out clipped and tight.

"You don't sound 'never better.'" She grinned, her smile wavering when he didn't meet her eyes, instead looking past her and over her shoulder. "Talk to me."

He sucked in a breath and studied her face intently. She'd never seen the stress lines around his mouth so pronounced. Not even when he was working on a difficult contract.

"This is between you and me. Got it?"

Her gut tightened. "Got it."

"My business partner, best friend of fifteen years, your brother, just informed me that if I don't leave you alone, he'll dissolve our partnership and make my life hell. At least in the business sense."

She stepped back, her heart skipping a beat. "He what?" But she didn't need him to repeat what he said, and he must've known that, because he didn't even try.

All the anger and annoyance of a lifetime settled in her chest. As usual, Nick had decided he'd play decision-maker in her life.

She was so over his controlling ways. He might mean well, but he needed to let her live her own life. Complete with her own decisions and choices. No matter if they meshed with his or not.

"I'm sorry, Jared. I'm sorry for the way my brother is acting. And I'm sorrier still that I got you involved in all of this."

"Al—"

"No. I need to make a few more changes. And these don't have anything to do with my confidence or my looks." She touched his cheek, letting her fingers slide over his jaw.

At that moment she knew she loved him. She'd do

whatever it took to make him happy, even if it didn't make her happy.

"We need to talk." Allison gripped Nick's upper arm. After she'd left Jared, she made her way back into the reception area to find him. Thankfully, the task had been easy, because he'd found his way back over to Roy.

He glanced at her from over his shoulder. "Give me a minute, I'm going to—"

"You're going to come with me right now, Nick."

His mouth hung open, and he narrowed his gaze, then pasted on a smile before turning toward Roy and the others. "Excuse me, gentlemen, it looks like my sister has something urgent to share."

She smiled at the group she'd left minutes ago, and then tugged Nick through the lobby and out the front door. She rounded on him, pushing him in the chest. Not that it had much effect, but it made her feel better. "What the hell are you thinking, Nick?"

"Are you kidding me? Did Jared come crying to you?"

"No, I saw you two arguing and went after him." She closed her eyes, fighting back the tears of frustration that burned her eyelids. "After all these years, how could you threaten him like that? How could you let his interest in me, my interest in him, come between you two?"

"He's going to hurt you."

"The only one hurting me is you."

Nick stepped toward her, reaching out to take her in a hug, but she slapped his hand away.

"I love you, Nick, but sometimes you're an idiot. Don't you dare give up your best friend, your business, for something as ridiculous as Jared and me..." She couldn't continue, didn't know how to describe whatever had taken place between her and Jared. But whatever it had been, this feud between them ended it.

"You and Jared, what?" Nick's eyes turned to steel again.

She punched him in the shoulder. "You know, Nick. It doesn't matter. You don't need to know how I run my life, who is in my life, anything about my life. Unless I decide to share. You need to take care of yourself, your friendships, and your business."

"Al." His voice held a stern warning, but she was done listening.

"I'm not going to sit by and watch you and Jared destroy each other. If I hadn't asked for his help, none of this would be happening." She flung her hair over her shoulder. "You know, I'd have thought you'd want me to hook up with your best friend. Fuck, you love him. Our entire family loves him—"

"Do you love him?" His jaw softened, and he touched her shoulder with the first show of warmth she'd seen from him in weeks.

She sighed. "It doesn't matter. I've come to a decision."

"And that is?"

She shook her head. "Nope. I owe Jared the same courtesy. Tomorrow, meeting in your office. Ten a.m. You'll find out then."

She turned on her heel, brushing his hand off her shoulder when he tried to stop her. "No spoilers, Nick. I'll see you in the morning."

Allison stared down at Jared and Nick as they sat in the two chairs before her. She purposely remained standing because it seemed the only source of power she had when it came to these two. "I'm glad you both can be in the same room long enough to hear me out."

"Al—"

She raised her hand as they both spoke in unison. "I'm not here for either of you. I'm here for me. I have something to say, you can listen, and then it's over. No questions, no attempts to change my mind. Because my mind is made up."

"What the hell is going on?" Nick demanded, his gaze locked with Jared's as if he were to blame.

"Why don't you give her a minute to explain before you start jumping down her throat?" Jared snapped.

"Why don't you—"

"Both of you shut the hell up. Did either of you hear what I said? I'm here to tell you something, and I don't need a fight to break out. I'm giving you the courtesy of being the first to know. Since you are both technically my bosses."

Their heavy breaths filled the gap of silence, and Allison ran her palm down the front pleat of her skirt. "Now, are you going to stay quiet long enough so that I can speak my piece?"

They nodded, but she didn't miss the black glare they exchanged. The look shriveled her heart, but also gave her the courage to continue, knowing she'd made the right decision.

She cleared her throat. "I miss you two getting along. I miss your jokes, teasing, and laughter. I miss seeing you work toward a goal. I miss you being friends."

"Allison—"

She silenced Nick with her hand and shook her head. "You two have been at each other's throats, all because of me. It made me realize that if I hadn't forced Jared into helping me, if I wasn't around, you two would still be fast friends. You could remain in the same room long enough to run your business. The break room wouldn't be buzzing with trouble brewing in upper management, employees wouldn't be in fear that some big changes are coming down the pipeline that might shake up their livelihoods."

"People are talking?" Nick actually sounded bewildered, and she furrowed her brow.

"Of course they are. See, you two used to be on top of things in this company, but your stupid feud has clouded both your heads. And it's all my fault."

She raised her hand again when Nick opened his mouth, refusing to make eye contact with Jared because she feared she might back out of her decision. For certain he'd be looking at her with those soft eyes that weakened her knees.

Her strength didn't quite extend to the point where she could handle that. Not right now.

"I've decided that I'm resigning my position here at Firstline."

Jared shifted in his seat, and Nick stood. Allison pushed him down none to gently with her hands on his chest.

"Because of Jared. You son of—" Nick twisted in his seat, making a grab for Jared, who shoved his hands off his chest.

"Listen to me," she yelled. Her heart pounded against her ribs as they both locked eyes on her. "Jared had nothing to do with my decision and is hearing it for the first time, too. He can't make me do anything any more than you can. I decided this on my own. I refuse to come between you two. If I'm not around, you'll both have a chance to mend your friendship. Your partnership."

"Al, I don't—"

She shook her head. Jared's soft voice became more than she could handle. She closed her eyes, swallowing down the tears burning a path up the back of her throat.

"This is for the best. Not only can you two patch things up, but I need a change. I'm becoming stagnant here. I need to keep my mind moving forward. Learn something new. Change my surroundings. Take on more responsibility." She tried to make her voice sound bright, excited, but deep down most of what she was saying wasn't anywhere near how she felt. She'd been happy at Firstline. Sure, she wanted to do some side work, but she'd never planned to leave her job.

But if it would help Jared and her brother rebuild their friendship, she'd move to another country if need be.

"Are you going to work for Roy?" Jared's clipped tone cut at her chest.

She nodded. "He's made a wonderful offer. One that I really can't refuse. He's going to exceed my current salary, I'll have my own team—that's right, I'll be the boss of a department—and my benefit package is pretty much comparable."

Jared pushed himself out of his seat. "Allison, you don't—"

"I do." She gave them each a stiff smile.

"I don't want you to leave." Nick still sat in his chair, but defeat lined his face. He leaned forward, resting his elbows on his knees, dropping his face into his hands. He jerked his attention back to her after dispelling a long breath. "Listen, you made a decision in the heat of the moment last night. I never wanted any of this"—he spread his arms out to his sides—"to result in something so drastic."

"My mind's made up. I can't work here anymore. Consider this my notice." As the words left her lips, the weight she'd carried on her shoulders for the last several weeks dropped off. But what she needed to say next almost killed her. "And as for our friendship, Jared, I appreciate all your help. You'll never know how much. But in order for you and Nick to rebuild your friendship, ours has to be over."

"We don't want to lose you," Jared mumbled.

Her chest ached as if her heart had broken into a thousand pieces. If he'd said the magic words—*he* didn't want to lose her—she'd have stayed.

Allison took a swallow of her wine as she made her way to her apartment door. Whoever was on the other side knocked again, this time more insistently.

"I'm coming." *Geesh, hold your horses.* She wasn't expecting anyone. And if truth be told, she didn't want to see anyone. Today had been one of the hardest days of her life.

She pressed her face up against the door and looked through the peephole. The label from her favorite bottle of wine filled her view, and she laughed, pulling open the door.

"Nicely done, Coll. How did you know I needed wine?"

"Because when I called you sounded like you were about two Hersheys shy of a meltdown. What's going on?" She sauntered past and headed straight for the corkscrew in the kitchen.

Allison lifted her glass. "I already opened a bottle."

"And I have a feeling this is a two-bottle kind of night."

"But I work tomorrow."

"So do I." Colleen pulled the corkscrew out of the bottle with such force she stepped back, bumping her butt on the counter behind her. "How damn strong do you gotta be to pull out a corkscrew?"

"It might work to your advantage if you weighed more than a hundred pounds and stood a few more inches over five feet."

Colleen flipped her off good-naturedly. She'd always been teased about her size but managed to take it in stride. Just like she took everything in stride.

"Okay"—she pushed aside the wineglasses and went straight for a twenty-four-ounce tumbler—"tell Aunt Colleen your troubles. Not that I can imagine you having any. You've done a complete one-eighty when it comes to your wardrobe and makeup. You look fine. And when I say fine, I mean *fine.* I know you weren't interested in the friend of Jerry's I wanted to fix you up with a few months ago, but even if you were, you are now so far out of his league you might as well be on another planet."

Allison laughed. After the vendor appreciation fiasco, and then giving her notice this morning, she wasn't sure she had a laugh in her anymore.

"I quit my job."

"Whoa. Thanks for not leading into it. I like how this new self-assuredness of yours has you laying things on the line."

"I'm glad someone likes it."

"Are you telling me someone doesn't?" Colleen came around the bar and plopped down onto the stool beside her.

"Nick."

Colleen rolled her eyes. "No surprise there. He doesn't like a lot of things. Did you finally get tired of him trying to run your life?"

Allison nodded. "It's a long story."

"I got all night, sista." She spun her barstool around and propped her feet on the back of one of the dining room chairs.

Colleen stayed uncharacteristically quiet, and Allison relayed the entire story, from A to Z. When she'd finished, she downed her entire glass of wine and groaned. "I'll regret that later."

"Life is all about regret."

Allison snort-laughed. "You're drunk."

Colleen waved her words away. "So, you and Jared, eh?"

She nodded, the sip of her wine turning bittersweet.

"I can definitely see you two together. I mean, he's a looker, you're a looker, he's funny, you're funny, and— "

"And you can forget about seeing us together, because it's not happening."

The silence stretched between them, and then Colleen cleared her throat, fluffing her hair. "What you're saying is that you're changing your job, basically your life, so that the man you love will be happy." Colleen gushed as she held her hand to her heart. "You know I'm not huge into romance, but that kind of grabs my heart."

"Don't forget I'm doing this for Nick, too."

Colleen rolled her eyes. "Yeah, whatever. I like the romantic version better. I get that you don't see a future with Jared, and I'm sorry, but what are you going to do about this Roy guy? I mean, he's interested…"

"I'll take it one day at a time. It's not like I'm going to just get over Jared in a day." *Or a week, month, or year. Years?*

She might have changed her looks, but her change of heart had her seeking a new environment. Heck, a new employer. Someplace away from her overprotective brother. Someplace away from having to see a man she'd let herself grow attached to when she knew better. Someplace away from the man who'd never see her as anything more than his partner's little sister, a friend, an employee—

Someplace away from the man she'd fallen in love with.

But all that mattered was that it'd be worth it if Jared and Nick didn't hate each other because of what she'd done.

# Chapter Fourteen

*The only way I'm going to get her out of my head is by getting out there and dating.*

Jared skimmed through the names in his phone. All the beautiful women he'd come to know over the years. How come he couldn't find anyone who interested him? Every time he closed his eyes, Allison's face came into view.

Had she only been gone from Firstline one week? It was the longest fucking week of his life. His empty shell of a life.

Maybe he'd become melodramatic, but he missed her. More than a friend should miss another friend. She invaded his thoughts, dreams, every damn waking moment.

Even now, if he closed his eyes, he smelled cherry blossoms. He could lick his lips and taste her. Feel the soft pressure of her hand in his. He was going to end up going insane if he didn't get out there and socialize.

The days leading up to her departure, he'd nearly worn a trail in the carpet between her office and his. He wanted to catch a glimpse of her, because she'd made it perfectly clear—by not answering his phone calls and keeping emails strictly professional—that she wasn't interested in seeing him.

His thumb flicked across the screen of his phone again. The names rushed by in a blur. He needed to concentrate. Of all the women he'd met over the years, there had to be one who he'd want to take to dinner.

He had no choice but to pick someone, before he lost his mind. If he wanted to get Allison out of his head, he needed to spend time with another woman. And soon.

Maybe he needed to take some of his own advice and hit the bar, make himself talk to a woman he'd never met.

He raked his hands through his hair. Thoughts of things he'd done with Allison were what kept her in his head. He needed to stop.

He slid his phone across his desk until it hit the vintage mantel clock that had belonged to his grandfather. He instantly sat forward, rubbed at the wood, and grabbed his phone.

*Let's try this again.* The screen on his phone came into focus, and he moved his thumb slowly as he read the names. An endless list of wonderful women, all fun, flirty, and beautiful. But none of them were Allison.

*Just pick one.* He flicked his thumb across the screen as if he were spinning the *Price is Right* wheel. Whoever it landed on he'd call.

Not that he was proud of the way he planned to choose his next date, but he had to take the easy way out. Make that first step.

*Lynne Grant, you're the next contestant…*

•••

Allison tried to hold her smile and keep her mind on what Roy was saying, but all she could see—over Roy's shoulder—was Jared and some tall, slender redhead taking a seat at a cozy table.

She should've chosen another restaurant. This was one of Jared's favorites, and for some reason coming here kind of gave her a connection to him. If only she'd considered the possibility he might show up as well.

Jared leaned over and whispered something into the beautiful woman's ear as he helped her into her seat.

Allison's belly flipped, and the green-eyed monster sat on her chest. The last couple of weeks she'd made a huge effort to avoid any mention of Jared, and now that she'd seen him, she couldn't look away.

She wiped her mouth and set her napkin beside her plate.

"—then he hit the wrong key and everything he'd just spent the last hour configuring disappeared." Roy's dry laughter pounded against her brain.

She could tell herself all day that Roy was a great guy, and he was, but that didn't make his endless conversations about work any easier to take. They'd started out with so many of the same interests, but the more they talked the more his conversations began to bore her.

She hadn't wanted to accept when he asked her out on another date. Wasn't one enough to know? But at the same time she wanted to give things a try. She needed to start somewhere if she were to get Jared out of her mind. Roy was interested. A great guy.

*But not a great guy for me. My great guy is sitting with a buxom redhead with a throaty laugh and a perfect body.*

Her chest pinched as her attention drifted back across the room to Jared. When would the pain in her heart ease up? She might have left Firstline two weeks ago, but that hadn't lessened the vivid memories of him. She swore she heard his voice at the office, his smell when she was alone in her apartment, the way he touched her in her dreams.

Her life had become empty. Her days all the same.

Nothing held the magic as it had when Jared had been in her life.

She met Roy's gaze with a smile, wishing she could focus on his drone. What would he do if she took him to a burger joint in the seedy part of town, or if she suggested they play darts in a bar, go out drinking, take up ballroom dancing?

He tossed his napkin onto his plate. "Are you ready? I thought we'd walk back to my apartment and grab an ice cream on the way. It's the perfect night."

*At least that's something different.* "Ice cream sounds good. And a walk even better. Maybe we could stroll along the lake, or by the museum?"

"Or maybe both." His playful wink gave her hope. He could be fun. Maybe he just needed to loosen up a little.

She dragged her gaze away from Jared, biting her lower lip when the redhead threw her head back and laughed.

Roy helped her out of her seat and steered her toward the door with his hand at her back. She moved ahead so that he didn't quite touch her, but she could feel the heat of his palm. For some reason she wasn't ready for that intimacy, even though it wasn't all that intimate. The small of her back and her elbow still had Jared's name tattooed on them. Not Roy's.

She turned her head to listen to whatever Roy was saying as they neared Jared's table. *Keep walking, keep walking…*

Roy nudged her on the shoulder as he slowed his pace, dropping his arm over her shoulders. "Hey, isn't that Jared?"

*Damn.*

…

*Damn it all to hell.* He pasted on a smile as Roy and Allison weaved their way past a few tables in their direction. Lynne spun in her seat, her smile already lighting up her face as she turned toward them.

Jared stood as they stopped at their table, and a quick round of introductions were made. Allison shifted her weight from foot to foot, and he couldn't keep his eyes from constantly returning to her face.

He'd thought he'd missed her before, but having her within arm's reach pushed him over the edge. He had to fight to breathe. To keep his hands at his side instead of reaching out to touch her.

"Are you Roy West, from the aquarium?" Lynne's eyebrow shot up.

Roy nodded, his face beaming. "The one and only."

How come Jared had never noticed how annoying this guy could be? Especially when he hugged a somewhat reluctant-looking Allison to his side.

"How's it going, Jared?" Roy asked. "Is Firstline surviving without the amazing Allison in the realm?"

Allison laughed, but it sounded forced. "I'm sure they're all fine. I hardly ran the place."

"You are missed, Al." He shot her what he hoped was a relaxed smile, though relaxed was the last thing he was. Especially as he watched Roy's fingers draw lazy circles on her shoulder. He shoved his fist into his trouser pocket. "If you ever want your old job back, say the word."

"Hey, hey," Roy said around his laughter. "Are you using my tactics and trying to steal back my new employee?"

"If that's what it takes." Jared grinned as he reclaimed his seat. He folded the corner of his menu to give his hands something to do. What they wanted to do was shove Roy's hand off Allison's shoulder.

Did she like the way he touched her? She looked uncomfortable. Or maybe that was wishful thinking on his part.

He shook off his thoughts and tried to focus on Lynne's

recommendation of the new restaurant across town that served the best prime rib, and Roy commenting that he'd already made reservations for him and Al next week.

"Maybe we could make it a foursome?" Roy quirked his brow.

Just what the hell Jared needed. He'd end up decking Roy for sure, and then he'd not only piss off Allison, but Firstline would lose a valuable client.

Jared didn't miss the surprised rise of Allison's brow, or the way her jaw ticked as she held her smile in place. God, how had she managed to become even more beautiful in two weeks? She lit up the room. But, hell, when didn't she?

"That'd be fun. What do you say, Jared?" Lynne shot him a questioning gaze.

"I'll have my people call your people," Jared said, making light of the situation. Hell would freeze over before his people did any such thing.

"Sounds good." Roy shook his hand again. "Well, we won't keep you. We're on our way for ice cream and a walk."

"Sounds lovely," Lynne said.

Jared gripped his menu tightly, not noticing until the paper was on fire that he'd held it over the large candle in the center of the table.

"Oh, Jared." Lynne stood, stepping away from the table at the same time he grabbed his water glass and tossed it on the fire. Not only did he put out the fire, but he got Lynne wet in the process.

"Shit. I'm sorry, Lynne." He stood to help dry her off and tripped into the table, knocking it over as Roy looked like the hero and pulled Allison out of harm's way.

Jared landed on Lynne, and the table landed on him.

Wait staff rushed toward them from every nook and cranny. Before he could get out another word, Lynne huffed and pushed herself up off the floor with the help of a waiter, grabbed her purse, shot him a look that nearly threw him to the floor a second time, and stormed out the door.

Allison snort-laughed. "Oh my God, Jared. Are you okay?" She grabbed his elbow and looked down into his face. Her eyes sparkled, and he couldn't stop from laughing. He'd missed laughing with Allison, and for a moment he let himself forget that Roy hovered nearby.

Then the other man cleared his throat. A somber expression filled his face. "You might want to make sure your date is okay." His gaze shifted from Jared to the door and back again.

"I'd say she's halfway home at this point."

Allison stooped to pick up some of the debris, and a waiter came up beside her. "I have this, miss."

"You sure?"

He nodded and smiled as two other staff members righted the table and swept up the mess.

"You two better make an exit before I knock something else down." Jared ran his hand through his hair. He felt like an ass, but at the same time he couldn't stop laughing. And he couldn't get Allison's snort out of his head. He loved how she could laugh at life, even in the most uncomfortable of situations.

"Are you sure?" Roy asked, but he was already pulling Allison away.

Jared nodded. "I've got this covered. Enjoy your walk and ice cream."

He watched them leave. His eyes trained on Allison's back as if he'd never see her again. She turned when they reached the door, a helpless look on her face. One that said she didn't want to leave him. And he didn't want her to, but what could he do? Beg her to stay when Roy obviously wanted to get out of the restaurant before they drew any more attention to themselves? Or until Jared knocked over another table and ruined someone else's date?

He laughed at the role reversal. He'd suddenly become the klutz who tripped over his own feet and could hardly talk in a social setting. Allison had morphed into the confident social butterfly.

Shit, he missed her. Loved her.

*Loved her?*

Hell yes, he loved her. What kind of idiot was he? If he didn't love her, why couldn't he get her out of his head? Every thought focused on her. If that wasn't love, what was?

His heart raced with excitement—for all of twenty seconds—that's the amount of time it took for the words to sink in. He loved her, but she didn't love him.

And that hurt like a motherfucker.

If she loved him, or even had a glimmer of feelings for him, she'd never have wanted to leave Firstline. She wouldn't be with Roy. She wouldn't have left him. But she'd made it clear in her actions and words she didn't share his feelings. That they could never be together.

At least together like he wanted.

Damn it. His wish about finding love had finally come true. He'd figured out what love was. But the woman he'd fallen for hadn't fallen for him.

•••

Allison's face hurt from smiling. Nick swaggered across the bar toward her. She'd been gone from Firstline less than three weeks, and he wanted to meet to see how she was settling in at her new job.

Her new life.

Her failure.

Not that she'd tell him that.

He planted a kiss on her forehead and slid onto the

barstool beside her.

"I ordered you a beer," she said.

"Great. Thank you." He took a swallow and leaned forward with his elbows on the bar. "Dad wanted me to tell you that dinner is back to normal next Sunday. He's so sick of the kitchen he's made plans to barbecue outside."

She laughed. "Sounds perfect. I stopped over to see Gramps the other day after work, but Dad was at the hardware store for some part to attach to the sink."

"The job definitely turned into more than either one of them expected."

She nodded, sipping her wine.

"So, how's the new job going?" Nick watched her from the corner of his eye as he took a slug of beer.

She laughed, but the sound rang hollow in her own ears. "It's going. But I haven't been there long enough to dish any dirt."

"But you have to know if you like it."

"It's okay." She found it hard to work up any enthusiasm as she dropped a straw into her glass of wine. She now understood why Colleen preferred the straw method to her drinking. The buzz came quick and hard. There were definitely times when that was a much-needed benefit.

"You don't sound happy."

That was the last thing she wanted him to think. "No. No. It's just that it's all too new. I've barely had time to settle into a routine yet."

"And how are things going with Roy? I know he's your boss, and it might be kind of awkward that you're dating, too, but everything okay?" His probing gaze had suddenly become too much. What if she couldn't hide the truth?

"He's a great guy."

"But?"

She knocked his shoulder with hers. "But nothing."

"Hmm." He downed a mouthful of beer. "I know I've been ordered to stay out of your life, but you have to remember I know you way too well to believe 'but nothing.'"

She didn't want to get into this. Especially now. Especially with Nick. She feared an ugly crying scene if she started revealing her feelings. All she could think about was the emptiness stretching before her. How everything in her colorful world had turned to black and white.

Like a penguin. And this was a penguin she wanted no part of.

"How's everything at Firstline? Did Kenny get that code figured out? How is— " She caught herself before she asked about Jared. "If you need me to help out Kenny or Nate, I don't mind." God, what she wouldn't give for her old job back. The old people, even Glenda the not-so-good witch. But mainly Jared.

"Everything is fine." He drew out the words as he studied her. "What's up, Al?"

Tears burned her eyes, and she took a long draw on her straw. What could she tell him? That she wasn't interested in her new job, even though she got to eat lunch by the penguin exhibit every day? That she missed her coworkers at Firstline who, for the most part, hadn't known she'd existed? That she was in love with Jared but didn't want to come between him and Nick and their business?

"It's all good. I'm just adjusting."

"You'd tell me if you weren't. Right?" He tweaked her nose.

"You'd be the first." Not only was she unhappy, but she'd become adept at lying.

•••

Jared hadn't slept more than three hours a night since Allison broke the news of her resignation. All he could picture in his head every time he closed his eyes was her smile, all he could hear was her laugh, and all he could smell was cherry blossoms.

He'd pretty much given up on dating. Not that it mattered because, more than likely, Lynne had already tarnished his name in the dating pool. He didn't have the drive or energy to try to score an evening out. Unless it was with Al.

His psyche had sunk to a new low. Not only did he barely sleep, but he had to remind himself to eat. He seemed to like to torture himself with images of Allison and Roy. The thought that Roy touched her, kissed her, made love to her, drove him over the edge.

As for work, he didn't even give a shit at this point. He was so miserable nothing mattered. All he wanted was Allison.

He sat back in his desk chair and scrubbed his hands over his face.

*If all you want is Allison, then do something about it.*

How could he let the woman he loved go without a fight? All because he didn't try. Didn't tell her how he felt.

He brought up Google on his laptop and punched in penguins. Had he become so desperate for some connection with Al he'd turned to stalking her addiction? He laughed into the empty office. If Maureen heard him, she'd probably call to have him committed. Not that he cared. At least then he'd be on a schedule, so he'd know when to eat, and maybe they'd give him some type of meds to knock him out so he could sleep a mindless sleep.

He scrolled through several sites. Reading portions aloud, tapping his pen on the surface of his desk.

Maureen came to the door. "Did you need something, Jared?"

He shook his head, and as she turned to leave he called her back. "Did you know some penguins mate for life?"

She grinned. "If we're going to trade penguin trivia, did you know the king penguin sings to his mate?"

"Hmm." He slouched over his desk, thrusting his chin into his palm. "I wonder what he sings."

"A love ballad, I'm sure."

"Classic rock, maybe."

They laughed.

"My son actually went online not long ago and purchased a special stone to give to his girlfriend before he proposed. He'd read that one kind of penguin will search the beach for the perfect stone to present to a female penguin. If she accepts, they are mates for life."

"Hmm. Did she accept?"

"She certainly did. Wedding is planned for early next year." Maureen walked across the room and typed a few words into the search bar, and several penguin sites came up. She scrolled down to one in particular and clicked the link. "Here it is."

Jared continued reading as Maureen peered over his shoulder. "Hmm." Did Allison know all of this? More than likely.

He smiled when he learned that the penguin known for doing this was Allison's favorite, the gentoo.

All of a sudden he missed her even more.

The phone on Maureen's desk rang, and she excused herself. Jared spun around in his chair, gazing out the window without really seeing anything.

Would Al want to give them a shot?

"Maybe you should bring her a fucking pebble." He laughed.

He and Al obviously had an attraction, or neither of them would've been able to make love the way they had. He'd never felt such a physical and emotional pull.

She had to have felt it, too.

To hell with this business. And Nick.

If his friend wanted to sever their friendship and give up their lucrative business, then so be it. Allison meant more to him than anything in the world. He would fight for the woman he loved. Even if he lost, he had to try. For the first time in weeks his blood pumped through his veins with purpose. He pushed himself up and away from his desk, yanked open his office door, and was greeted by Maureen's wide-eyed stare.

"You okay, Jared?" she asked.

He nodded. "Is Nick in his office?"

"He is."

Jared didn't even bother to knock. Instead he pushed open Nick's door and stormed across the room. Nick looked up from his desk, his pen poised in his hand. "What's up?"

"What's up? I'll tell you what's up. I love your sister. I miss her. I don't care if our friendship is over, if you want to dissolve the business… Fuck, I don't care at this point if we go belly up, some natural disaster takes place, or the world ends tomorrow. All I know is that I want to spend every second of the rest of my life with Al." He cupped the back of his head. "I don't even know who I am anymore. Since she left, I've tried to go about my life like nothing has changed, but *everything* has changed. I can't do this anymore. I'm going after her, and if you have a problem with it you can—"

"Don't even say it." Nick stood, hands low on his hips. "She's just as miserable as you look. I don't know what happened between the two of you, and I'm sorry I got in the way, but if you love her—really love her—then go get her."

"You're not shitting me, are you?" Jared didn't know if he could take it.

Nick shook his head, a slow smile spreading across his face. "Go get the girl."

A lightness filled Jared's chest that he hadn't felt in weeks. "I will."

He practically ran from Nick's office, smiling as his friend's laughter followed him out of the room.

"Go get her, Jared," Maureen stood from her desk and shouted as he raced out the door.

He'd go get her, all right.

...

"I can't apologize enough for telling you like this, Roy. I hope you'll understand." Allison balanced the box containing everything from her desk on her knee as she extended her hand toward Roy. He gripped it in a firm handshake as they stood just inside the entrance to the aquarium. All the confidence in the world didn't prepare her for this difficult task. Not only had she given her resignation—and Nick had promised her old job was hers for the taking only an hour ago—but she'd told Roy she wasn't interested in him, either.

He grinned, and his shoulders sagged. "I'm sorry that the job didn't work out for you, Allison, but I understand. And no hard feelings about giving notice. If your place is back at Firstline, then I won't hold you here to serve out two weeks that will only make you unhappier than you already are."

"I can't thank you enough."

"As for you and me, well, I can't say my heart is broken, and I don't mean that in a bad way…"

"No. That makes me feel a little better, too. I didn't want to hurt you, Roy. You're a great guy. Just not my guy."

"Who is your guy?"

Her gaze shifted to a commotion in the parking lot, and excitement zipped through her. She lost her balance as her head became dizzy, and she needed both hands in order to hold on to the box, as if that would keep her upright. "I'd like it to be that guy."

A bubble of laughter escaped her lips. Was she seeing

things?

Roy spun around, a large smile brightening his eyes. "I can't say I'm surprised."

Allison swallowed, her eyes trained on Jared as he crossed the pavement. A small group of tourists and a busload of students watched his progress, too. Several phones were pulled out and photos snapped. But who could blame them?

He was dressed in his black tux complete with a red-orange bow tie and peach-colored shoes.

She snort-laughed. Where the heck did he find peach-colored shoes?

His outfit wasn't lost on her. He looked like a penguin. Not just any penguin, but her favorite: the gentoo.

Roy opened the door, and she stepped just outside the threshold. The cool morning breeze kissed her face, and she shook her head in order to clear the hair from her eyes.

Jared moved closer. Several people nearby shouted, pointed, but she blocked out all the sounds with each step he took. Her heart beat out an erratic rhythm, and she wasn't sure she'd be able to stand upright much longer as all her blood left her head.

He stopped in front of her. The warmth of his body surrounded her, and she breathed in his wonderful sandalwood scent. God, she'd missed him.

"Allison Hall, I've searched high, low, aboveground, and below in order to find you the most perfect, smooth pebble. Perfect like you."

She waved her hand in front of her face. "You're going to make me cry."

He grabbed the box from her hands and placed it at their feet, then took her hand and kissed it. "Not yet. You need to hear me out since I've worked so hard to get this right."

She snort-laughed and covered her face.

"I've heard from a reliable source you're not happy. And

I'm not happy, either."

"Nick?"

He nodded.

"Al, I love you. And I know you feel something, too. I'm asking you to give me a chance. Let me take care of you, but without smothering you; let me protect you, and you can protect me, too. Let me shower you with pebbles for the rest of our lives, but let this pebble be the first of many." He pulled a velvet jewelry box from his front pocket and snapped it open.

Inside the most beautiful princess-cut diamond ring winked at her, and she gasped.

"Jared…" She could hardly breathe, barely speak.

"If you accept my pebble, we'll be linked for life. Partners, mates, lovers, friends…"

"The whole nine yards," she whispered.

"And then some."

She laughed, and her heart swelled when he gave her a shaky laugh. Allison took a step toward him and touched his cheek. "Oh my God. I love you, too. I never dreamed you felt the same. Nick gave me my job back an hour ago. I was going to hunt you down and—"

He shook his head, grazing his lips against her forehead. "I don't even need you to finish that sentence. All I needed to hear was that you love me."

She pressed her mouth to his for a quick kiss and then put her hand out so that he could slide the diamond onto her finger. A perfect fit. Several patrons wandered out of the building, and the people from the parking lot stood back at a distance. More cameras clicked, and applause followed. Allison could feel her face heat, but she loved that she could see a tinge of color rush over Jared's face, too.

"With this pebble I promise to always love you. To make you happy, laugh, and smile. And if we're ever separated by ice barges or storms, I'll stay true and search for you forever."

She covered her face with her hands and laughed before reaching up to caress his cheek. "I love you so much. And I promise the same." She bared her soul as she held his gaze, her entire body on fire as he pulled her into his arms.

With his arm draped around her shoulders, he lifted his free hand toward the crowd. "I love this woman."

The crowd cheered, and Allison patted him playfully on the chest. "Can we have our engagement party here at the aquarium, maybe a penguin theme?"

He pulled her into his arms for a soft kiss. "Whatever you want, babe. I'll even agree to honeymoon in Antarctica if that'll make you happy."

"You make me happy."

# Acknowledgments

As always I want to thank my amazing editor, Karen Grove, who defines the word awesome. She's been such a powerful influence on my writing and a great support. I can't thank you enough, Karen.

I also want to shout out to all the peeps behind the scenes at Entangled Publishing. You're an amazing place to be, and I appreciate every day how lucky I am to be a part of the Entangled family.

Thank you to all my wonderful readers and my amazing street team who take the time to read my books and help me spread the word. Writing is such a huge gift, and I'm thankful every day to be able to do what I love.

Thank you to all the people in my life who have interesting quirks, phrases, habits, and looks that I've "borrowed" to help make my characters come to life. And finally, thank you, Sue Stevens, for allowing me to put your name in my book. I can hear your laughter when you read it in print for the first time, and that makes me happy. You're a true friend and I love you.

# About the Author

Christine Warner is living her dream in Michigan along with her family, three laptops (she might have a slight addiction, or maybe it's a fear of one imploding from overuse), and a much-loved assortment of furry friends.

Besides laughing and a good round of humor, she enjoys spending time with her family, cooking, reading, and writing, but no arithmetic. A confessed people watcher, she finds inspiration for her stories in everyday activities. She loves to read and write about strong heroes and determined, sometimes sassy heroines.

A girl gone wild, at least where social media is concerned, she enjoys meeting other avid readers and writers on Facebook, Twitter, Instagram, Goodreads, and her website at christine-warner.com.

*Discover the* **Friends First** *series…*

A Friendly Engagement

A Friendly Arrangement

***Also by Christine Warner***

Bachelor's Special

Made in the
USA
Middletown, DE

75943491R00146